AARON HARTZLER

HAPPY DEATH DAY & HAPPY DEATH DAY 2U

Aaron Hartzler has written stand-up comedy, one-man shows, billboards, books, essays, screenplays, and a great number of tweets. He is the author of the memoir *Rapture Practice* and the novel *What We Saw*. He lives at the beach in Los Angeles with his husband, Brant, and their two rescue dogs, Charlie and Brahms.

www.aaronhartzler.com

HAPPY DEATH DAY
&
HAPPY DEATH DAY 2U

HAPPY DEATH DAY & HAPPY DEATH DAY 2U

Adapted by Aaron Hartzler

BASED ON CHARACTERS CREATED BY SCOTT LOBDELL

BLUMHOUSE BOOKS | ANCHOR BOOKS

A Division of Penguin Random House LLC

New York

A BLUMHOUSE BOOKS/ANCHOR BOOKS ORIGINAL, FEBRUARY 2019

This work is a novelization of the motion pictures *Happy Death Day* (2017) and *Happy Death Day 2U* (2019).

The Cataloging-in-Publication Data is on file at the Library of Congress.

Anchor Books Trade Paperback ISBN: 978-1-9848-9772-5
eBook ISBN: 978-1-9848-9773-2

Book design by Debbie Glasserman

www.anchorbooks.com

Printed in the United States of America
10 9 8 7 6 5 4 3 2 1

CONTENTS

HAPPY DEATH DAY

■

Do not go gentle into that good night.
Rage, rage against the dying of the light.

—DYLAN THOMAS

1

Even before she opened her eyes, Teresa "Tree" Gelbman was certain that today would be a total nightmare. Someone seemed to be hitting her in the head with a sledgehammer, and each blow had a vaguely musical tone. Also, there was a trombone involved. Somewhere in the haze, she heard a voice yell, *Fuck off!* and the trombone abruptly stopped, but not the pounding in her head—or the ringing bell.

The bell tower. That's what it was, tolling out the hour from the middle of campus.

The more Tree came back into her body, the worse her head hurt. She pulled a pillow over her ears to try to drown out the noise. *What time is it even?* That damn bell had to stop ringing soon. Finally, it did. In the moment of stillness that followed, she bravely made the decision to open her eyes.

What the hell . . . ?

First of all, this was not her room at the Kappa house. There were posters for old movies and TV shows covering every inch of the wall above the bed: *They Live, Back to the Future, Repo Man*—whatever that was. She was in Nerd Central. And whose T-shirt was she wearing?

Oh. Probably his.

The likely nerd in question was about six feet away, digging around under a desk. *Ugh. How did this happen?* She groaned at the thought, and the guy turned around.

"Oh, hey. You're up! I wasn't sure if you wanted to sleep in or not."

"Am I in a . . . *dorm room*?" she asked.

"Uh . . . yeah."

At that moment, her phone burst to life. It was a weird ringtone she didn't remember downloading and that she now regretted more than . . . well, whatever had happened last night:

Yeahhh! It's my birthday, and I ain't gotta pick up the phone!

Tree snatched her phone off the nightstand. It was 9:00 a.m. and, naturally, her father was calling. She sent him to voice mail and looked around for her stuff.

"Where are my clothes?"

"On the dresser."

Taking a deep breath, she mustered the strength to stand. She had to get out of here before the combination of horror and dorm room nerd funk overpowered her.

"I folded your pants . . . last night. You know, I wasn't sure if that material gets wrinkled."

"Great." Tree whipped off his T-shirt, revealing her black bra.

The guy wheeled around to give her privacy, but he still looked like his mom had just caught him watching porn. It would've been charming under other circumstances, but clearly he'd seen more than her bra last night. Tree didn't really care why he was pretending to be shy now. Nerds were confusing because they had no game. At least with frat boys and jocks, you knew where you stood. All this emotional stammering was exasperating. Waiting for boys to figure out their feelings was exhausting. Plus, it bored her.

"D-Don't know if you remember my name or not," the guy stammered. "You got pretty wasted last night. My name is—"

"Tylenol?"

"No. What?" He turned back around, confused.

"My head is killing me," she snapped. "Do you have any *Tylenol*?"

"Yeah. Yeah, I do." He scrambled toward his desk, pleased, it seemed, to have a task, and unzipped a toiletries bag. Tree pulled on last night's outfit as he bumbled around and finally produced some painkillers. "It's right here."

She sighed and slid her feet into patent red stilettos, then took the bottle from his eager, outstretched hand. "Thanks," she said.

She popped two pills into her mouth, and he almost tripped over himself racing to get her a water bottle from his dresser. She'd already gulped the pills down dry by the time he got there. This was not her first rodeo.

"I'm Carter, by the way."

"Not a word of this to *anyone*." Tree meant it exactly as it sounded: a threat. "Got it?" She handed the Tylenol back to him.

Carter nodded. "Yeah. Sure."

It was sort of cute how crestfallen he looked when he figured out this was *Never. Happening. Again.* Handsome, even. All he really needed was a little hair product and some decent jeans. Tree knew she was as far out of his league as Carter was ever likely to get, but she also wasn't the kind of girl who took on a project. She had big plans, and one of those was *not* to become the laughingstock of every Greek on campus—or the legendary one-night stand of every geek on campus.

She grabbed her purse and turned to go. As she reached for the door, it flew open and she saw a guy with bleached-blond hair, already midsentence.

"Dude! You hit that *fine vagine* or wha—" He froze as soon as he saw her.

She turned to shoot daggers back at Carter. In the awkward silence, she shouldered her bag and stalked out down the hall, followed by Carter's hushed voice to his roommate.

"Nice one, dickhead."

Tree stopped at the front door of the dorm and sighed, bracing herself for the trek across campus in last night's outfit.

Let's get this over with, she thought, and charged ahead into the morning sun.

2

Tree had hoped that perhaps she could sneak back to the Kappa house unnoticed, but her stomach sank as she walked across the quad in her red stilettos and slinky sequined tank. Bayfield University was already in full swing, and this would be a walk of shame, pure and simple.

A guy she always saw hanging out in front of the art building passed her, giving her an up-and-down look that could only be interpreted as judgmental.

As she hurried past him, a girl with awful hair and zero makeup tried to stop her, holding out a clipboard.

"Stop global warming?" she asked.

Tree shook her head and pushed past her. In truth, she'd never wished more fervently that she could accelerate the certain demise of the ice caps. If only sea levels would rise immediately and cover the campus to end her embarrassment. If she saw anyone from her sorority—or worse, if a Kappa Pi saw *her*—she knew there'd be hell to pay.

As Tree approached a couple studying on the lawn, the sprinkler system *whooshed* on, drenching them both as they scrambled to gather up their notebooks and flee the spray.

The siren of a car alarm broke through the morning air and jarred her headache back to life. She picked up her pace. All she wanted was to be back in her room.

She shielded her eyes from the bright morning as she approached a group of frat pledges standing on the grass. One of them held a sign that read TWENTY-SIXTH STRAIGHT HOUR, while the rest of them sang, bleary-eyed, "Sixty-three bottles of beer on the wall . . ." Their frat brother shouted at them through a bullhorn: *"Twenty-six hours? Is that all you got? I can't hear you!"* Tree watched as one of the pledges collapsed onto the ground in exhaustion. In response, the frat brother yelled, *"Keep going!"*

She checked her phone as she cut across a section of lawn toward a series of brick arches that shaded a sidewalk near the bell tower. No new messages, but where had that weird birthday ringtone come from? Had she downloaded it in a blackout?

Then, as she reached the relative privacy of the covered walkway, Tim Bauer stepped out from behind a pillar.

"Hey."

Crap. Tree glanced around, annoyed, but there was no escape. She was caught.

"Hi."

"You haven't returned any of my texts."

"Sorry," she said with a sheepish smile. "I've been really busy."

She moved to go around him, but Tim blocked her way. He nodded down at her party look. "Yeah. I can see that."

She didn't have the bandwidth for this. It was time for a truth-down.

"Okay, Tim. We went on *a* date. *One.* I don't have to text you back. We're not, like, a thing."

"I just—you know, I figured we had a nice time . . ."

His voice trailed off, and Tree felt a flush of anger. Tim

was nice enough—handsome even. He was muscular and athletic, but he just didn't get it. She had to nip this in the bud.

"*You* had a nice time," she said. "I was *miserable*. I mean, who takes their first date to Subway? It's not like you have a foot-long."

Tree rolled her eyes and stepped around him. She could feel him there, staring at her, long after she walked away.

Sorority row at Bayfield University spoke to the long and storied history of the school, and the Kappa property was the jewel in this crown. Kappa Pi Lambda was housed in a sprawling, historic pink mansion with a perfectly manicured lawn and flower boxes overflowing with freesia. The porch ranged across the front of the house, ringed with purple hydrangeas. Jasmine and wisteria climbed up the walls at each corner, framing the grandeur in fragrant elegance.

The Kappa Pi Sisterhood was one of the most prestigious on campus, and the meticulous upkeep of their dwelling spoke to the privilege of belonging. The money they spent on landscaping alone could've run a small country, and their formal mixers were the stuff of legend. On the walls inside hung countless pictures of women who had gone on to become leaders in business, science, academics—even a couple of Hollywood stars. On any other day, Tree might have stopped to bask in the pride of being a member of such an exclusive club, but not today.

One of her sisters, Emily, sat on the wraparound porch, enjoying the morning sun and listening to music on her headphones. She smiled and waved, but Tree blew right past her, swiftly and quietly swinging open the beautiful old front door, its leaded glass panes catching the light and spilling a prism of rainbows across the foyer. Tree threw a quick look around, then slipped inside. Thank god, the coast was clear.

She eased the door closed without a sound and tiptoed up a couple of stairs toward her room when a voice from behind stopped her cold.

"Oh. My. *God*. You sneaky little bee-yotch."

Slowly, she turned to find Danielle Bouseman, her best frenemy and Kappa president, looking rested and magnificent in head-to-toe designer workout gear. Danielle's flowing honey-brown hair was pulled up, and the chiseled abs beneath her yellow sports bra were as sharp as her tongue. She put her hands on her hips and smiled expectantly.

"Who was it?" she asked.

"Nobody," Tree said.

"Sisters don't keep secrets."

"Seriously. It was *nobody*."

"Well," Danielle said primly, "I hope 'nobody' used a condom. We don't want 'somebody' looking like a whore."

"Thanks, Danielle." Tree laughed and turned to climb the stairs. "Super helpful."

"What are sisters for?" Danielle called after her. "Oh! And don't forget. House meeting at lunch."

"Living for it!" Tree called back.

When she swung open the door to her room, Tree felt like she had already been awake for a month. Her roommate, Lori, was sitting at the vanity, writing in her journal, dressed in the scrubs she wore to her work-study shift at the campus teaching hospital. She glanced up as Tree closed their door behind her, collapsed onto her bed, and cuddled up with the stuffed bunny she'd brought to college—the only trace of childhood that she allowed herself.

"She finally rolls in." Lori closed her journal and slid it into the vanity drawer.

"Did I totally embarrass myself last night?" Tree asked her.

"Not at all," Lori said. "Unless you consider dancing on a

table, starting two fights, and barfing pretzel chunks all over the bar embarrassing."

Tree groaned. "Please tell me you're kidding."

"Oh, and also you rammed your tongue down Nick Sims's throat right in front of Danielle."

Tree burst out in a laugh. "Oh god! But she was so nice to me this morning."

Lori took a sip of her coffee. "I think she was as drunk as you were last night. Consider it collective amnesia."

"Thank god for that."

Lori laughed with her for a moment as Tree looked over to check her clock: 9:20 a.m. She jumped up and flew into action. "Crap! I'm so late for class." In a flash, she kicked off her heels and threw a shapeless sweatshirt over her sparkly tank. Grabbing her backpack, she rummaged around in the general disaster area of her desk.

"I can't find my damn book!" she said in a panic, knocking over a pile of mail topped by a black envelope with only her name scrawled on it in bright red strokes. "Ha!" she shouted triumphantly. She pulled the textbook from the pile and shoved it into her bag.

Tree heard Lori clear her throat and turned to find her holding up a single cupcake. A lit candle flickered in the center of the frosting. Tree froze and felt a familiar pang of sadness in her chest.

"Did you really think you could keep it a secret from me?" Lori smiled at her sweetly as Tree stared at the cupcake.

"How did you find out?" she asked.

Lori beamed at her, victorious, and very pleased with herself. "Driver's license. Not the best picture of you, I might add."

Tree nodded. "I assume you changed my ringer, too?"

Lori smiled with a sly glint in her eye. "Who, *me*? Never."

This was why Tree loved having Lori as a roommate—the

thoughtful notes, the simple kindness. For weeks, she had hounded Tree about her birthday, and even when Tree had refused to divulge a single detail, she hadn't seemed upset, only confused.

How could Tree explain why she didn't want to celebrate this day? How could she articulate that all she really wanted was to skip her birthday for the rest of her time on this planet? But here was Lori, all smiles and excitement, having figured out how to give her this simple token of their friendship—exactly the thing a sister would always do.

Tree felt herself trembling on the edge of a sadness she would be unable to contain and made a decision not to allow the grief to overtake her. Reluctantly, she took the cupcake from Lori, closed her eyes for a moment, and blew out the candle.

"What'd you wish for?" Lori was all smiles.

Tree arched an eyebrow at her. "A new roommate."

Lori laughed. "Wench!"

Tree considered the cupcake for a moment, dropped it without ceremony into the trash can by her desk, and opened the door to go.

"Hey!" Lori called after her. "I made that from scratch!"

Tree turned around and resumed her normal tone of bitch on wheels. "Sorry. Too many carbs." She ignored Lori's hurt look and headed into the hall. "Toodles!"

The look on Lori's face made it clear she was disappointed, but Tree didn't have time for anyone else's disappointment. Her own sadness was too big—too threatening—and she had to keep paddling in her own direction to avoid being swept away by it altogether. There was one surefire way to keep it at bay, and that always began with a trip to the science building.

Dr. Gregory Butler was already well into his lecture when the door at the back of the classroom squeaked loudly, announcing Tree's arrival. She was pleased to see he wasn't wearing a lab coat. The way his snug, gray trousers hugged his butt was something that should never be covered, in her opinion. As she slipped into the back row, he turned his perfect, chiseled jaw her way and raised an eyebrow, his ice-blue eyes burning into her with an intensity that made her instantly weak in the knees. Tree was unsure if the look he gave her was a smile or a sneer, but she could work with either. He ran a hand through his perfect hair and continued to talk without missing a beat—something about extreme agitation and the acceleration of locomotive response across the quantum plane.

Tree could never be sure what he was talking about exactly, but she felt agitated and ready to respond—that much was certain. She was hopeless at science. It was why she'd started going to visit him during his office hours across campus at the Bayfield University Hospital in the first place.

She'd pop by this afternoon for a refresher.

3

When class let out, Tree walked toward the outdoor dining patio near the cafeteria where Danielle liked to hold their house meetings. On the way, she passed Keith Lumbly sweating it out in the Bayfield Baby mascot costume. The mask was pulled off his face and resting on his head as he hawked souvenirs for the Bayfield Booster Club.

If there was one downside to Bayfield University, it was their mascot. Whoever had once thought that a baby was a great idea for a college team representative must never have seen a horror movie. The mask resting on top of Keith's head looked like Porky Pig with a human nose and an oversize baby bucktooth. The wide eyes and blank smile took on a bizarre, terrifying feel when worn on the face of a grown person. There was something deeply unsettling about it, and Tree hurried past the merch table, which was full of the weird baby's face emblazoned on everything from T-shirts and flags to your very own masks. You could be a Bayfield Baby at games—or for whatever weird stuff you happened to be into.

Keith's voice droned on in a bored monotone as she

passed. "Get your school spirit on before the big game. Ten percent off with your student ID."

He sounded as over it as she was.

Tree spotted her sisters gathered around a couple of tables with Danielle calling them all to order. Tree hurried over to take her seat. Danielle ran their lunch meetings with an iron fist. You would've thought they were all members of the UN Security Council. One of the pledges passed each of them a bottle of zero-calorie, fruit-flavored water. This was "lunch," and Tree tried not to think about the fact that her father was probably sitting down at the country club, where she was supposed to be meeting him right this second.

Some things were more important than small talk with Dad over lunch, and putting in an appearance at the house meeting was one of them. Danielle could make your life a living hell if you missed one. Lori was nowhere to be seen, which probably meant she was still at the hospital. Danielle didn't make exceptions—especially for work-study programs.

After a quick, cool welcome, Danielle called the meeting to order. The first item on the agenda was choosing this year's charity.

"I can say right now, there is no way we're doing the Special Needs Art Fair again," Danielle began. "It totally freaked my shit out. Thoughts?"

Before anyone could answer, Becky Shepard plunked a lunch tray down next to Tree and slid in beside her. Every eye fell on her tray, which held a sandwich, a side of pasta salad, a fruit cup, and a tall glass of chocolate milk. Feeling the weight of their collective stares, Becky looked up with a confused smile.

"What's wrong?" she asked.

"Oh, I don't know," Danielle said sarcastically. "What's wrong, Tree?"

"Nothing," Tree said, turning to Becky. "Except for the cat-lady buffet you just dumped on our table."

Tree saw Becky look at her tray, then notice that everyone else was not eating. The look on her face turned to panic, but Danielle wasn't done with the public shaming.

"And is that chocolate milk I see?" she asked.

"I missed breakfast."

"What *is* breakfast, Becky?" Danielle's question was a dagger thrown with precision. As it hit its mark, Becky jumped to her feet, grabbed her tray, and tried to escape from the torrent of shame.

Tree was barely able to snicker to herself before she felt an impact right behind her, followed immediately by the cold and sticky fingers of Becky's chocolate milk splashing across her neck, head, and hair. She leaped to her feet and wheeled on Becky, yelling, "You *asshole*!" as she came face-to-face with Carter—the apparent cause of the collision.

Danielle was cackling at the scene. Becky fled in tears as Carter grabbed napkins from a dispenser on the table and attempted to dab at the mess all over Tree. Tree stood there, stunned, a sinking feeling gathering in her stomach.

"I'm so sorry, Tree!"

The minute the words left Carter's mouth, Tree knew she was doomed. Danielle's laughter stopped instantly, and her eyes narrowed.

"You two *know* each other?"

"No!" Tree shouted at the same moment Carter said, "Yes!"

Tree shot nuclear warheads with her eyeballs at the dweeb from the dorm, and she was relieved to see that he clearly remembered her threat from earlier. Carter froze, a fistful of napkins in mid-wipe, and started stammering.

"We, uh . . . we had a class together. Last year."

Seemingly satisfied, Danielle continued giggling as the

rest of the girls joined her, relieved that they weren't in the crosshairs of the ice queen for once.

Tree used the moment to step behind Carter and out of Danielle's direct view. She huffed and snatched the napkins from him, dabbing at the chocolate milk still running down the back of her neck into her sweatshirt. Carter leaned closer to her and held out his hand.

"I just came by to return this," he whispered.

Tree glanced down and saw the gold bracelet her mother had given her for her birthday a few years ago. *Shit.* In her haste to escape this morning, she must've left it in his room.

"I didn't know where you lived." Carter's voice was pleading and apologetic.

Tree snatched the bracelet out of his hand and looked around to see if anyone had noticed. Luckily, they hadn't. She felt a strange emotion well up inside her. She didn't know how to say thank you. This bracelet was so important to her, and Carter could just as easily have tossed it in the trash instead of taking the time to track her down and return it. The relief that washed over her made her eyes well up, but she couldn't let on. Not here. Not now. Not in front of Danielle. Still, Carter lingered hopefully, waiting for the thank-you Tree could never deliver.

"Can I *help you* with something?" Her voice was hard as nails.

The cloud that darkened Carter's eyes made her feel like a jerk, but now was not the time or the place. He backed away from her and shook his head, amazed by her coldness. Finally, he shrugged and stepped back.

"Sorry again about the mess."

Tree watched him go, forgetting for a moment where she was. She wasn't usually this person. Or was she? He had done something kind, and she was unwilling to acknowledge it. Was there ever a way to make him understand?

"What a douchebag." Danielle's voice pulled her back to the present.

Tree went back to her seat at the table. It took everything in her not to jump up again and chase Carter down. She wanted to explain that she couldn't risk Danielle knowing what had happened between them. She didn't know how to tell him that once she'd lost more than a bracelet on her birthday, but this was the same sorrow that made her lash out at his kindness. It was the only thing she could see.

As Danielle continued the house meeting, Tree knew there was only one thing that would get her through this terrible day. As soon as the meeting adjourned, she made a beeline for the Kappa house to get cleaned up.

4

A hot shower did wonders for Tree's spirits. And by some birthday miracle of fate, Lori wasn't back from her shift at the hospital yet, so Tree could bask in the luxury of having the room all to herself.

With Becky's chocolate milk and last night's eyeliner finally scrubbed away, Tree applied some fresh mascara and just a touch of lip gloss. By the time she'd finished a fresh blowout, she felt nearly human again.

It was still warm outside—an Indian summer in full swing—but a light breeze blew through her hair as she walked across campus through the ancient oaks, elms, and maples. No color yet, but within a few weeks or so the sky at Bayfield would be on fire with an explosion of yellows, oranges, and reds.

Autumn had always been her favorite time of year, and she couldn't help but think about the first time her mom had taught her how to rake the fallen leaves in their front yard into fluffy piles—and then how to charge across the fading grass and dive into them. How old had she been? Four or five? She'd thought that they were doing an important chore, that her mom wanted a tidy yard without a single stray twig or a blade of grass out of place. It had been a surprise to her that, in the end, all that effort was about having fun.

That was her mom in a nutshell: she'd do anything to make Tree giggle.

As Tree walked into the lobby of the campus hospital, her cell phone jarred her back to reality.

Yeahhh! It's my birthday, and I ain't gotta pick up the phone!

She checked the screen and hit Ignore on the call from her dad. She had to remember to change her ringtone as soon as she got back to the house. *Goddamn it, Lori.*

She pushed the button for the elevators in the lobby. As if on cue, the bell dinged, and Lori stepped out.

"Oh! Lori." Tree was startled to see her still here in her scrubs.

"Hi." Lori stopped short, but she didn't smile.

Tree frowned. "I thought your shift was usually over by now."

Lori shrugged. "Doing a double for Jen. She has the flu."

"We missed you at the house meeting today."

Lori rolled her eyes. "Didn't think I needed to be there to decide what color Danielle's hair should be this season."

Tree laughed, but Lori didn't join in. Tree felt a familiar heaviness descend between them. The fun was gone in a flash.

"So." Her roommate crossed her arms. "I guess I don't have to ask what *you're* doing here?"

Tree sighed. She wasn't about to get into this. "Gotta go."

She nudged past Lori and pressed the elevator button again. It had just been here. *Damn it. Where did it go?*

"Look, Tree . . ."

Tree closed her eyes and took a deep breath. She'd heard this speech a zillion times before, and she silently begged the elevator to hurry as she saw from the lit display above the doors that it had begun its descent: *4 . . . 3 . . . 2 . . .*

"It's none of my business," Lori continued, "but I think eventually something like this is bound to have some pretty serious consequences."

Ding.

Mercifully, the doors opened, and Tree stepped inside. She hit the button for the fourth floor.

"You're right," she said with a smile. "It's none of your business."

Tree tried not to register her friend's disapproval, but Lori looked like she'd sucked on a lemon. Finally, the old metal doors closed with a dull clunk. Tree attempted to shake off the weirdness with her roommate, trying to let her spirits rise along with the elevator.

It was her birthday, after all.

She could give herself any gift she wanted.

The Bayfield University Hospital had been built in the '40s, added onto in the '60s, and remodeled in the '90s. This series of projects had left behind a winding tangle of corridors that were virtually impossible to navigate without a map. The administration had recently begun a floor-by-floor construction project to simplify the layout, but the layers of ancient steel and concrete meant the cell reception came and went, and GPS—for those who needed directions—was spotty at best.

Luckily, Tree knew her way around almost every inch of the fourth floor. She smiled as she approached the nurses' station outside Dr. Butler's office. Deena, the charge nurse on duty, was whispering something to her coworker.

Tree heard her say, "Well, I'm not comfortable with it,"

and saw the other nurse nod, a frown creasing her forehead with concern. Both of them straightened up and smiled when they saw Tree walking by. She waved as she blew past. Deena was always bitching about something—the amount of paperwork the morning charge nurse left her to do; the cost of a Diet Coke in the vending machine; the distance of her son's preschool from campus. Her complaints were endless, and Tree, for one, had decided months ago that the best course of action was to ignore her.

She rounded the corner and passed a police officer posted outside a patient's room. He nodded as she walked by, and Tree smiled back. No doubt the Sigma Nus had gotten a pledge so drunk he'd tossed himself through a window. Now, poor Officer Schmuck Face had to wait until this idiot kid came to so a report could be filed about all the details he'd never remember in a million years.

At the end of the hall, she stopped at a door marked DR. GREGORY BUTLER and cautiously threw a glance over her shoulder. Then she turned the knob without knocking and slipped inside, closing the door behind her with a soft click. Professor Butler wasn't here yet, but Tree didn't mind waiting. He was probably just finishing up his morning rounds.

She closed her eyes and took a deep breath. The scent of this place always made her heart race: leather-bound books, the dust on their spines, the sweet chemical smell of the disinfectant the staff used to mop the floors in the hall. The office was cramped, but Tree always thought of it as cozy.

She walked over to the desk and noticed a photo in an inscribed frame: *Gregory & Stephanie*. There he was with his wife, the two of them resplendent on their wedding day. Still, even under glass, his bright blue eyes beckoned Tree toward him. She laughed to herself and tipped the frame facedown on the desk.

As she did, she heard Dr. Butler enter behind her, and

she turned around. When he saw her standing in his office, he closed the door as fast as he could.

"We can't do this. There's too much going on in the building today."

Tree walked toward him slowly without saying a word. She took his car keys out of his hand and dropped them in a dish on his desk.

He continued to protest—something that Tree would never admit excited her just a bit. "I have patients—"

"Yeah," she interrupted. "And I'm losing mine."

Tree grabbed his belt, jerking him toward her, and unzipped his fly. She slid one hand into his pants, threw an arm around his neck, and pulled his mouth to hers, kissing him hard.

That was all it took. She felt his arms slide around her waist, lifting her as if she weighed nothing, spinning her around, and putting her down on his desk. She wrapped her legs around his and pulled him in closer.

This was what she had wanted all day. *It was all I wanted last night, too,* she thought. College boys were so boring compared to this—so simple and petty—headed nowhere but back to the keg in a hurry. There was only so much fun she could have with a frat boy who really just wanted to get off so he could get another drink. But this . . .

This was *exciting*.

Gregory kissed his way down her neck, and she ran her hand from his shoulders up into his hair.

His lips grazed her ear. "This doesn't mean you're passing my course." His voice was sly and teasing.

Tree pulled his hair gently, making him tilt his head back and gaze at her with those perfect baby blues. "Do I look like I care?"

When he kissed her again, she felt a chill of pure pleasure run down her spine. Her right leg kicked out by reflex, knocking a desk chair on rollers across the small room with a bang. Both of them jumped, laughing as the chair slammed to a stop, wedged between the door and filing cabinet.

It was perfect timing.

The knob turned without warning, and someone pushed open the door, stopped short by the back of the chair jammed beneath the knob, the rollers caught on the filing cabinet.

A woman's voice called out from the hallway, "Gregory? Are you there?" and Tree felt her heart leap to her throat as the rest of her leaped into action.

Perhaps it was what her mother had called "a woman's intuition," but Tree knew in an instant it was Gregory's wife. The speed with which he zipped his fly, smoothed his hair, and made it to the chair lodged against the door was truly impressive.

In a flash, Tree maneuvered into the chair behind the desk. She grabbed a pen and a legal pad, flipped to a blank page, and set the frame back up. A split second later, the woman from the picture walked through the door. Stephanie was still pretty, but plainer now, and fragile somehow.

Gregory kissed her lightly on the lips. "Hey, sweetie."

"What's with the door?" she asked, looking at Tree, then back to Gregory again.

Gregory shook his head and laughed. "Stupid chair got stuck. Just wrapping up here."

Tree flipped the top pages back over the legal pad and smiled, returning it to the desk as she grabbed her bag. She squeezed past Stephanie and forced a smile—one that was not returned.

"Thanks for your help, Dr. Butler," Tree said. "I think I get it now."

"Glad to hear it." Gregory was all business. "See you next week in class."

She hurried away down the hall. When the elevator doors

finally slid closed behind her, Tree mouthed a silent curse. *Shit.*

All the way to the Kappa house, she couldn't stop wondering whether Stephanie suspected anything—and also how she possibly couldn't.

5

Later that evening, Tree sat on her bed painting her toenails and watching a *Teen Mom* marathon for the umpteenth time. Something about this show made her feel marginally better about herself. Whatever her hang-ups were, Tree had made it to college without an unplanned pregnancy, and on days like today, these were the tiny victories to which she clung.

There was a light knock on the door, and Tree called out, "Enter."

Danielle appeared, makeup perfect, hair in giant juice-can curlers, already dressed for tonight's party. Tree glanced up at her and frowned.

"Is that my top?"

Danielle struck a pose. "How cute is it on me?"

"Whatever. Just don't get anything on it, please."

"You mean like Nick's *nutter butter*?"

Tree laughed. "Wow. Classy, Danielle."

"What time are you going to the party tonight?"

"I don't know. Later."

The truth was that Tree was hoping to ghost on this mixer

altogether. She hated her birthday as a general rule, and this one already had been exceptionally trying. Her hangover had finally begun to fade, and it seemed unwise to pour more booze on top of that. Of course, the thought of being sober at a Bayfield Greek social of any kind made her want to run screaming into the night. Even at its most scintillating, the conversation at these events left a great deal to be desired, and once the campus gossip of the past twelve hours had been thoroughly examined and exhausted, there would only be dancing, beer pong, and endless photo-booth selfies left as entertainment.

Inevitably, the evening would quickly dissolve into a race to see which new pledge brother would puke first and which new pledge sister would drink enough to insist on going home with him anyway. Two weeks ago, a couple of frat boys had been discovered by their girlfriends making out with each other in an upstairs utility closet at the Sig Ep house, but even the novelty of that moment had barely energized the party. Tree just wanted this day to end, and it seemed to her that the shortest distance between now and waking up tomorrow was certainly not a kegger at Chi Sigma Epsilon.

Danielle would definitely demand a better explanation than "I don't feel like it," and just as she was working out what that might be in her head, the power flickered and the room was plunged into blackness. Tree groaned.

"Our tuition dollars at work." Danielle huffed in the darkness.

"It's like nine thirty," Tree agreed. "The timing seems more and more random."

The rolling blackouts had started a few days after they'd arrived on campus. It had been unseasonably warm so far this semester, and the administration had chalked up the outages to the enormous strain of hundreds of window-unit air conditioners on the campus's aging electrical grid. But now the blackouts had begun happening during off-peak hours like this—sometimes accompanied by power surges that would shatter lightbulbs and send sparks showering from utility poles and streetlamps.

As they waited in the darkness for a few moments, Tree held her nail polish brush in midair, trying not to get lacquer on her toes or comforter. Finally, the lights flickered back on, and Danielle instantly turned to check her makeup in Tree's mirror, as if the darkness itself might've sullied her appearance. Satisfied with what she saw, she turned to go.

"Anyhoo, don't be too late, or all the cute Sigma boys will be taken." Danielle winked at her and headed out the door, reaching up to start pulling curlers out of her hair.

"Okay, byeeeeee," Tree said.

"Byeeeeee!"

"Crazy bitch," Tree whispered to herself with a smile. She loved Danielle, but that girl was *a lot*.

She went back to examining her pedicure, relieved. Maybe she'd be able to bail on this party without too much fuss. One of her toes, on the other hand, was a disaster, hemorrhaging with red gloss. Tree growled, reaching over to grab the nail polish remover off her nightstand, promptly spilling the open bottle on her bedspread.

"Damn it!"

She jumped up to grab a towel hanging on the back of the chair at her desk. Before she could turn back to the mess at hand, something caught her eye, peeking out beneath the stack of her unopened mail.

Tree knew what it was. She also knew better than to pick it up—especially today of all days. There was no sense in putting herself through it. *Don't do it,* she commanded, but her body seemed to be on autopilot. What was it about not being able to stay away from things that were bad for her? It was like that time she bit her cheek at junior prom in high school. For a week, she couldn't keep her tongue off the little sore bump in the side of her cheek. Before she could stop her own hand, she reached down, pushed away the envelope on the top of the stack, and pulled the dog-eared picture out of the pile.

The photo cut straight to her heart. The pang in her chest was almost instant. There she was the morning of high school graduation, beaming at the camera in her cap and gown. Her father smiled so proudly it appeared his buttons might literally pop off his shirt. Her mother's smile was identical to the one she'd given Tree by genetics—delicate lips upturned in delight, eyes dancing with a quiet excitement. It had been so long since Tree had seen herself make that face in the mirror that for a moment she doubted if that was actually her in the picture.

Did that really happen? Was I ever truly that happy?

Carefully, she brushed her finger over the image, absently wishing that by touching the faces of this happy family just so, she could return to who she had been in that moment. But the joy captured in the photo was no match, it seemed, for the weight in her chest, and the image went blurry as her eyes filled with tears. Before a single one could fall onto the picture, she marshaled control of her emotions once more. She yanked open the top drawer of her dresser and buried the photo under a pile of clothing.

Wiping at her eyes, she grabbed the towel and the bottle of remover and attacked the puddle of polish. By the time everything was scrubbed and rinsed, Tree had recalled how good it felt to take action. Maybe the Chi Sig house wasn't her dream destination, but anything was better than sitting here crying over pictures from high school.

A balmy puff of air from the open window carried a whisper of jasmine into her room. Tree rummaged around in her closet, pulling out a flirty white dress with spaghetti straps covered in tiny black polka dots.

Today would get better, she decided. She couldn't go back and get a do-over, but she could start fresh from this moment, right now. There were still a few hours before midnight, and she was going to turn things around.

Who knew what the evening might hold?

With any luck, it might turn out to be her first happy birthday in a long while.

6

The night was warm and lovely.

As Tree walked to the party along the ambling, well-kept sidewalks of Bayfield University, she felt better than she had all day. A light breeze rustled the leaves in the canopy of old trees over her head, dappling the way ahead with moonlight. The campus was mainly quiet now, with just a few students here and there, hurrying to meet friends.

Tree's high heels made a pleasing click on the pavement, and even the Bayfield Babies banners hanging from each of the old-fashioned streetlamps somehow didn't seem so menacing. The mascot was ridiculous.

The Bayfield Babies? For a college? That was the best they could do? Talk about a serious lack of imagination.

She quickened her pace toward the little footbridge ahead where several paths intersected and looped over and under one another. Each one headed off on a different level toward a different location. Her phone buzzed, and a new voice mail flashed onto the screen from Gregory. She hit Play and listened as she walked. His voice was so sexy it made her blush.

Hey, it's me. I'll text you later about meeting tonight. Not sure if I can get away, but I'll do my best. By the way, that was close this afternoon. Too close, actually. But . . . also kinda hot.

Tree laughed and tapped the screen to play the next voice mail. This one was from her dad, and she knew he'd be pissed even before she heard his voice. She wasn't wrong.

Teresa, it's your dad. I sat in that restaurant waiting for you for over an hour. I can't believe you would do this to me—today of all days!

Tree sighed and hit Delete, but somehow even her annoyance with her father had softened. He didn't get it. How could he? He was just doing things the only way he knew how. She glanced down at the gold bracelet on her wrist and made up her mind to call him back tomorrow. He might not ever understand, but that was the point of being a family, wasn't it? You didn't have to "get" each other to love each other. They'd figure it out and find their way through it. They always did.

She walked over the bridge and down a short incline toward the sprawling center park in the middle of campus. A rowdy group of students headed her way, going to a party or a game in the opposite direction. They were buzzed and amped up—girls laughing too loudly, a couple of guys with foam fingers that read *#1*, shouting school chants—each of them dressed in Bayfield crimson and with *B*s on their sweaters and wearing or carrying their Babies masks. Tree laughed at their over-the-top school spirit and shook her head as she passed through the middle of the bunch.

A curved staircase took her from the upper level of the path down to a loop that crossed under the bridge through a short tunnel. Tree stopped as she reached the bottom of the stairs and found the pathway under construction. It was being upgraded and had been cordoned off. Orange-striped sawhorses with yellow flashing lights and diamond-shaped Caution signs blinked out a warning about the torn-up path. She looked back up the stairs, but this was the quickest way to cross the quad, and she wanted to get there already.

She stepped in between the two sawhorses and noticed something ahead sitting on the ground in the dead center of the tunnel. It had been placed directly in a pool of light that came from one of the eerie LED lights that had been hung on the bottom of the bridge. As she stepped toward it, she heard a soft tune begin to play.

It was a music box.

And it was playing "Happy Birthday."

Tree stopped again and rolled her eyes. *Oh my god.* This was too much, but *bravo* on Danielle and the gang for trying. She turned to look back to see if she'd missed where they were hiding. Undoubtedly, they were going to try to jump out and scare the living shit out of her.

"Hey!" she called out up the stairs behind her. "You guys are hilarious. You can come out now."

Nothing made a sound except the music box.

Losers. She walked directly into the center of the tunnel, bending down to get a closer look at the music box. Three ceramic children at a birthday party leaned in to blow out the candles on a cake. Anchored to a carved wooden base, they were doomed to spin forever to "Happy Birthday."

If that isn't my worst nightmare . . .

Something *clicked* behind Tree. Startled, she spun around, expecting to catch her friends mid-scare. But it wasn't Danielle. Someone was standing just outside the mouth of the tunnel wearing a Bayfield Baby mask. Tree made a mental note, correcting her earlier thought: the mascot was not at all harmless and amusing.

Whoever it was wasn't moving and just stared at her through the eyeholes in the plastic. It must've been one of those morons she'd passed upstairs a minute ago.

"Yo," she called out. "I think your friends went the other way."

There was no response. The person just stood there, stock-still.

"Can I help you?" Tree asked.

Nothing. Just the yellow caution lights blinking off and on, illuminating the wide-eyed baby face of the mask with its single white tooth.

"Look, weirdo, I'm not scared." Tree was losing patience. "Why don't you go try this with one of the heifers at Delta Gamma? They're into cosplay."

Another long pause with no movement or sound from the creep in the mask. Tree decided it was time for a new tactic.

"Okay!" she said, turning up the volume. "I'm calling the cops."

That seemed to do the trick. After a split second, the Bayfield Baby turned and ran—though not back up the stairs as Tree had expected. Instead, she watched him lumber up the embankment leading to the upper level of the bridge that formed the tunnel. She could hear loose dirt underfoot and the sound of plants being trampled.

After a moment, everything was quiet. Slowly, she started walking toward the Chi Sig house again, looking behind her several times to see if the masked creep was back. A few seconds later, as she stepped out the other end of the tunnel, she checked once more to make sure she wasn't being followed. Satisfied that her threat to call the police had scared off the prankster for good, she turned at last in the direction of the party.

Behind her, the music box sprang back to life, close and awful like something sharp on the back of her neck.

She wheeled around, heart racing. She could hear her own breathing, and now she was pissed that she'd gotten afraid. She was about to run back into the tunnel and kick the damn music box against the wall when she felt a shadow fall over her.

As she looked up, the masked Bayfield Baby came crashing down from the top of the bridge, almost crushing her. At the last possible moment, she stepped to the side and pushed, knocking her attacker off balance. The glint of a long silver knife flashed in her eye, and she screamed as she scrambled away.

Tree had never run so far or so fast in heels, but she sure as hell was not going to look back. The path on this side of the tunnel was even more torn up, with double the barrels and cones blocking the way, and lights flashing caution in every direction.

Just when she could see the grass up ahead, the toe of her shoe caught on the edge of a wooden frame prepped for the crew to pour concrete tomorrow. Tree tumbled onto the bed of gravel, jagged rocks cutting into her palms and knees as a gash grew across her toe. The terror numbed her pain, and she rolled over, sitting straight up and frantically searching for any sign of the psycho with the knife.

A hand grabbed a fistful of her hair from behind, pulling it hard, yanking her eyes up. There above her was the Bayfield Baby's unwavering smile. She screamed as the knife was raised, up, up, up over her exposed neck and bare clavicle. With a flash, it entered her, and Tree felt the searing pain of the cold steel severing bone from tendons and muscle, slicing ribs away from her sternum, puncturing her lung, cutting into her heart.

She couldn't see anymore. The darkness came so suddenly that she felt a spasm of panic shoot through her. It was her last surge of strength. Flailing in the inky night, she pushed her attacker up and away—one final, desperate attempt at escape.

To her amazement, the weight holding her down disappeared. Tree shrieked at the icy fire of pain that engulfed her as the knife sliced back out of her chest the same way it had entered.

Choking and crying, she bolted upright, clutching the wound that ran nearly all the way through her body. With a gasp that felt like her lungs were filling with lava, she dared to open her eyes, terrified the masked lunatic was standing over her, toying with her, waiting to plunge the knife in once more and finish the job.

But she didn't see anyone with a knife.

Just a guy digging around under a desk in his dorm room. He turned around when he heard her sit up, gasping and wheezing.

"Oh, hey. You're up!" he said with a smile. "I wasn't sure if you wanted to sleep in or not."

7

Tree stared at the guy from a bed in a dorm room, still clutching the front of her shirt. Just moments ago, a knife had been lodged in her chest, but somehow she wasn't in pain now. Or in her own clothes. This wasn't her shirt.

What the hell?

She heard the bell tolling out the hour across campus, and out in the hall, a voice yelled, "Fuck off!" and somebody stopped practicing the trombone.

Her heart was still beating like she'd just sprinted across a parking lot to the sale rack at the back of Barneys. She took a deep breath and let the relief that she wasn't being murdered settle over her. *Jesus,* she thought. *What a fucking nightmare.*

Her phone started buzzing on the nightstand, and she heard that stupid ringtone again:

Yeahhh! It's my birthday, and I ain't gotta pick up the phone!

She grabbed it and looked at the screen. 9:01 a.m. September 18. One missed call from Dad.

Ugh. My birthday.

The call from Dad was typical. Still, Tree couldn't shake

a weird feeling that was gnawing at her stomach. Where had she heard that ringtone before? And hadn't her dad left her a voice mail . . . yesterday? Wait—wasn't it yesterday? She ran a hand over her face.

Pull it together, Tree.

The guy with the goofy grin was staring at her. She had to get out of his bed. God only knew what had happened there last night, and she wasn't about to let it happen again. Just in case that's where this was headed, it was time to move, and now.

She threw off the covers and stood up, reaching over to grab her pants off the dresser as he took a step forward to show her where they were.

"Oh . . . right," he mumbled as she pulled them on. "I folded your pants for you last night. You know, I wasn't sure if that material . . . gets wrinkled."

As she whipped off his T-shirt, he turned around. "Ahh—" he said, like he'd been caught. Tree didn't give a shit. She just wanted to get out of here, but he was still trying to exchange pleasantries.

"Don't know if you remember my name or not. You know you were . . . pretty wasted last night, but uh . . . I'm—"

"Carter."

Tree froze as the word came out of her mouth. He turned around, surprised. The goofy grin was back.

"You remembered!"

She stared at him for a second, her brain trying to put the pieces together. Had they met? Why did he seem . . . familiar? After a second, she reached down to pull on her heels.

"Oof. Tylenol."

"What?"

"My head is killing me," she explained. "Do you have any Tylenol?"

"Oh! Uh . . . yes." Tree watched as he turned toward the

drawer, then back to the dresser, as if he were trying to put his finger on where it was. He started to rummage around on the dresser. "Um . . ."

Her eyes narrowed. "It's over there." She pointed to the desk by the door.

"Right!" He hurried over to the desk and started digging around.

She sighed as she pulled down the zipper on the ankle of her pants. "It's over there, under your clothes."

"Right!" he said again, reaching under his stuff and pulling out the dopp kit. He retrieved the bottle and brought it over to her.

"Thanks," she said.

"Oh, and . . ." He reached over to grab a bottle of water, but she ignored it as she unscrewed the pill bottle's lid. "It's like you've been here before."

There was a joke in his voice, but Tree froze when he said it and looked up at him. It felt like that to her, too, but she had no idea where she was. The expression on her face must've given her away, because he stopped smiling and took a long look at her.

"Are you okay?" he asked.

She frowned and looked around the room, really taking it in. Her eye was drawn to the back of his door. Under the mini basketball hoop, there was a hodgepodge of stickers—music stores, comic book shops, a puffy hot dog with a googly eye. In the center was a bright blue bumper sticker that read TODAY IS THE FIRST DAY OF THE REST OF YOUR LIFE.

She couldn't take her eyes off it. Something about it made the butterflies in her stomach turn into Ping-Pong balls.

Carter was saying her name, asking again if she were okay. But she stared at the door as if she knew that something was about to happen.

Then it did.

She heard someone yell, "Dude!" just outside and saw the knob turning. A guy with bleached-blond hair burst through the door asking Carter a question. "You hit that *fine vagine* or wha—?"

He froze at the sight of her, and now her heart was racing again. She put the open bottle of Tylenol down on the dresser, grabbed her bag, and headed out the door as Carter stuttered apologies.

"I'm . . . I'm sorry . . ."

As she walked down the hall, she heard Carter's voice once more: "Nice one, dickhead."

Tree's head was killing her. She made a beeline for the lobby of the dorm, and as she pushed through the front door, she decided she had to stop overdoing it at parties. This whole thing was too weird.

What the hell happened last night?

As she walked toward the quad, she passed a guy who gave her a very judgy look. He was an art student, for sure, but she felt like she'd seen him someplace besides hanging around in front of the art building. She rubbed her eyes and kept going.

A girl pushed a clipboard in front of her and asked her to stop global warming. Tree had a fuzzy memory of seeing that bad hair somewhere else, but she couldn't place it.

She held up a hand and hurried on by. "Sorry," she said. "No, thanks."

Hurrying on, she saw a couple studying on the lawn. They got drenched as the sprinklers came on, scrambling to save their textbooks. Any other day, she'd have probably laughed, but today, it just seemed odd.

And familiar.

Oddly familiar.

She heard a car alarm going off and somehow knew it was coming from a red SUV even before she looked over and saw it. A group of pledges was singing "Ninety-Nine Bottles of Beer" on a patch of grass nearby. One had a sign that read TWENTY-SIXTH STRAIGHT HOUR, and their frat brother yelled at them to keep going. Tree felt a strange certainty that they must be on the verge of passing out from exhaustion.

Then one of them did, right onto the grass.

Tree watched him go down and slowed her walk. *Why does this day feel so weird?* she wondered. *Probably just too much booze. And whatever else had happened.*

Shaking it off, Tree decided she wouldn't give in to the anxiety in the pit of her stomach. Her head hurt from squinting in the sun with no shades, so she made straight for the covered walkway by the bell tower. Tim, this guy who'd been blowing up her phone lately, stepped out from behind one of the pillars. She stopped short.

He had a tight body, good hair, and a great jawline to boot. Even if their one and only date had been terrible, he was also kind. When he blocked her way and asked why she hadn't returned any of his texts, she just stood there for a second, blinking at him.

"Tim," she finally said. "What day is it?"

He frowned and glanced down at his watch, like maybe this was a trick question and he just wanted to double-check.

"Uh . . . Monday the eighteenth," he told her.

She squinted at him. "You're *sure?*"

"I'm pretty sure."

Nice one, Tree. For the love of Christ. Who walks around asking people what day it is?

"I . . . um . . ." Tree searched in vain for a plausible explanation for her crazy question, but after a second she gave up.

He took you to Subway *on your first date,* she reminded herself. She didn't owe him an explanation. That was for damn sure.

"I gotta go," she said and kept on walking.

"Call me?" he yelled.

She didn't turn around.

Quickening her pace toward the Kappa house, she couldn't shake the feeling that something was majorly *up*. What was it, though? It was like someone had shuffled all the memory cards in her head. She recognized her life, but it wasn't in the right order—like her brain had been shrouded in a fog that came from someplace other than a bottle of Cabo Wabo tequila.

Tree ran up the stairs to the porch, barely noticing Emily, who was sitting in the sun and listening to music on puffy white headphones. It felt like she was being chased, she decided—like in that fucked-up dream from the night before—only she didn't know what she was running from.

She burst through the front door of the house, rattling the ancient lead glass in every pane. As she darted up the staircase, she heard a voice that stopped her cold.

"Oh. My. *God*. You sneaky little bee-yotch."

I knew this was going to happen, Tree thought. *I knew it.* She was gripped by the sudden fear that maybe she had permanently damaged her brain at last night's party. *Am I still drunk?*

"Who was it?" Danielle demanded.

Tree turned around slowly and opened her mouth to say something, then closed it again. There was Danielle, glistening from whatever yoga class she'd just done in a bright yellow sports bra. *Exactly the way I pictured her*, thought Tree. Whatever the look was on her face, it must've alarmed Danielle, because her friend's tone suddenly turned serious.

"Sisters don't keep secrets."

After a second, Tree laughed. This was crazy. "I'm totally having déjà vu right now."

"Oh." Danielle crossed her arms like that was *nothing*. "I have it all the time. It's supposed to mean someone's, like, thinking about you while they're masturbating," she said matter-of-factly. "I have it at least five times a day."

Tree shook her head and pressed her fingers into the bridge of her nose. It felt like her brain was starting to liquefy inside her skull and perhaps she could stop it.

"Seriously," she said, trying to play it off. "I've been having it all day. It's so weird."

Danielle raised an eyebrow, and her tone changed to Big Sister. "Maybe you should switch to water next time, hon."

Tree sighed and slowly turned to head upstairs. "Thanks. I'll keep that in mind."

"What are sisters for? Oh! And don't forget . . ." Danielle waited until Tree paused halfway up the staircase. "House meeting at lunch."

A chill ran up Tree's spine. *Didn't we just have a house meeting . . . yesterday?*

Before she could ask, Danielle waved a hand at her.

"Hell*ooooooo*," she said, clearly exasperated. "It's been on the board since, like, last Thursday, Tree."

"Yeah . . . I remember," Tree said with a nod, but she suddenly wasn't sure if she did. Was she remembering something that had never happened? How had it all seemed so real in her dream? She tried to cover her confusion with a smile at Danielle and hurried up to her room.

Lori was ready for her shift at the hospital and writing in her journal at the vanity. Tree barely noticed her sitting there until she spoke.

"She finally rolls in."

Jarred out of her thoughts, Tree looked over at her roommate. This feeling was getting stronger, not disappearing. She wanted to try to explain it to Lori, but all she could muster was, "That's so *weird* . . ."

Lori eyed her for a moment, then closed her journal.

"You okay? You were kind of a mess last night."

A frown passed over Tree's smiling face. Doing both felt strange. So did everything else. She was on the verge of spilling it all to Lori when she looked at the clock on her bedside table: 9:20 a.m.

"Oh, shit!" She immediately pulled off her heels. "I'm so late for class."

Tree tossed on a sweatshirt over her shiny tank from last night, reached under a stack of mail to grab her book, then tossed it into her bag.

"Did you really think you could keep it a secret from me?" Lori asked her.

She turned around and saw her roommate holding a cupcake with a single candle burning in the center. Lori handed it to Tree.

"Don't you want to know how I found out?" she asked.

"Driver's license?"

"Clever girl." Lori smiled. "That picture, though—"

Tree interrupted her. "I gotta go."

Without waiting, she put the cupcake down on her nightstand and started to leave.

"But you didn't even blow out the candle!" Lori protested.

Tree closed the door behind her with some extra *umph*. If that didn't take care of the candle, Lori could blow it out herself.

8

Under typical circumstances, watching Dr. Butler's ass while he wrote physics equations on a whiteboard could make Tree feel better about anything.

These, it seemed to her, were not typical circumstances. After class was over, she didn't wait around to flirt like she usually did, and she could feel Gregory's eyes following her out the door. By the time she sat down at the house meeting on the dining patio, he'd already sent her three texts and left a voice mail.

Tree, on the other hand, was too concerned that she might be taking leave of her senses to give a shit.

As Danielle parsed the options for the charity drive, Tree sat sipping on her fruity zero-calorie sparkling water and mulling over the day's events. Were they this *particular* day's events? Why did everything seem so familiar? Like that voice . . .

"Get your school spirit on before the big game. Ten percent off with your student ID."

She turned to find Keith Lumbly sweating it out behind the merch table. Her eyes fell on the masks for sale. Those wide plastic eyes seemed to bore a hole right through her soul. She tried to think about something else—anything else—but scenes from last night's dream kept flashing into her memory. The longer she stared, the more paralyzed she felt.

"What's wrong, Tree?"

Danielle's question cut through her stupor of fear, and Tree was finally able to take her eyes off those damn masks.

"Um . . . I'm just . . . a little tired, I guess," she said.

"No, dumbass." Danielle rolled her eyes. "What's wrong with *that*?"

Danielle pointed at the lunch tray Becky had just plunked down on the table next to Tree.

"*So* not Kappa cuisine," she said with the air of a French aristocrat telling peasants to eat cake. "And is that *chocolate milk* I see?"

"I missed breakfast," Becky said quietly.

Danielle sighed. "We *all* miss breakfast, Becky."

Becky jumped up in a mushroom cloud of humiliation, picked up her tray, and turned to leave in a hurry.

It hit Tree in a flash. "Becky, look out!"

Tree was already moving when she said it, but it was too late. She felt the impact of Becky's collision with Carter behind her, and even though she ducked, Tree was still drenched with chocolate milk.

As Danielle sent peals of laughter across the quad, Carter scrambled to grab napkins from the dispenser on the table.

"I'm sorry!" he said. "I'm so sorry, Tree."

Danielle stopped laughing immediately. "You two know each other?"

Carter said, "Yes," just as Tree said, "No," and she slowly turned to look him in the eye. Something passed between them, some little understanding, and she could see that Carter had been able to translate her look of abject terror.

"We had a class together last year," he said. "That's . . . all." He was still dabbing at her with napkins. Tree took them from him to finish herself.

"Sorry again," he said, and he started back toward his dorm.

"Hey!" Tree jumped up to stop Carter, pulling him a few feet away from Danielle's prying eyes. Carter looked at Tree like she'd lost her mind until he glanced down and saw her open hand in front of him.

"My bracelet?" she whispered.

"Oh. Yeah."

Carter reached into his pocket, pulled out Tree's gold bracelet, and dropped it into her hand. He could barely look her in the eye, but Tree saw him steel himself against the embarrassment. He gave her a grim smile.

"I'm sorry again . . . about the mess."

As she watched him walk away, Tree closed her fingers around the bracelet. She was happy to have it back, but the only thing Tree could hear was the question tumbling over and over in her mind: *How did I know he had this bracelet on him?*

Finally, she turned back to the table.

"What a douchebag," Danielle pronounced judgment on Carter as she watched him walk away.

Tree decided she'd had enough house meetings to last a lifetime. She slipped the bracelet into her pocket, took a play out of Carter's book, and left the scene of the accident. She wasn't sure what was wrong with her. Was it psychological? Was it all in her head? Could it be medically diagnosed?

Regardless, she was going to see the doctor.

Tree paced back and forth in Gregory's office while she waited for him to arrive. Something about today didn't add up. It was like she could sense what was about to happen before it happened—maybe not exactly what was going to happen but that *something* was about to. It felt like she'd dreamed this entire day last night, and if that were true—if she'd dreamed this day moment by moment—did she already know how it would end?

When Gregory came in, Tree hurried over to meet him. As he quickly closed the door behind him, she reached around him to lock it.

"We can't do this," he said. "There's too much going on in the building today."

"I need to talk to you."

Gregory walked over and dropped his keys on his desk, then turned around and sat on the edge of it. "Tree, I know what you're going to say."

Tree felt a surge of hope as she walked over to him. Maybe he was more intuitive than she'd realized. Maybe he had an answer to this weird déjà vu moment she was having.

"You do?" she asked.

He took both of her hands in his and stared into her eyes. For a moment, she forgot where she was, or what she was worried about, or that she very well might be hurtling toward her dream-foretold death at the hands of a knife-wielding psychopath who ran around in a Bayfield Baby mask.

Gregory sighed. "It's normal for a young girl to have feelings for an older man. But you can't let it cross that line. You can't fall in love."

Record scratch. Tree frowned. "I'm not falling in love with you."

To her great annoyance, Gregory actually seemed relieved. "You're not?" He asked this with a bit too much glee.

"No," Tree said. "I've been having the weirdest day, and I—"

Gregory leaned forward and stopped her mouth with a

kiss. She leaned into the safety and security that she always felt with him. It was the thing that kept her coming back for more. It wasn't safety or security in their relationship; it was the knowing that he provided her. There was no doubt that he was turned on by her, and that was the thing that she needed to know, that no matter what the circumstances of their relationship, she was desirable. It turned her on to know that she turned him on.

His lips moved from her mouth to her neck, sending a frisson of excitement racing through her, but just before things went any further, she felt the overwhelming sensation that something was off—something she sensed was about to happen. Nothing was less sexy than a sudden sense of dread.

"Your wife . . ."

The words were a breathless whisper, and as soon as they left her lips, Tree felt Gregory stop—halted cold in his tracks.

"Okay. That's kind of a buzzkill," he said.

No sooner had the words left his mouth than they both jumped as the doorknob rattled. Stephanie called out from the hallway.

"Gregory? Are you in there?"

Gregory's eyes were the size of cafeteria dinner plates. "Thank god you locked the door!" he whispered.

Tree realized in this moment that Gregory thought this whole thing was a game. It wasn't that he didn't find her attractive (he did) or that he thought she was stupid. (Well, maybe, but who really cared? She didn't.) It was that he would always be this guy. Even in a crazy scenario where Tree actually loved him, and he actually left his wife for her, Tree realized that this was who he was: the guy who cheated.

Gregory swung the door open, and Stephanie peered into the office.

"Hey, sweetie! Didn't realize I locked the door," he told her. "Just wrapping up here. Have you met my student Teresa?"

He said it all a little too fast. Stephanie walked into the room, giving Tree the up and down.

"No," Stephanie said coolly. "I haven't."

Tree was already moving, her bag slung over her shoulder. "Nice to meet you," she said, blowing past Stephanie as fast as she could.

As she stepped into the hallway, she turned back and caught a glimpse of Gregory. He was smiling at his wife, playing off what had just happened by doing the loop de loop with his index finger at his temple—the international sign for crazy.

Tree wanted to turn around and yell, "I'm not the crazy one here, you thirsty asshole!" but she had to keep moving. There were bigger issues to deal with and not very much time before the clock struck midnight.

One of those issues was the party at the Chi Sig house tonight. She had a vague feeling that it was a bad idea. She wasn't sure why, specifically—only sure that she'd woken up from a dream this morning in which she was being murdered on the way to a party at the Chi Sig house.

Isn't that enough of a reason not to go?

Tree asked herself this question several times as she walked back to the Kappa house. When she got to her room, she clicked on the TV. *Teen Mom* was running (another) marathon on MTV. The title card made her think of her own mom, and she scrolled back to her favorite video on her phone. It was from Tree's birthday exactly three years ago. She was a senior in high school. Her dad was filming.

They were standing at the island in the kitchen. Her dad had brought home a birthday cake frosted with yellow flowers and green leaves. They sang, "Happy birthday to us!"

Sometimes people told Tree that it was crazy that she and her mom had the same birthday, but Tree had always considered it a special gift of fate—as if the universe had willed it so. Her mom always said that Tree was the most perfect birthday present she'd ever received.

As the video danced across the screen on her phone, Tree felt the stab of longing that only comes from being far from home on a special day. She watched as they blew out the candles. She could hear her dad call them his "favorite girls" in the background, and then her mom asked her if she'd noticed how great the cake smelled, and when she leaned down to sniff, her mom pushed her face into it.

She'd sat up sputtering frosting as her mom and dad giggled and yelled. She was laughing and scooping frosting off her own face and throwing it at them. It was a cake fight—the perfect picture of the woman that her mother was, of the woman that her mom had taught her to be. Fun first. No matter what.

Tree wiped away a single tear that was sliding down her cheek. That was when it became clear she had to go to the party. She could almost hear her mom's voice in her head: "Life is supposed to be fun. Fun first."

Fun first.

That was her mom's motto—and Tree would be damned before she sat around on the night of her birthday waiting to get killed by a dude in a baby mask.

Danielle strode through the door at that moment, picture-perfect except for the juice-can curlers in her hair. Tree frowned as she approached. Danielle was wearing her top. Before Tree could say anything, her friend read her mind.

"I know. I'm just borrowing it for tonight."

It was all too much. Overwhelmed by her déjà vu, Tree let her eyes wander to the TV screen.

"What time are you going to the party tonight?"

Danielle was saying something, but Tree was fixated on *Teen Mom*. There was something so familiar about all of this. *Was this show in my dream, too?*

"Hello? Earth to space-bitch."

Tree snapped back to attention. "Huh?"

Danielle did a super-mean imitation of a deaf person—voice and everything. "I said, 'What time are you going to the party?' "

Tree frowned. "I don't know. Later."

Just then, the lights went out. Tree yelled, "Oh my god!"

Moments later, they flickered back to life, but Danielle was having none of it. "Our tuition dollars at work."

There was something deeply unsettling about all of this. Danielle must've been able to see it in Tree's eyes.

"Chill out!" she said. "It's just another rolling blackout, sweetie."

"It happened before?" Tree felt confused. Had it happened in real life? Or her dream last night?

"Yeah, like two weeks ago," said Danielle. "Anyhoo, don't be too late, or all the cute Sigma boys will be taken."

Tree watched Danielle go, a mounting sense of dread making her stomach queasy.

She had to snap out of it before she left for the party. Maybe the dream had been just that, and the day was a total coincidence. Tree wasn't sure, but she wasn't going to take any chances. She had to get to that party. If the dream was real and somehow telling the near future, the next two hours were make or break—the difference between life and whatever the hell this was.

She went to her closet and pulled out a flirty little white

dress with polka dots. This would be perfect for tonight. She loved the way she looked in this dress—and the way people looked at her when she wore it. Maybe people had dream hangovers. Maybe that's what this was.

Fun first. If Mom had taught her nothing else, it was how to show up fashionably late and make an entrance.

9

Tree would've been lying if she'd said this didn't feel familiar.

As she walked to the party, she knew she'd been here before somehow. There was the warm breeze and the manicured sidewalks, the Bayfield Baby banners on every old-fashioned streetlamp. There were the voice mails:

Gregory: *That was close!*

Dad: *Today of all days . . .*

She saw the walking bridge up ahead and slowed for a moment. Everything was a little hazy. She tried to remember what had happened in her dream, but she couldn't get a clear picture. A group of students coming from or going to a game passed her. There was something about them she couldn't quite put her finger on. Several of them were wearing Bayfield Baby masks. She paused as they passed, then turned to watch them. One of them, dressed all in black, mask over his (her?) face, turned back and noticed her.

Tree's pulse quickened. Was this the killer? Was this the masked psycho who was about to make her dream a reality?

Someone in the group beyond yelled a name she couldn't make out, and whoever it was turned and followed along, hurrying to catch up to the group.

Tree took a deep breath and kept walking. Across the walking bridge, down the stairs, she turned right and—

Holy. Shit.

There it was. The tunnel. The path under construction. The music box sitting in the center playing "Happy Birthday."

She froze—but just for a moment. It all came flashing back to her. The music box. The masked psycho running up the embankment and dropping on her from the bridge above.

"No way." She whispered these words—perhaps to the unseen nutjob in the mask, perhaps as a prayer for safety. And now she was talking to herself.

Jesus, Tree. Pull it together.

She ran back up the stairs and took the long way around to the Chi Sig house. It only took another couple of minutes, and the paths were well lit. Still, when she arrived, every window in the house was dark. If this was a party, it was truly a slumber party, and someone had declared Lights Out.

Tree felt the queasiness return to her stomach as she approached. Had she gotten the house wrong? Had Danielle decided to play a trick on her for leaving the house meeting early today? She walked up the porch stairs to the front door and tried the knob. It was locked.

What the actual fuck?

She stepped back from the door and turned to check the yard on either side. Nada. This was super weird. She turned back to the door to knock one more time, except the door was open.

And the psycho in the baby mask was standing there.

Tree felt a flood of adrenaline she'd never experienced race through her body like a drug. Her scream was loud, and shattering, and perfectly timed with her punch—a right hook to the jaw. The killer in the baby mask went down.

And the lights came up.

Standing just inside the door was Danielle, along with every friend Tree had made at college. Behind them, the membership of every frat and sorority on campus. They'd all just seen her freak out and punch someone. At first, Tree didn't understand why they were all standing there in the dark, holding blue plastic cups and not making a sound. Then someone toward the middle of the crowd offered a half-hearted, "Surprise?" and she saw the banner above them that read HAPPY BIRTHDAY.

Nick Sims got up off the floor, rubbing his red, swelling cheek. "What the hell, Tree?"

Tree rushed inside to help him up. "Oh my god! I thought you . . . I thought I was . . . I'm so sorry!"

In the awkward silence, Danielle stepped forward, turned toward the assembled, and raised Tree's hand in the air like the victor of a prizefight.

"Don't mess with a Kappa bitch!"

When she shouted this, the crowd roared back to life. Someone cranked up the music, and there was a general rush forward to give high fives and hugs.

Tree was overwhelmed and so relieved. Her heart was racing, and she thought that she could've just had an actual stroke. But Danielle pulled her into a hug, and she hugged Danielle back. Something about it made her feel better, and invincible, and also, slightly silly.

Of course Danielle was going to throw you a surprise party, you moron. She chided herself, but only for a moment. She could feel her mother's approval beaming through every smile in the room. Life *was* supposed to be fun. Tree decided that for the next two hours, that's what she was going to have: as much fun as she possibly could.

She laughed and hugged Danielle and followed her to the bar for a blue plastic cup of her own.

Cocktails achieved, Tree and Danielle walked back to the center of the party. The two of them held court. They were, after all, the reigning leaders of the Kappa house, and Tree laughed so hard at one point that she had the conscious realization that she was having fun.

As she watched the guys play foosball and poker and with other girls' emotions, Tree realized that she belonged here. Danielle was a great friend—probably her best friend—and Tree didn't take that lightly. True, Danielle was a little psycho around the edges, but for the most part, the tallies landed in the "pro" column, not the "con" column.

And my god, Tree thought. *Who gets the entire Greek population on campus crammed into one crappy house for the birthday party of a girl they've hardly noticed walking to class?*

So, she took her place next to Danielle in front of the fireplace mantel that seemed to serve as HQ here at the Chi Sig house. They laughed and surveyed the scene, discussing the guys who sauntered by trying to curry privilege. After a little while, Danielle took a short lap around the ground floor of the party. When she returned, Tree could tell she was annoyed.

"That slut."

"Who?" Tree asked.

"Lori. She said she'd be here." Danielle shook her head. "She's so out of the house next year."

"I think she had a double shift," Tree said. She checked her phone. No new messages.

"Whatevs." Danielle was over it. "She's been boning some mystery guy."

Tree laughed. "What?"

Before Danielle told her who Lori was sleeping with (or how she knew this), something else caught her eye. *That's my girl,* thought Tree. *The shiniest object wins.*

Danielle nodded toward the hallway. "There's your stalker," she said with an evil grin.

Tree followed Danielle's nod and saw Tim, his triceps about to snap the sleeves off his V-neck. He took a sip from his beer and stared Tree down.

"He's so hot," Danielle whispered.

"Danielle!" Tree laughed. "That's so gross."

"Oh, okay." Danielle rolled her eyes.

Before Tree could protest any more, Nick appeared with a fresh drink and a charming smile, as if to say Tree's right hook to the jaw was forgiven—and he was ready to see what she had in mind for Round 2. Danielle took a step forward, wedging herself into the circle, but Nick didn't seem to notice her.

"Truce?" he asked Tree.

"Fine." She smiled back at him. "Why were you wearing that stupid mask, anyway?"

Nick shrugged. "Just showing a little school spirit. Didn't think I'd get clocked for it."

Danielle laughed loudly at this. Too loudly, Tree thought. Her friend was coming off as a little desperate. Tree waited for Danielle to finish flipping her hair and settle down.

"I really am sorry," she told Nick. "Did you ice it?"

"It's fine," Nick said, stepping between her and Danielle so they were face-to-face. He gave her a devilish grin. "You can make it up to me later." He gave Tree a knowing wink and then headed off into the crowd.

Tree watched him saunter away for a moment. She wasn't mad about his dimples or the way his butt looked in those jeans. When she turned back to Danielle, she saw the look of the ice queen fixed upon her.

"What?" she asked.

"Don't 'what' me." Danielle was pissed. "You know exactly what you're doing, Tree."

"Danielle—" Tree tried to stop her, but it was no use, and her friend stormed off in a huff.

Tree felt her phone buzz and checked the screen to find a text from Gregory:

Sorry . . . can't get away tonight. C U tomorrow?

Tree sighed and put her phone away. Glancing around, she realized she was surrounded by two kinds of people: the ones she hardly knew and the ones she hardly wanted to know. Maybe trying to salvage her birthday wasn't such a good idea.

Tree polished off her drink and put the cup on the mantel. At least she wasn't having weird premonitions about what was going to happen next. The vodka made her feel a little sleepy, and as she surveyed the party, she realized that she was tired of being alone in rooms like this, surrounded by people, and still, somehow, all by herself.

She started making her way to the front door. As she pushed through the crowd past the stairs, she glanced up and saw Nick just standing there, looking right at her. He flashed her a smile and jerked his chin up in the direction of the second floor.

Tree paused and smiled back.

The message was clear as day: *Follow me.*

Maybe it was the booze or just the confidence that came from feeling like she was on her own. Whatever the reason, she changed course and followed Nick Sims up the stairs.

10

The second floor was as crowded as the first, people making out in the hallway and running in and out of the bedrooms that lined the hall, doing god knows what.

She searched the crowd and finally spotted him waiting for her in a doorway at the end of the hall. As she started toward him, he flashed her a smile and disappeared into the room.

Tree walked down to the open door, crossed the threshold, and froze in her tracks. The entire place had been Frat-Brah'd to the max. A black beaded curtain and a white skull and crossbones hid the door to the closet. A fraternity paddle was mounted next to a dresser, which held a careful display of at least thirty empty Jägermeister bottles—each one kept as a trophy of individual triumph, in a living monument to blackout drinking.

Posters covered wide swaths of the wall space—athletes, cars, women in bikinis, and a surprising number of roosters in various shapes, sizes, and styles. Beneath one of the roosters over the bed, a full-size blow-up doll wearing a sombrero languished in the space by the window, her open mouth a permanent red *O* peeking out from behind the headboard. A light-up sign nearby glowed with the word *Applause*.

Tree was unable to stifle a laugh. Never before had she seen home décor so clearly penis-themed—definitely the work of a guy whose chief concern was crowing about his cock.

A blue glass bong caught her eye on the bedside table. She walked over and picked it up. It must've been over three feet tall and was surprisingly heavy.

"Wow," she said aloud.

The whole place was a veritable temple of peak fraternity brother. It was a shrine to a very specific college experience, the kind that cropped up years later with hashtags during confirmation hearings. In Nick's defense, she noticed his bed was made. Perhaps he wasn't a total lost cause.

There was still no sign of him. Tree guessed he must be in the bathroom or maybe the closet doing whatever it was he did before he tried to put the moves on a girl. Hopefully it didn't involve a scented body spray. She'd gotten hives once from making out with a guy on the swim team who was doused in that stuff. That would be a hard pass on her end.

She stepped over to the mirror above the dresser and checked her lipstick. She flipped her hair forward to give it some lift, and when she flipped it back up, she almost jumped out of her skin. Someone wearing that damn baby mask was standing right behind her.

Tree wheeled around, stumbling up against the dresser, the Jäger bottles clattering in protest.

"Shit, Nick! You scared me!"

She laughed, putting a hand to her chest where the knife had landed in her nightmare. Nick just stood there, still and silent.

The wide-eyed Bayfield Baby totally freaked Tree out.

"You want me to punch you in the face again?" she asked.

He didn't move a muscle or make a sound in response. Tree laughed, then took a couple of slow steps toward him. She pulled the mask up slowly to reveal Nick's boyish smile, the ever-present mischief dancing in his eyes.

He leaned in like he might kiss her, but instead, he said, "Welcome to the Pleasure Dome," and hit the button on a remote Tree now saw in his hand.

Instantly, the room was blasted with electronic dance music so loud that Tree thought her heart might stop. Flashing club lights mounted to the ceiling sprang to life shooting LEDs in every color at a mirrored disco ball. (*How did I miss* that *earlier?*) It was an all-out assault on the senses, and if that weren't enough, Nick started dancing. Or, rather, flailing around, looking insanely pleased with himself. Tree stood there mesmerized by how bad he was at this—not just dancing but also hooking up. She really thought he'd have more game. Instead, he seemed to be losing himself in the beat. Was she supposed to join him? That was not happening.

"It's a little loud, don't you think?"

Tree tried to yell over the music, but it was no use. Nick tried pulling her toward him to dance, but Tree's phone buzzed, and she saw the texts from Danielle:

Where R U?!

R U w/ him right now?!

She turned around and stepped over to the dresser to give Nick some space while she answered. He kept dancing behind her as she texted back:

No! I would never do that 2 U.

It was only a tiny lie, Tree decided. She technically was "with" Nick right now, but thanks to the Pleasure Dome, she would never be *with* Nick. Ever.

Another text from Danielle popped up:

I hope you both die!

Tree rolled her eyes as she read that message. When she turned around, all she saw was that Nick had stopped dancing and put that goddamn mask back on. That was it. She was out.

"Okay!" she yelled. "I'm officially over this. Have fun in the Sahara Tent." She walked over to Nick and got up right in his face so he could hear her through the mask and over this god-awful music. "C'mon!" she said. "Like, seriously, Danielle is freaking out."

His arm moved up, and there in his hand, where the remote had been, was a knife wet with blood.

Tree gasped and took a step back and stumbled over something. It was Nick. That was impossible, but there he was. His lifeless body was sprawled across the floor, a pool of blood growing under him so rapidly that Tree couldn't make sense of where all of it was coming from.

She looked back up. Whoever this was wearing the mask now had the knife raised in her direction. With a scream that even she couldn't hear above the music, she ran to the dresser, grabbed the fraternity paddle off the wall, and swung back as hard as she could. It was a direct hit right in the baby mask, and the psycho went down. The knife clattered away under the bed.

Tree ran for the door, but just as she had the knob in her grasp, she felt strong arms rip her backward, flinging her onto Nick's bed. She tried to crawl off the other side, but it was no use. The killer was on top of her now, pinning her down.

Tree screamed and kicked and felt the killer pause. She turned to see one of Nick's frat brothers standing in the suddenly open doorway.

"Get help!" she screamed, but her cry was lost to the blaring beats and he just stood there, holding his drink and swaying in the doorway. A slow, goofy grin spread across his face as he surveyed what he clearly thought was her and Nick getting it on.

"*Yeaaaaaaaaah!*" He raised his glass and turned back into the hall, closing the door behind him.

"You asshole!" Tree screamed, struggling to keep the killer's hands off her neck, squirming and kicking, scratching and biting, until she saw a hand reach over and grab the blue glass bong off the side table. Suddenly, the bong crashed down onto the edge of the headboard above her, shattering the end. The skunky smell of bong water flooded the room as the killer in the baby mask raised the broken end of the cylinder into the air high over his head.

Tree screamed one last time as he brought it down, closing her eyes tightly as the jagged edge of the glass ripped into the soft skin of her neck, just above her collarbone. Her whole body jerked and seemed to contort. She choked as her own blood filled her windpipe, the panic of not being able to breathe now added to the searing pain of a white-hot poker in her throat.

She grasped at her neck, trying to cough or gasp. Gagging and retching, Tree bolted upright, forcing her eyes open one last time to search for any sign that someone out in the hallway might possibly have heard her and come to her aid.

As the room came into focus, the music stopped. There were no lights or disco ball. No blow-up doll or applause sign. No Jäger bottles on the dresser.

Just some guy, rummaging under a desk in the corner.

11

Tree's scream brought Carter scurrying out from underneath his desk in the corner. She was crying and clawing at her throat. She could still feel the sharp point of the broken bong severing her arteries, but now a new terror overtook her.

There was Carter. And her pants folded up. She heard the bell tolling outside, and the trombone player getting told to *Fuck off!* in the hallway.

Carter rushed over to her, his mouth hanging open. "Is everything okay?" he asked, just as her phone started to ring:

Yeahhh! It's my birthday, and I ain't gotta pick up the phone!

Tree grabbed it and sent her dad's call to voice mail, then leaped out of Carter's bed, found her pants on the dresser, and started pulling them on as fast as she could.

Carter frowned. "Don't know if you remember my name or not. You were—"

"Pretty wasted?" Tree cut him off.

He paused, looking at her funny. "Yeah."

She pulled off his T-shirt, and he turned around shyly to avert his eyes. "And your name's Carter?" she asked him.

He turned back around. "Yeah."

"And we've *never* met before?"

He shook his head. "No. I mean, not until last night."

The tears were streaming down Tree's cheeks now. "My god," she said softly. "This is a nightmare."

Carter was insulted. "I'm sorry," he said sarcastically as Tree pulled on her sparkly tank from the night before. "*You* were the one who wanted to come home with *me*."

Tree didn't respond. There was no way to explain to Carter what was happening. She grabbed her phone and heels off the floor, tucking them under her arm, and raced for the door barefoot. Just as she opened it, the kid with the bleached hair came barreling in, still asking about her "fine vagine." She yelped as they almost collided with each other. He froze in the doorway, and Tree charged past him into the hall as Carter said, "Nice one, dickhead," behind her.

Stepping into her red patent heels in the lobby, Tree raced through the front doors of Williams Hall. Blowing past the judgmental art student, she pushed away the clipboard from the environmental activist girl, who was deeply offended.

"A simple 'no, thanks' would do!" she shouted, but Tree was already dodging the sprinklers as they soaked the couple on the lawn.

She felt like strong, murderous hands were about to wrap around her neck at any moment. Her heart raced and a cold sweat trickled down her neck. The car alarm made her jump even though she knew it was coming, and she raced by the pledge who collapsed on the grass as the fraternity brother shouted into the bullhorn.

When Tim stepped around the pillar to block her path, she shrieked. Was he the one? Was he the killer who had just stabbed Nick to death, all because he was angry she had blown him off? Had he killed her, too? He certainly had the arms to break a bong over a headboard.

"You okay?" Tim asked her. "Why haven't you returned any of my texts?"

Tree could only sniff and stare at him, her face wet with tears and mascara. After a moment, she raced around him without speaking, half running to get back to the Kappa house. She glanced back to see if he followed her. He didn't, but she still picked up her pace.

Finally back in her room, she swung the door closed and leaned against it. She closed her eyes and took a deep breath, trying to slow her pulse.

"She finally rolls in."

Tree ignored Lori and walked over to her bed, sitting down and doing her best to catch her breath. Lori closed her journal at the vanity and looked over at her with concern.

"Hey. You okay?"

Tree stared straight ahead, her mind racing. When she didn't answer, Lori called her name again and came over to her.

"Tree? Tree, what's wrong? Say something."

Tree looked up at her for a moment before she spoke. She felt like something was breaking open inside her.

"I feel like I'm losing my mind. I don't know what's happening to me."

Lori sat down on the bed next to her and put a reassuring hand on Tree's back. "Just calm down," she said softly. "Tell me what's going on."

Tree turned toward her and grabbed Lori's warm hand to keep her own from shaking.

"Lori," she said, her voice quivering with panic. "I know this isn't going to make any sense, but I have already lived through this day. Twice."

Lori frowned and looked up at the ceiling trying to formulate a response. "Tree . . ."

"No! Believe me, I know. It sounds crazy, but this is happening to me. I swear to god."

"I'm sure it *feels* like you're living through—"

"Okay, okay!" Tree interrupted her. She was desperate for someone—*anyone* to believe her. "You made me a cupcake for my birthday. Right? You're about to give it to me, and then later on tonight, there's a surprise party."

Lori wilted with disappointment. "Who told you? Was it Becky?"

"Nobody told me!" Tree was almost shouting now. "That's what I mean. Don't you see? I know what is going to happen before it happens!"

"Jesus," Lori whispered as Tree leaned in toward her, frantically whispering. The fear was overwhelming.

"Lori, somebody's going to kill me tonight."

Lori looked at her in total shock, and Tree felt the slightest tinge of hope that maybe, just maybe, she had gotten through. Then Lori's face cracked into a smile.

"Okay, I get it," she said with a laugh. "Who put you up to this? Danielle?"

"No!" Tree was sobbing and frantic now. "This isn't some stupid joke! This is actually happening to me. I don't know who's going to kill me tonight, but someone is. I just don't know who it is. I—"

"Tree! You're starting to freak me out."

"How do you think I feel?" she yelled at the top of her lungs, the frustration and the fear finally commanding her fully. Tree didn't care how crazy she sounded. Maybe she was losing her mind. Right now, the only thing that mattered was that Lori believed her.

Lori rubbed her shoulder. "Tree, look at me," she said in a soothing voice. "Nobody's trying to kill you."

Her response only made Tree more frantic. "Yes, they are!"

"Tree!" Lori raised her voice. "Look at me!"

A sinking feeling gripped Tree as Lori looked into her eyes and continued.

"I know today is hard with your mom and all," she said. "Why don't you skip class? Just take the day off and get some rest." Lori reached up with a gentle smile and wiped away the tears sliding down Tree's cheeks. "I promise you'll feel better tomorrow, okay?"

Tree gave up on trying to convince her friend. Finally, she nodded, and Lori finished getting ready for her shift at the campus hospital. Before leaving, she put the cupcake on Tree's nightstand and told her she was sorry that it wasn't a surprise.

Tree lay on her bed and stared at the ceiling. What had she thought was going to happen? No one was going to believe her. Maybe *she* was the only real psycho on the loose at Bayfield University. Her hand wandered up to her throat. She could feel her pulse hammering through her neck, right where the killer had stabbed her. Right where she imagined she'd been stabbed. How could it feel so real but be just a dream?

The helplessness that flooded through her at that moment threatened to paralyze her completely. Just before it did, Tree willed herself to sit up.

Maybe nobody would believe her, but that didn't mean anything was different. She'd lived through this day twice before, and no matter how things lined up, one thing was certain—someone was trying to kill her and would try again tonight. The only thing she seemed to be able to control was her own course of action. Something about that idea made Tree feel a little bit better.

She wiped her cheeks with her hands and stood up, looking around her room. She might not be able to change what was going to happen, but she could be ready for it.

12

Tree took Lori's advice to blow off her classes, but she didn't relax. After a trip to the local hardware store for a hammer and nails, she spent all afternoon in their room at the Kappa house, dismantling her IKEA nightstand. Several hours later, every window was covered with the boards she'd nailed over them. After pounding the last one into place, she stepped back to admire her work.

"Let's see you get in here now, asshole."

Next, she went about rearranging the furniture. Her dresser, not from IKEA, was as heavy as a tank. Groaning and grunting against the weight, she slid it across the door of the room, pushing it flush for good measure. As she did, a frame on top fell over. She picked up the picture and gazed at it for a moment. It was of Tree and her mom from the summer after senior year. They'd been out shopping for stuff to take to college. Her dad had found them relaxing on the front porch afterward and insisted on taking a picture. They were both smiling up at the camera. There was so much hope in her own eyes and so much love in her mom's.

Tree wished she could go to sleep right this second and wake up on that morning instead.

A hard knock at the door and somebody rattling the knob jarred Tree out of her thoughts.

"Tree?" Danielle's voice was loud and clear. "Why's the door locked?"

There was no way she could let Danielle in. She couldn't see the room like this. She'd never let Tree live it down. If she wound up living through this day at all.

"I just need some alone time."

"What time are you going to the party tonight?" Danielle asked through the door.

Tree grabbed her phone to check the time: 9:23 p.m.

"I don't know . . ." she began as the power surged and the lights went out, plunging the whole house into darkness.

"Our tuition dollars at work!" Danielle shouted her annoyance in the hallway. As the lights flickered back on, she continued, "Anyhoo, don't be too late, or all the cute Sigma boys will be taken."

"Okay!" Tree called back. "See you soon."

When Danielle's footsteps faded away down the hall, Tree glanced back down at the frame she was holding. She opened the top drawer of her dresser and put it on top of the clothes that hid her graduation picture. Then she flipped on the TV and took up her post on her bed. She wasn't going anywhere tonight.

As she'd boarded up the windows in the room, an idea had taken shape in the back of Tree's mind: If she survived the night, maybe she wouldn't wake up on the same day again. If she could avoid dying, she'd get a new tomorrow. It was worth a shot, anyway, and her room felt like a fortress now. If a killer was coming for her, well, good luck getting in here.

She snuggled in on her bed to watch some TV and picked up the cupcake Lori had left on the nightstand. Red velvet was her favorite, and it smelled delicious. Peeling off the paper wrapper, she started to take a bite but paused when she realized she was watching the same episode of *Teen Mom* for the third time (day?) in a row. Tree sighed and looked for the remote. It wasn't in any of the usual spots within arm's reach, and she dug around in the pillows and blankets for a second. No dice.

She put down the cupcake and crawled off her bed. Sometimes having a roommate really drove her bonkers.

Where'd Lori put the freaking remote?

She went over to her desk and started digging through the piles of books, papers, and mail. The black envelope she'd seen a couple of days ago when she'd found her graduation photo slid out of the stack, her name scrawled across the front in what looked like red crayon. Something about the fact that there was no stamp or postmark piqued her curiosity. She picked it up and flipped it over. There was a sticker on the back seal that read IT'S YOUR BIRTHDAY.

Tree tore open the envelope and pulled out the card.

ANOTHER YEAR OLDER AND YOU'VE STILL GOT GAME.

She flipped it open and saw that the inside was covered in illustrations of bingo cards. It was one of those talking cards, and a recorded voice called out bingo numbers: "G 48!" Something was set up to spin in the middle of the card, too, but it had been altered. The spinner, which it appeared was supposed to point to the numbers printed on the card, had been replaced with a picture of the Bayfield Baby. Its freakish smile whirled around and around, finally coming to a stop over the words *Have a lucky day.*

Beneath that was a handwritten scrawl that made Tree's heart pound in her chest:

Enjoy today . . . because there is no tomorrow.

Then, with no warning, the television behind her suddenly went dark. An icy stab of fear pierced her chest and tightened its cold grip around her stomach. Slowly, Tree put down the card and walked over to the TV. She turned the TV back on manually and reached down to flip the channel away from *Teen Mom*. The next channel was in the middle of a breaking news story, reported by a female reporter standing outside the emergency room of Bayfield University Hospital.

—where suspected murderer Joseph Tombs is being treated for a gunshot wound following a violent shoot-out this morning that left one officer dead."

The mug shot of a menacing killer with long, stringy hair wearing an orange jumpsuit flashed across the screen as the reporter continued, "Tombs had been the subject of a nationwide manhunt—

The screen went black again, and Tree jumped in panic. She looked around the room, noticing the bathroom, then the closet. Slowly, she took a couple of steps back to the bookshelf until she was close enough to grab the hammer she'd just used to seal herself inside.

A cold wave of nausea and anger swept over her as she walked with slow, quiet steps toward the closet, trying not to breathe. She cursed her own stupidity.

Damn it, Tree. Did you really not think to check the closet before you barricaded yourself inside your own room?

She raised the hammer and threw open the closet door. Nothing but clothes on hangers. Sighing with relief, she closed the door, but as she turned around, her eye was drawn across the room to a tiny movement through the open bathroom door.

Did the shower curtain just move a little?

This time, she walked even more cautiously across the room, hammer raised, her free arm outstretched. Her blood was roaring in her ears, and Tree wondered if this time she might just die from fear. She stepped into the bathroom and extended her shaking hand to the floral shower curtain, praying for the nerve to pull it open. Just as her fingers brushed the fabric, the TV blared to life, screaming a commercial into the room.

Tree jumped and spun around, running back into the room.

Who was turning on and off the TV?

The fact that the killer had the remote didn't hit her until she heard the breathing through the mask behind her.

Tree spun around to find the familiar figure wearing all black and the Bayfield Baby mask smiling in homicidal glee. Before she even screamed, the knife was raised and coming at her. She narrowly escaped the strike with a dodge to one side, and the blade dug into her mattress.

Swinging the hammer with everything she had in her, Tree cracked the killer on his shoulder blade and watched as he stumbled over the bed, disappearing in a heap on the floor. She ran to the door, pushing and pulling the dresser away, inch by inch until she could yank the door far enough open to escape, but it was too late. As she grabbed the knob, she saw the deranged Bayfield Baby charging at her, knife raised. She felt the blade rip all the way through her chest and splinter out the door behind her, pinning her to the wood. As she slumped against the steel blade impaling her in a white-hot pain, she let out a bloodcurdling scream that echoed in her own ears until everything went dark.

Even in the blackness, she could hear her own screaming, and it continued as she sat bolt upright in Carter's bed, tearing at his T-shirt in hysterics.

13

Tree couldn't stop screaming, and she saw Carter jerk up under the desk, hitting his head hard and joining her with his own yell of shock.

"What's wrong?" he asked, shooting out from under the desk. "What's going on?"

Tree had no words. She was frantic and jumped out of bed too quickly, doubling over in pain.

"Tree!" Carter reached for her. "Are you okay? Are you sick?"

Her cell phone started playing that ringtone, drowning out the last of the 9:00 a.m. bell chimes outside. Tree grabbed her phone and shouted, "Shut up! Shut up! Shut *up*!" before throwing it against the wall in rage. She grabbed her head, sobbing and shouting, "Oh my god! Oh my god! Make it *stop*!"

Carter ran over to her, alarmed. "Are you okay?" He tried to touch her, but she pushed him back.

"Get away from me!" she bellowed at him.

"All right!" He took a step back.

She pulled on her pants, still wearing the T-shirt Carter

had given her to sleep in, then raced to the door, flung it open, and ran into the hall. His roommate with the bleached hair flattened himself against the wall as she passed, and by the time she got out the front door, Tree was crying uncontrollably.

As she raced past all the events and people she knew would be waiting for her, she could barely see or hear them. Art student, activist, couple at the sprinklers, car alarm, pledge passing out . . . it was like she was getting tunnel vision. The world seemed to get smaller and smaller. She felt herself begin to hyperventilate. She was light-headed now, and her peripheral world was beginning to spin. She could feel the eyes of everybody on the quad staring her down. Every face was a frown. Every look one of disgust or of menace. She must look like a crazy person, but she didn't care. Who could she trust? Who would believe her? How could she ever make this end?

Tree was so dizzy, the ground shifting beneath her, that she felt herself pitch backward, right into someone who was walking behind her.

She looked up and saw it was Carter. He held out her shoes, her bag, and her shiny tank with the spaghetti straps.

"I'm sorry," he said. "You forgot your stuff."

Something about the kindness in his voice made Tree begin to cry. As everything spun around her, she collapsed into his outstretched arms that were full of her stuff.

"Help me," she pleaded.

As she sobbed against his green plaid flannel shirt, Tree felt his arms slowly close around her. She wasn't sure how long he held her there in the middle of the campus, letting her ugly cry all over him.

All she was sure of was that, for the first time in four days, she felt safe.

An hour later, Tree sat at a table in front of the huge windows in the Bayfield cafeteria. The glass went floor to ceiling, and the soft light that spilled through the lovely green trees cast a beautiful glow over the room. Midterms were approaching, and the place was mostly deserted; only a few tables had students wearing headphones and feverishly typing on laptops.

Tree stared down at the table and sucked the last few drops of her Diet Coke through a straw. She'd finally stopped crying, but she knew she wore the face of a raccoon beauty queen, smeared with a mask of melted mascara. At any other moment in her life, she'd never have agreed to come to a public place looking like this. She was still wearing Carter's T-shirt over her skintight black pants from last night's party, but she was unable to locate a single fuck to give within her. It was funny what you suddenly no longer cared about when the stakes in your life were turned up a notch.

Carter sat across from her, eyes wide and mouth hanging open in disbelief as he tried to process what she had just explained to him three times in a row.

"Would you stop staring at me like I took a dump on your mom's head?" Tree asked. She couldn't even bring herself to look him in the eye.

"I'm sorry," he said. "I'm just trying to wrap my brain around this."

"How's that going for you?"

"Assuming I believe any of this is even remotely possible, there has to be a reason you're stuck in this day. Okay? Out of all the other days in your life, what makes this day special? What gives this day meaning?"

Tree shook her head and shrugged, finally gathering the courage to look at him. "Nothing," she said.

The moment the word left her lips, her phone began to ring:

Yeahhh! It's my birthday, and I ain't gotta pick up the phone!

Carter pointed at the phone as Tree let her father's call go to voice mail.

"It's your *birthday*?"

"Yeah," Tree said like it was no big deal.

"Hel*lo*!" Carter was incredulous.

"So? Birthdays are just an excuse to eat cake and open presents. There's no real meaning behind a birthday."

Carter rolled his eyes. "It's *symbolic*. Whoever's killing you knows it's your birthday."

Tree wasn't convinced. Carter could tell.

"All right, look." He pulled a napkin out of the dispenser in the middle of the table and a pen out of his shirt pocket. "Give me a list of names of everybody who knows it's your birthday, and we can find whoever's trying to kill you."

"Well, thanks to my sorority, pretty much the entire school knows it's my birthday. They're throwing me this stupid surprise party tonight. I mean, it literally could be anyone."

"Who has *motive*?" Carter wasn't letting this go.

Tree thought about it for a minute. "Okay, maybe it's Danielle."

Carter nodded and started the list. "All right."

"I mean, I made out with some guy she liked right in front of her last night."

Carter paused and looked up at her briefly. "Oh." He nodded to the side and gave her a half smile. "Must have been before we met. Busy night."

Tree rolled her eyes. "Okay, Mr. I'm-Gonna-Take-This-Drunk-Girl-Home-and-Take-Advantage-of-Her. Don't judge."

"For the record," Carter leaned in, suddenly serious, "I didn't take advantage of you last night, okay? I slept on Ryan's bed."

Tree stared at him. "We didn't have sex?"

"No!" Carter seemed offended by the suggestion. "You

were wasted last night. I was afraid you were going to fall or choke on your own vomit like Janis Joplin."

Tree was tempted to smile at this last part, but she realized two things that made her pause: 1. Carter might be the sweetest guy in the world, and 2. he was kinda cute.

The guys she typically went to parties with were all after one thing and one thing only. She stared into Carter's eyes, and he held her gaze and stared right back. After a minute, he gave her a small smile. Suddenly, the awkwardness of shared attraction became too much for them both. Tree glanced out the window, and Carter looked back down at their one-name list.

Flustered, Tree wiped a hand across her cheek. "What were we—?"

"Suspects."

"Right! Suspects. So, Danielle. Gregory? His wife. Creepy Tim. Oh!" She leaned forward and pointed at the list as Carter scribbled down names on the napkin. "That tiny girl from T.J. Maxx that I got fired." She nodded and continued thinking. "Maybe the Uber driver I spit on last week. I think his name was—"

Carter looked up at her, a pained expression on his face.

"What?" Tree said. "Nobody's perfect."

He rolled his eyes and put down the pen.

"All right, look," Carter said. "The way I see it is, you have an unlimited number of lives, so you have unlimited opportunities to solve your own murder."

Now it was Tree's turn not to believe her ears.

"So, I'm just supposed to keep *dying* until I figure out who the killer is? That's your genius plan?"

Carter shrugged. "Do you have a better idea?"

Tree thought about it for a minute and discovered that she didn't.

As they left the cafeteria, Carter offered to walk her home.

"I'm fine," Tree said. "But thank you. Besides, I want to get started on the list."

"You'll be okay?" he asked.

Tree shrugged. "If I'm not, I'll see you in the morning."

Carter laughed and nodded. "And you'll have to explain this to me all over again."

Tree smiled. "Well, I guess it's a plus that you're such a good listener."

She couldn't tell for certain, but she was pretty sure Carter started to blush. He stuffed his hands in the pockets of his jeans and looked down at his sneakers.

"I do what I can." After a second, he looked up at her. "Good luck tonight."

As Carter turned and headed back to Williams Hall, Tree stood for a minute and watched him go.

Carter wasn't at all what she'd expected, and if it hadn't been for this damn time loop she was stuck in, she never would've spent more than those first few minutes of the day with him. Tree never would have given herself the chance to get to know Carter under normal circumstances, and something about that gave her pause.

How many people had she blown right past based on something annoying she saw on their outside: their hair, their clothes, the music they listened to, the car they drove, their body fat percentage, or the way they did their eye shadow?

Four days ago, she'd woken up for the first time in Carter's bed and had been horrified to be sleeping in a dorm room. She'd judged him instantly as not having enough money to live anywhere else, had decided he was a nerd because of the posters on his wall. She'd cut him off when he tried to introduce himself, refused to take the water he'd offered her when he'd brought her the Tylenol. He'd just been trying to be friendly, but she'd shut it all down because she'd been afraid she'd spent the night with a guy who wasn't up to her standards.

But now, she realized, she'd been wrong.

Not only was he "up to her standards," Carter was far more interesting than any of the morons she usually went out with. He was smart, funny, and patient. Who else would've ushered the campus basket case into the cafeteria mid-meltdown, gotten her a soda, listened to her insane story, and actually talked through how to deal with it in the event that it were true? Most of the people she called friends wouldn't have lifted a finger to help her once they saw the mascara running down her chin and the bizarre outfit she was wearing—let alone sat with her in the cafeteria while she sobbed and begged them to believe her unbelievable story.

As Carter turned the corner at the end of the courtyard, he glanced back at her and stopped for a second. He raised his hand in a little wave and smiled at her.

Now it was Tree who was blushing.

As he slipped out of sight, Tree realized that she'd never been caught staring after a boy like that. She was the girl who had game. She was the one who called the shots and never, ever gave a compliment first. She never let boys see her cry. She didn't let anybody know if she was feeling afraid, or sad, or . . . well . . . that she had any feelings at all, really.

That just wasn't who she was.

As she turned to walk back to the Kappa house, a new thought came to her: *Maybe that's who I'm becoming.*

For the first time in four days, she felt the slightest glimmer of hope.

14

Tree put Carter's plan in motion as soon as she got back to her room. After cleaning and organizing her desk so that she could actually sit at it and work, she made a list of the main suspects:

1. ~~**NICK**~~. (She crossed his name off immediately because, well, if he'd already gotten killed, he couldn't be the killer.)
2. **TIM**. Stalker-like tendencies. Mad I don't return his texts. Saw me making out with someone else. Judgmental every morning when he sees me walking home from Carter's.
3. **STEPHANIE**. Has caught on I'm sleeping with her husband.
4. **DANIELLE**. Mad that Nick likes me more than he likes her. I made out with Nick. Still angry about that guy freshman year.

It was something. That night, Tree started with Tim. She knew from previous parties that his room was on the ground floor of the frat house and had a window that looked out into the driveway. Of course, it was a long shot that he'd even be there, or that the blinds would be up, or that she could learn anything by looking at him through a window, anyway. Then again, that any of this was happening at all was a long shot, and Tree figured it was worth a try.

If Tim caught her snooping around, all the better. If he was the killer, he'd come after her and she'd either kill him, or at least wake up in Carter's bed knowing who she was after. If Tim wasn't the one, then the real killer would still come for her and Tim wouldn't even remember that she'd stalked him when today started all over again tomorrow.

She waited until it got dark and headed out when she saw Danielle beginning to put the curlers in her hair. Across campus, she crept up the driveway and found both Tim *and* his window blinds were *up*.

She couldn't see anything but his face, but he was kicked back with his laptop open, jerking off with a fervor that Tree found both impressive and a little nauseating. She felt totally gross spying on him, but there was something wildly titillating about watching a guy do something so intimate. The dudes she'd had sex with always tried to act like porn stars. It was rare that anybody was interested in pleasing her as much as they were into getting off themselves. What Tim was doing seemed so vulnerable. He wasn't putting on a show for anybody, and—

Bang, bang, bang.

Tim froze. Somebody was knocking on his door. Tree jumped in the darkened driveway like she was the one who'd been caught with her pants down. Tim yelled, "Hang on a sec!" and scrambled to put on underwear and shorts. It looked sort of painful as he crammed everything into his underwear and cracked open the door. Tree had to put a hand over her mouth to stifle her own laughter.

She crouched down under the windowpane for a bit. She didn't want anybody at the door to be able to see her. When she heard Tim close the door again, she slowly peeked up over the sill. Tim was at the sink in his room washing up, but that wasn't the thing that made her mouth fall open.

The screen of his laptop was facing the window now. He must have batted it in that direction as he'd scrambled for the door so nobody could see it from the hall. The porn he'd been watching was still playing, and now Tree could cross one more thing off her bucket list: watching two military men have sex.

Seeing gay porn on Tim's computer was like having the lights turned on in a dark room.

Tim had one of the best bodies in the school. He was smart, handsome as hell, had great hair, perfect eyebrows, wore T-shirts that actually fit him, and smelled nice. With all those things in place, Tree had been totally stumped as to why he seemed to have zero game with girls.

She thought of how offended she'd been that he'd taken her to Subway.

"What kind of place is that to take a first date?" she'd asked Danielle, who had collapsed in a puddle of laughter across Tree's bed.

Why wouldn't he take her there? *It wasn't a date at all.*

She felt a little wave of embarrassment that she existed in a world where she just assumed that everyone was straight. Of course they weren't. She'd seen movies from the '80s where being gay was this big shameful secret and coming out was a horrible ordeal. Even in the reruns of *Dawson's Creek* she'd loved as a kid, after poor Jack came out all he seemed to do was cry about it. But things had changed. There were kids in her class back in junior high who had come out, and nobody seemed to care. She certainly didn't, so she'd never considered that it might still be a difficult thing. Tree understood all at once, no questions asked, that it would be a *huge* deal for Tim. Sure, marriage equality was the law of the land now, but for a guy coming out to his fraternity brothers at Bayfield University? That was not an easy conversation.

The thought crossed her mind that just because Tim was watching gay porn didn't mean he was for sure gay, but . . . well, he certainly seemed to be enjoying himself, and it definitely made some puzzle pieces fit. Everything about their "date" was illuminated in different colors now—as if someone had applied an Instagram filter to the entire night and now she could see the whole picture.

When Tim had hugged her good night after they'd gotten back to campus, she'd actually been offended. Because he didn't try to make out with her, she assumed he was saying something was wrong with her. She'd tossed and turned half the night, imagining the shit he was saying about her to other guys. But it hadn't had anything to do with her. Was she so stuck on her place as the center of the universe that it had never crossed her mind that their lack of chemistry might mean something other than *Tim thinks I'm ugly*?

No *wonder* their conversation had been so stilted and lame while she'd watched him eat a meatball sub. He'd seemed so nervous—like he wasn't talking about anything he really wanted to be talking about. Now Tree understood why he hadn't.

Instead of actually talking to him like a human, she'd sat there sullen, pissed that she was on a date at a Subway. The more he tried, the more she shut him down until finally he was a stuttering pile of mush and disappointment. He couldn't have come out to her then. Nobody wants to divulge something personal to a total asshole. She was no different from the meatheads in his frat house.

Tim wasn't her killer. He wasn't mad because she'd been making out with somebody else. He wasn't texting her because he wanted to take her out again or try to get in her pants. The guy just needed a friend. Somebody who wouldn't blow his cover just yet but that he could trust with his secret. Maybe he'd just wanted to go drink rosé and cruise guys together at the mall while they hunted for bargains at Barneys.

Along with a twinge of guilt that she'd bungled the whole thing so badly, Tree actually felt some small blush of pride that she was the one Tim had tried to tell. Maybe she wasn't such a bitch on wheels after all.

Her smile didn't last long. As she took a step forward, a dark figure in the Bayfield Baby mask stepped out of the shadows and rammed a knife up to the hilt in her abdomen. She didn't even have time to scream.

Tree stumbled backward and coughed once, spraying the mask with a mist of her own blood. The killer stood there with his permanent one-toothed grin, watching as she slid down the brick wall beneath Tim's window, then turned and disappeared into the shadows.

The pain was a bright, hot fire in her stomach, but it wouldn't be long now. Tim turned up the music in his room, and she smiled. As the darkness closed in, she heard Carly Rae Jepsen singing "Let's Get Lost" and Tim singing right along with her.

At some point, the music changed, morphing into the ringtone she now hated more than any sound in the world.

Tree reached over and grabbed her phone off Carter's nightstand as he stood up from under the desk. Without saying a word, she pitched the phone directly into his trash can, then rolled over and tried to get a little more sleep.

15

Later that afternoon, Tree decided it was time for a makeover. She'd always been secretly jealous of girls who dressed and styled themselves for their own pleasure as opposed to anyone else's. Tree had always wanted to try a different hairstyle, but everyone always fawned over how great her hair was. She was a natural blonde, after all, and most of the girls she knew would have killed her in cold blood by carving her heart out with a spoon on a street corner in broad daylight if they thought they could have her hair.

The idea was that guys loved long hair and especially preferred blondes like her, but Tree saw all kinds of girls all over campus who seemed to get plenty of attention from guys and had all sorts of different looks. *Maybe,* she thought, *the problem is the kind of guys I'm trying to please.*

On the way back from Carter's dorm room, she made a quick detour to the beauty supply store. An hour later found her grinning into the mirror in her bathroom at the Kappa house. She went to work with a pair of scissors and a jar of bright pink Manic Panic. The result was the chunky, uneven punk layers she'd always wanted to try, strategic swaths of fuchsia layered around her face. Danielle was mortified when she stopped by the room to ask what time she was coming to the party, and a crowd gathered at her door to gasp and laugh as Danielle begged her to at least wear a hat when she showed up later.

Tree told her to get bent. “If I want to try something new, I will. I don’t owe anybody anything.” As Danielle stormed off, Tree added, “And don’t get anything on my top!” to laughter and a smattering of applause from the assembled sisterhood. One of the girls from down the hall had smiled and said, “See you tonight.”

“Only if you’re lucky,” Tree said. Then she pulled on an all-black outfit and grabbed the night-vision goggles she’d picked up at the army surplus store after she’d left Sally’s Beauty.

Tonight was Operation Stephanie, and Tree was going full military mode. She painted her face in greens and blacks and sneaked out the back stairwell of the house on her way to the hot teacher’s mansion.

Gregory was a teacher but also a doctor, and Stephanie clearly came from family money. The good doctor would be at the hospital tonight, so Tree parked several blocks away and crept through the hedges of the neighbor’s backyard.

She stationed herself at one of the two enormous fountains that flanked the circular drive at Chez Butler. She wasn’t sure how long she’d be there or what exactly she was looking for. She didn’t have to wait. Dressed to the nines in a designer dress and cape, Stephanie descended the front stairs to the car that had arrived. She paused briefly, turning back to the house, then dug a phone out of her clutch. Something about her demeanor suggested to Tree a woman who thought she was being watched—or perhaps was watching someone else.

Regardless, there wasn’t much more to see. Stephanie

ducked into the car and was carried out of sight, probably to a fund-raiser where she'd donate the cash for the wing of a building or a shelter for at-risk youth.

Tree groaned and pulled off the goggles as Stephanie's car turned out of the drive. This was a total bust. She turned around and walked down the two steps ringing the fountain's shallow pool, steeling herself for the scratchy journey back through the neighbor's hedge. She wondered if there were another way back to her car.

The answer presented itself in the form of her killer, who burst out of the hedge at that precise moment. She screamed because that damn baby mask scared the shit out of her every single time. The killer flew at her across the short yard and tackled her directly into the fountain. Strong arms closed around her throat as she kicked and thrashed in the two-foot pool beneath the tinkling Gothic spray. As she choked on the water that flooded her lungs, she remembered her mom saying once that babies could drown in six inches of water. *Turns out babies can also drown someone in two feet of water.* She might even have laughed if she hadn't been dying.

She came to, with long, blond hair once again, coughing, gagging, and heaving in Carter's bed.

"Oh, hey. You're up!" was all Carter got out before she vomited a torrent of fountain water all over his floor.

While they mopped up the mess with every towel that he owned, she explained to him that it was not tequila, and why. It took a while for him to get it, which was fine. It was a big mess.

This was the shape of her days now, it seemed. Or, well, her *day*. She'd spend a few hours with Carter, explaining what was happening to her and convincing him it was real. She'd tell him that the idea to figure out who the killer was had been his, and she'd fill him in on her progress with the suspect list.

She hated the part where it was time for her to go find the next suspect. Each time she left, she carried with her new memories of Carter—his likes and dislikes; the lines from movies he liked to quote; the things she said that had made him laugh—but knew that if she woke up here again tomorrow, he'd only remember her as the drunk Kappa Pi from the bar last night.

In the midst of days that all ended the same, over and over, Carter was the one constant Tree had come to rely upon. It was a revelation to her to meet a guy "for the first time" without having to employ any of the defenses she'd developed over the years. She didn't have to worry that he might be a jerk, or a dummy, or take advantage of her in any way. Each time he pulled his head out from underneath that desk, doing whatever he was doing under there, she already knew that she wouldn't later have to tell him to pull his head out of his ass. She realized somewhere along the way that this lack of fear—this lack of being forever on guard—changed the way she related to him.

She didn't have to fear that he'd treat her like an infant or an idiot (like a great number of her dates). She didn't have to fear for her physical safety (as she had on more dates than she cared to count).

Instead, she was able to relate to him in a way she'd rarely related to any man in her life: as an equal.

It was magical.

Tree began to wonder what the world would be like if every girl on campus could have the experience of *knowing* that the guy she was meeting for the first time would treat her with respect and do her no harm.

What might the world look like then? How would that change her relationship with other women?

Tree already knew it had started to change her relationship with herself.

She helped Carter haul the wet towels down to the laundry room on her way out.

"Thanks for the help," he said, then offered to walk her back to the Kappa house like he did every day.

She told him she'd be fine and that she'd see him tomorrow.

He frowned. "Not if it works."

"What do you mean?"

"If you kill the killer, then tomorrow will be tomorrow, not today, and you won't wake up in my bed."

She smiled. "Carter, I know where you live."

He did that thing where he stuffed his hands in his pockets and looked at his sneakers.

"Okay, then," he said. "Good luck out there tonight."

16

Danielle was the next name on the list of possible suspects, and Tree's attempt to determine if the president of Kappa was more enemy than friend left her feeling as muddled as their relationship.

After the house meeting on the patio, she walked with Danielle back to the house. Danielle was speaking exhaustively about how exhausting something was, and Tree let her mind wander. There had been a time when she'd hung on every word Danielle had to offer, but now she seemed to find less and less of interest in things that Danielle found endlessly fascinating.

As they walked, a basketball player Tree recognized passed by and bumped into Danielle, who dropped every single book she was carrying. He kept walking, even after Danielle yelled, "Asshole!" at him. Or maybe, Tree thought, *because* she yelled, "Asshole!" at him.

Regardless, Tree bent down to gather up the textbooks, folders, and notebooks that Danielle insisted on carrying to class in her arms instead of a backpack.

Danielle's disdain for book bags of any kind was well

known. "I will not have the straps of a JanSport ruin the line of my top." And so she carried her books against her chest like Sandy in *Grease!*—waiting, no doubt, for her Danny Zuko. *Or, more likely*, Tree thought, *her Kenickie*.

As Tree gathered up the books, a black envelope fell out of one of them. It didn't yet have Tree's name scrawled on the front in red crayon, but otherwise, it was exactly the same card she'd found on her desk three days ago. Or, on this same day, three times ago. *Oh, fuck it*. Tree stood up with the card in her hand and grabbed Danielle's hair.

"You *bitch*!" she shouted.

Danielle screamed as Tree started punching her in the face. Danielle grabbed Tree's hair, too, and both of them ended up on the ground. Tree wasn't sure what had come over her except perhaps the rage of someone who was face-to-face with her killer.

She and Danielle tumbled into the grass by the sidewalk, trading wild blows. Tree rolled to the curb, and as Danielle scrambled to keep a grip on her, both of them fell out into the street.

"I knew it was you!" Tree straddled Danielle and hit her in the nose.

Danielle grabbed Tree's hair to hold her there and screamed back, "I'm going to *kill you*!"

Which was when they both heard the horn blaring and looked up to see the blue city bus speeding toward them.

The horn blaring in her ears was quickly replaced by the toll of a bell, and Tree let loose with a full-body spasm of rage. Carter leaped from his place under the desk and arrived at his bed to find Tree screaming into a pillow.

Tree was furious with this process. She had so little to go on. Was that the same card she'd found on her desk? Did Danielle scrawl her name across it later and leave it for her?

Or was that what the invites to the surprise party looked like? Had everyone gotten one of those?

Does it even matter if I find the killer?

But there was no guarantee that identifying and killing her killer in the Bayfield Baby mask would free her from this day. What if she was doomed to live this day on repeat for the rest of time, regardless of what she did about her killer? What if that person would always be stuck in this loop, too?

Chances were high that it didn't matter at all.

Maybe nothing did.

While Carter did that charming thing where he tried to find her Tylenol, Tree pulled off the T-shirt he had loaned her. But this time, her own interior existential crisis took over, and she didn't put on her own shirt. Instead, she kept stripping clothes off. As Carter stood there with his back to her, being chivalrous and offering her privacy, she unhooked her bra, took off her underwear, and flung open the door to the freshman with the bleached-blond hair who was now both paralyzed and, for the first time, speechless. She spoke for him:

"Check out my fine vagine for yourself, dickhead."

She smiled sweetly and walked down the hall to an electric guitar only she could hear.

Pushing through the front door of Williams Hall in her birthday suit, on her actual birthday, was one of the most liberating things she'd ever experienced. As she walked naked across campus, Tree understood that she could live a life where there were no consequences. She could do anything that came into her head. What if the campus police came running over and arrested her right now? Hell, she could be put in a maximum-security federal penitentiary, and the killer would still come for her, mask and all. There was no stopping it. Tomorrow morning would always be another version of today, and she'd find herself right back in Carter's bed at 9:00 a.m.

As she marched up the Kappa stairs, Danielle, alive and well again, appeared behind her and gasped. Tree turned around on the stairs and stood there, letting the Kappa president drink it all in. For a few moments, Danielle was completely speechless. Finally, she managed to utter the words, "What are you doing?"

Tree shrugged as several other girls gathered in the hallway inside the front door.

"I didn't feel like walking across campus in last night's going-out clothes."

She waited for a second as everyone took this in, and then Danielle busted out laughing.

"Holy shit!" she yelled, then charged up the stairs, wrapping Tree in a giant bear hug. Turning to face the girls downstairs, she raised Tree's hand just like she'd done at the party the other night.

"Don't mess with a Kappa bitch!"

Tree smiled and looked at Danielle, who leaned over and whispered in her ear, "Girl, you're my hero."

Tree kissed her cheek and marched up to her room to find some sweats. Danielle wasn't a killer. Maybe she would hire a hit man, but even that seemed like a stretch. Danielle was like Vegas—she had a particular bent toward things that really weren't that shocking. Just like Vegas was the place where good Christian folk went to get "sinful" but saw topless dancers you could find anywhere, so, too, Danielle was as basic and as harmless as they came. Sure, her tongue was a razor and she could slice up your self-esteem if you let her, but cold-blooded murder? The girl just didn't have it in her.

That night, with all the suspects crossed off her list, Tree decided to see if she could just outsmart the killer without knowing who it was.

She grabbed a baseball bat that had been left in the hall closet and set out to the party tracing the exact route she'd taken that first night. She found a big tree to hide behind near the mouth of the bridge where the music box was playing and waited until she saw a large shadow darting toward her in the moonlight.

Tree sneaked up behind the killer from the opposite side of the bridge and swung the bat with every ounce of strength she could muster.

The body hit the ground with a thud, and Tree turned it over so she could pull off the mask and settle this once and for all.

Only there was no mask.

Just Becky.

Having to suffer through Danielle's house meeting food-shaming of Becky over and over again was one of Tree's least favorite parts of this endless day. And now, Tree had knocked her out cold.

Why was Becky darting around like that?

Tree dropped the baseball bat and got on her hands and knees. On the ground, scattered around Becky's body, were a dozen doughnuts and a crumpled pink bakery box. Girl was sneaking in sweets while everyone else was out of the house.

The remorse that coursed through Tree was overpowering. She started smacking lightly at Becky's face, begging her to wake up, and calling her name. She checked Becky's pulse to make sure she was still alive and that she was breathing. Then Tree pulled her phone out of her pocket to call 9-1-1, reaching around to find the bat so she could explain to the police.

But the bat was gone. Tree never saw it again.

The killer hit her with it from behind.

The blow knocked her so hard she seemed to fly high into the air, and the ground disappeared beneath her. As Tree fell back to earth, she saw Carter's bedroom far below her and dropped directly into his bed, her head landing gently on his pillow.

17

Tree opened her eyes and winced. The trombone. The bell. Carter's butt sticking out from under the desk.

Here we go again.

She sat up slowly, rubbing the side of her head, most recently bashed in by her own bat. Carter turned around.

"Oh, hey. You're up! I wasn't—"

"Your plan totally sucks." Tree stood up and grabbed her pants.

"What?" Carter asked.

Lately, this was where the explanation began. She'd get his attention by telling him where stuff was in his room, or what his roommate, Ryan Phan with the bleached-blond hair, was going to yell when he burst through the door.

But today, she was tired and sore, and standing up required no small effort. Tree felt like she'd been run over by a truck, repeatedly. As she pulled on her clothes, Carter gave his typical opening speech.

"Don't know if you remember my name or not. You were . . . pretty wasted last night, but, uh . . . I'm Carter."

A sharp pain hit her right in the stomach and Tree gasped, planting her hand on the dresser to steady herself.

"You okay?" Carter asked.

Tree bent down to get her shoes off the floor. "Never better."

She took a deep breath and started shuffling toward the door, but the pain shot through her again, and she stopped to grab at her stomach.

"Are you sure you're okay?" Carter asked.

"Fine."

Tree reached the door just as Ryan burst in shouting about her fine vagine. She saw him freeze and begin to apologize, but something was happening, and she couldn't understand his words. Then his face went fuzzy like the sounds that were coming out of his mouth.

As her legs buckled, Tree pitched forward into Ryan's arms, and everything went dark.

For the first time in what felt like years, Tree woke up someplace other than Carter's dorm room. A thick silence filled the air around her, punctuated only by the shrill and steady sound of:

Beep . . . beep . . . beep . . . beep . . .

Her vision was blurry, but across the room, a door opened, and a shadowy figure walked in. As he drew closer, Tree could see the mask of the Bayfield Baby covering his face. She opened her mouth to scream, but no sound would come out. Outstretched arms reached toward her, and then her vision focused on a face.

No deranged baby mask.

Only Carter.

"Hey," he said softly. "Easy there."

Tree felt Carter's gentle touch on her shoulder. She looked

around the room, saw the heart monitor beeping next to her, suddenly aware of her surroundings.

"What happened?" she asked.

"You collapsed this morning."

"What day is it?"

"Monday," Carter said.

Tree got more specific. "What's the *date*?"

"It's the . . ." He thought for a second. "It's the eighteenth."

Tree closed her eyes with a sigh. *Goddamn it.*

"We've been trying to get in contact with your parents," Carter said. "But for some reason—"

Carter stopped short as the hospital was plunged into a blackout.

Right on time, Tree thought. *Nine thirty-two p.m., anyone?*

A second later, the lights flashed back on, and she saw Gregory had stepped into the room behind Carter.

"Can I help you?" he asked.

Carter jumped as if he'd been electrocuted. "Jeez!"

"It's okay," Tree told Gregory. "He's a friend."

Tree saw Gregory narrow his eyes at Carter. *Was that suspicion?* The thought seemed ludicrous, but she'd been around enough guys to know how petty they could be. Gregory was jealous.

She watched Gregory's smug air as he announced that Carter had to leave. "Sorry. Visiting hours are over."

Carter nodded. "Got it."

He turned to go, and Tree was sorry he was leaving.

"Thanks, Carter."

Carter stopped in the doorway and turned around as the biggest smile spread across his face. Tree realized that he was pleased because she knew his name. He had barely introduced himself before she'd fainted that morning. He had no idea that they'd spent hours together for the past seven days. She knew far more about him than just his name.

"Feel better," he said. Then he disappeared out of the room.

"When am I going to get out of here?" Tree asked Gregory, who was leafing through a medical file.

"I'm having a hard time pulling your medical records."

"Why?"

Gregory flipped open an iPad and sat down in a chair next to Tree's bed.

"We just got these back from the imaging," he explained. He pointed at several different lines around her lungs on the images. "These are signs of major trauma. Given the severity of the scar tissue and the size of the lesions . . ." His voice trailed off for a moment, and Tree waited. "This is going to sound crazy, but you should be dead."

Tree felt the panic rise inside her. The *beeps* of her heart monitor got faster. She sat up and began pulling at her IV. Gregory was immediately on his feet.

"Hey, hey, hey. What are you doing?"

"I need to get out of here." Tree was not asking permission.

"No way." Gregory was adamant. "You need to stay here for observation."

Tree started to panic. "If I don't get out of here, I'm going to die."

"Tree, listen to me. You are absolutely safe here." Gregory shushed her as if she were a baby and brushed a strand of hair out of her face. "I won't let anything happen to you."

Tree licked her lips.

"I'm really thirsty," she told him. "Could you get me a soda?"

"Sure."

He leaned over and planted a light kiss on her forehead. Tree smiled at him as he made his way to the door.

The minute he was gone, so was she.

Tree rounded the nurses' station on the fourth floor without making a sound. The nurse, Deena, was working a night shift by herself, so there was no one to listen to her complaints. Instead, she lost herself in a book and only half turned around when Tree sneaked by on tiptoe.

As Tree reached the door of Gregory's office, she glanced down the hall. The police officer wasn't there. Wherever he'd gone, it couldn't be far. A steaming cup of coffee was sitting on the floor right next to his chair.

Tree pushed open the door of Gregory's office, closing it gingerly behind her. Once she was inside, she went straight to the old leather-bound cigar box where Gregory always dropped his keys.

It was empty, and Tree whispered a curse. Moving around to the back of the desk, she pulled open the middle drawer but found nothing. She tried again, yanking at the side drawer.

Bingo.

Gregory's keys were sitting in an upper tray. As Tree grabbed them, she looked down and saw something else. Pushing back the upper tray, she pulled something out of the lower compartment in the drawer.

A Bayfield Baby mask.

Tree instantly dropped the mask and slid the drawer closed. Her eyes filled with tears as the horror of the situation swept over her. At one point, she'd actually considered developing feelings for Gregory, and he was the one trying to kill her?

As quietly as possible, Tree poked her head out the door of Gregory's office to make sure that the coast was clear. Cautiously, she headed down the corridor toward the stairwell that led to the parking deck. She'd walked this way a hundred times in the past two years, but something about tonight made it terrifying. Perhaps it was dying and dying and dying this past week or just that someone kept killing her. She pushed past a swinging door in a darkened back hallway. She could see the light from the stairwell to the parking deck up ahead. Tree quickened her steps, and just as she did, Gregory opened the door to the stairwell and stepped into the hall.

Tree froze.

Gregory approached her slowly as if she were a rabid dog who might attack.

"Tree? Tree. It's okay. It's just me."

She was about to scream. She wanted to yell at the top of her lungs, *Why did you kill me?*

Before she could, the masked killer appeared behind Gregory. The frozen grin, still and menacing over the raised blade.

Tree pointed behind him, but she couldn't even shout his name.

His perfect blue eyes went wide as the blade disappeared in his back. Then they closed forever as he crumpled into a lifeless heap on the linoleum.

Tree screamed as the killer ripped the knife from Gregory's back. She was already running and could sense the killer chasing after her. He gained at every turn until that ghoulish mask with a menacing smile was floating just behind her. She cut a sharp corner around an empty nurses' station, and the knife flashed just past her, the killer tumbling with it into a whiteboard covered in medical orders.

At the next corner, Tree rolled a gurney into his path. It wasn't much, but it tripped him up before he could shove it out of the way. It bought her a few precious seconds as she reached the door of the fire escape and raced down the stairs.

Tree's lungs and abdomen were on fire. Her head pounded. Above her, the killer had entered the stairwell now and was flying down the stairs. Tree gave every last ounce of strength she had and finally reached the ground floor. She raced into the parking deck and immediately hit the button on Gregory's key fob.

The telltale *boop-boop* sounded one row past the stairwell door in the far corner. She raced down the ramp to that row and pressed herself against the back of a support pillar as the killer burst through the stairway door behind her.

All was quiet as the killer started creeping across the garage. She waited for as long as she dared before peeking around the column. She saw the baby mask, half a level up. Without making a sound, she bolted from her hiding spot, staying low behind the parked cars, peering through their windshields at the killer. Finally, she was close enough that she had to punch the fob button once more, or risk passing Gregory's car and never escaping this psycho.

The *boop-boop* brought the killer racing down the ramp to her level. Tree had one chance, and this was it.

She sprinted from behind an SUV for the silver Mercedes in the corner. The killer was on the other side of the same row and running full tilt, trying to beat her to the car. Tree wasn't going to make it, but as she rounded the front of the car and dove for the driver's-side door, the baby mask dropped out of sight. The killer had slipped and fallen in a puddle of oil behind the car. That was all Tree needed to leap into the car, slam the door closed, and lock it.

Immediately, the killer was up again, hammering the handle of his knife in the driver's-side window. Tree fumbled the key into the ignition, battling to turn the car on. Just as the engine growled to life, one final blow from the knife shattered the window.

Safety glass shards pebbled her face and body as she reached for the gearshift. The killer grabbed her by the neck, and as she pulled the car into reverse, Tree screamed and slammed on the gas.

The smell of burning rubber filled the garage as Gregory's Mercedes hurtled backward into another parked car. Tree threw the car in drive and stomped on the pedal as hard as she could. The car shot forward, and Tree raced down the ramps, sending the killer diving out of her way.

As she floored it out of the parking exit and onto the open road, Tree watched the rearview mirror. She was certain at any moment that the killer would come roaring up behind her.

But no one followed.

Tree felt a sense of euphoria whip through her unlike any happiness she'd known before. Tears coursed down her cheeks as she hurtled farther and farther away from the danger. This was the thrill of survival. It was the ecstasy of staring certain death in the face and finding an escape.

"I did it." She whispered the words aloud at first. They grew louder each time. "I did it! *I did it!*" She whooped at the top of her lungs, a long loud, "Waaahoooo! Catch me now, bitch!"

Tree slammed her foot down as hard as she could on the gas pedal and sped away into the night.

18

Tree's celebration lasted until the flashing lights appeared in her rearview mirror. As she eased Gregory's car onto the shoulder of the road, there was only one thing to say:

"Shit."

The cop sauntered up to her shattered window, and she flashed a smile. The name tag on his uniform read SANTORA.

"I know I was speeding, Officer." Tree thought that perhaps if she were cooperative, he'd let her off with a warning and she could keep driving into a new tomorrow.

"Turn the engine off, please."

Tree complied with a meek, "Yes, sir."

"License and registration."

Tree felt her stomach sink. This was not going to end well.

"I don't have them," she said.

"Pardon?"

Tree decided that if she were ever going to throw herself upon the mercy of anyone, it might as well be now.

"Someone is trying to kill me again!"

She blurted out the words and watched them have a less-than-ideal effect on Officer Santora.

He frowned and repeated the last word she'd said as a question. "Again?"

"Yes! I mean, no!" Tree reached for the explanation that would make the most sense. "He's tried before, but this time I got away; I didn't have time to grab my clothes, and my driver's license was in my pocket."

Santora grabbed the flashlight off his belt and shined it in Tree's face. She squinted back, unsure what was happening.

"Ma'am, are you under the influence of alcohol or any other controlled substance?"

"No! That is what I'm trying to—" Tree stopped short as an idea took shape. "If I am," she asked, "will you arrest me and lock me in a jail cell?"

Santora nodded. "That's usually how it works."

"I'm drunk!"

Tree almost shouted the words. The plan was genius. He could take her back to the station, and she'd be safer than she'd ever been. If she could just make it to midnight alive, she might see tomorrow. At least, that was Carter's theory. And he was smart.

Officer Santora eyed her a little suspiciously. She could tell he wasn't used to people confessing. "You are?"

Tree nodded and leaned in as if they were partners in a conspiracy. "Wasted! And I'm high. Pills, weed, you name it, I'm on it!"

Officer Santora hitched up his britches with two thumbs through two belt loops. "Well, then, I'm going to put you under arrest."

"That's a good idea."

Tree got out of the car and put her hands behind her back just to make things easy. She smiled as he cuffed her. "I've never been arrested before," she explained.

Santora only grunted in response and pushed her into the backseat.

"Thank you!" she shouted at him through the glass. If she hadn't been shackled, she'd have kissed him on the cheek.

As he closed the door, Tree heard the police radio crackle to life. The dispatcher was calling out a warning.

All units, we've got a 187 at the university hospital. Suspect is believed to be an escaped patient. Be advised—

Tree heard the roar of an engine somewhere behind her. She saw headlights growing larger at an alarming rate, and just as Officer Santora squinted in that direction, the car came barreling straight at him. Sparks crashed over Tree as the glass in every window shattered. Tree screamed as she saw Santora hit with a force that bent his body in ways that weren't natural, sending him flying into the air and then tumbling out of it twenty yards in front of the cruiser. His crumpled body lay lifeless on the shoulder of the road, illuminated by the unrelenting glow of his own cruiser's headlights.

Beyond the cop's body, the other car made a skidding U-turn, fishtailing into a 180 until it faced in her direction. The cop car was completely flooded with light. Tree shielded her eyes as she heard a car door open and close.

Footsteps came closer as the figure approached, backlit by the car behind him. The Bayfield Baby mask appeared in the window, just as Tree dreaded it would.

"What do you want?" she screamed through the glass. "Why are you doing this to me?" She was crying now, and angry. She shouted, "Who are you? Show your face!"

Without a word, the killer turned around and walked back to his car. Tree was dumbfounded.

What now?

He got into the driver's seat, and a black-gloved hand emerged from the driver's-side window of his car. Between the thumb and forefinger was a single lit birthday candle. It was only at that precise moment Tree smelled the gasoline hemorrhaging from a hole in the side of the cop car. She was locked in by handcuffs and police car doors that couldn't be opened from the inside. There was no escape.

"Holy shit!"

Tree looked out her broken window at the fountain of gas that was spraying onto the road beneath her. Then she watched in horror as the gloved hand of her killer dropped the lit candle out the window of his car. It tumbled end over end over end.

Whoosh!

A yellow-blue flame raced back toward the police cruiser. Tree could see her own reflection in the orange-red glow. She had just enough time to whisper, "No!" once and yell, "Oh, fuck!" at the top of her lungs before a massive explosion split her eardrums with a sonic boom, and she felt her skin and muscle melt away in the searing heat. Up, up, up she flew in a searing ball of fire.

19

The tower bell was ringing yet again as Tree opened her eyes. She was exhausted. Wincing in pain, she gradually pushed herself up to a sitting position.

Carter popped up from under the desk. "Oh, hey. You're up!"

Tree held up a hand. "Silence!"

Carter stopped talking and stared at her. She smiled at him, then rolled her eyes and hauled herself to her feet. She grabbed her phone and dismissed the call from her father, then shuffled over to Carter's desk and unearthed his toiletries bag. He watched as she poured out the entire bottle of Tylenol into her hand.

"I don't think you're supposed to take that many. You could die."

"If only it were that easy."

She tossed the entire fistful of pills into her mouth, then snapped her fingers.

"Water, *por favor.*"

Carter got her the bottle from his bedside, and Tree gulped it down, swallowing every last pill.

"Aaaaah!" She smiled at him, then put the water bottle down and strode over to the door, flinging it open as Carter's roommate, Ryan with the bleached-blond hair, appeared. Before he could say it, she cut him off.

"Hi. I'm the so-called fine vagine, and if that's the way you refer to girls, then you and your hand are going to have a very lasting relationship." She gave him a big smile. "Have a nice day!" she finished before gently pushing him back into the hallway and swinging the door closed.

She turned around to find Carter standing there with a confused look on his face.

"What?" she asked.

He smiled. "I mean, are you always this charming in the morning?"

"Just this one," she said, and she gave him a big silly grin, then dropped it and marched back over to his dresser, grabbed her pants, and started to get dressed.

"So, were you having a bad dream?" he asked.

"Sorry?"

"You were screaming before you woke up."

Tree reached down to pull on her shoes. "Well," she said, "I was dying. Again."

"What?"

Tree nodded. "It's a long story."

"You know, I've got time. I'm not doing anything today."

Tree paused with her hand on the doorknob, but the same damn sticker gave her pause.

TODAY IS THE FIRST DAY OF THE REST OF YOUR LIFE.

"Seriously," she told him, "I hate this sticker."

Then she marched out into the hallway.

Carter hustled to catch up. "Hey! Wait!" he said, falling into step with her.

"Why are you following me?" she asked without slowing down.

"I want to hear your story."

"Look, no offense," Tree said, "but the last time I explained it to you, it got me nowhere."

Carter stopped walking. "The last time?" He hurried to catch up with Tree as she took long, sure strides out of the dorm. "So you're having bad dreams? I took a course on neurocognition and dream content."

"Hooray for you," Tree said as they passed the judgmental art student. She bared her teeth at him and made a biting noise like a dog.

"I might be able to help you," Carter explained.

Tree didn't break her stride. "Can you stop me from reliving the same day, every day, only to be murdered by someone I may or may not know?"

Carter frowned.

"Yeah, thought so."

Tree kept walking as they passed the girl with the clipboard.

"Stop global warming?" the girl asked, thrusting the clipboard at Tree, who took it and handed it off to Carter. It stalled him briefly, and Tree felt him hustling up to her yet again. She had to give it to him—he didn't give up easily.

"Wait. You think you're reliving the same day? Literally?" he asked.

"Yup."

"And somebody kills you?"

"Yup again," she said.

"Come on. You're just messing with me, right?"

Tree stopped in the middle of the quad and turned to face him.

"Sprinklers." Tree snapped her fingers, and the sprinklers went off as if on her command. She turned and pointed at the parked car. "Car alarm," she said as the blaring sound filled the air. Tree grabbed Carter by the shoulders and turned him to face the frat pledges singing "Ninety-Nine Bottles of Beer."

"Now," she said. "See that pledge over there in the baseball cap? He's going to fall riiiiiiight . . . now."

The pledge went down on the grass with a *thump*.

"Any questions?" She thumped Carter on the shoulder and kept walking.

To his credit, Carter kept following her, and finally, Tree agreed to go with him to a diner just off campus. Carter sat and watched as Tree shoveled a giant burger into her mouth. She took a sip of her Diet Coke, then let out a giant burp.

Carter smiled. "That's impressive."

"That was *nothing*," she replied. She raised her hip off the seat of the booth and let out a massive fart that sounded like a trumpet. She grinned at him as he glanced around to see if anyone had heard.

"Did you get it all out?" he asked.

"Whatever," Tree said. "You won't remember it anyway."

Tree's phone sprang to life on the table. Her dad was calling. Again.

Yeahhh! It's my birthday, and I ain't gotta pick up the phone!

Carter glanced down at the screen. "It's your birthday?" he asked.

Tree nodded and sent the call to voice mail, then turned the phone over on the table.

"It's your dad," he said. "You want to get that?"

Tree stared at her plate in silence.

After a second, Carter kept talking. "I was never close to my dad," he told her. "Can't even remember the last time he called me on my birthday."

"Yeah," Tree said. "I'm supposed to be with mine. I couldn't bear the thought of sitting through another uncomfortable celebration while we both pretend that everything is awesome."

Carter frowned. "Are you closer with your mom?"

"Was," Tree said.

"What happened?"

Tree looked up at Carter, but she couldn't bring herself to say it. The look was enough.

"Oh."

"Yup." Tree was grateful that he hadn't actually said the word. "Three years ago."

"I'm sorry," he said. "That sucks."

"Yeah," Tree agreed. "We actually share the same birthday, though."

Carter smiled. "That's crazy."

"When I was a kid, I always got to skip school. We'd go to the beach." Tree couldn't stop herself from smiling as she told him the story. "My dad would buy us this huge birthday cake and put just one candle on it. We'd blow it out together."

"Bet you miss her."

Tree nodded. "You know, it's funny. When you relive the same day over and over again, you kind of start to see who you really are. If my mom saw me now, who I've become, I don't think she'd be very proud."

"Don't say that."

"It's true," Tree insisted. "I'm not a good person, Carter. Maybe this is karma. Maybe I deserve it."

Tree buried her face in her hands. Thankfully, Carter didn't insist on talking right away. They sat for a minute in silence, listening to the clanking of dishes and the line cooks calling orders in the kitchen on the other side of the counter.

Finally, Carter leaned in from the other side of the booth. "Look, I don't know you all that well," he said, "but it's never too late to change. Especially if what you're saying is true. Each new day is a chance to be somebody better."

"That's just it," Tree said. "I don't think I have that many chances left. I keep on getting weaker every time I come back. Maybe I'm like a cat with nine lives. Eventually, I'm going to run out."

They sat there in silence again, but Tree was surprised to see that it wasn't uncomfortable. Carter was just there. He wasn't bored or agitated. He wasn't constantly checking his phone. He was present. He was willing to be right there with her, no matter how real or vulnerable things got. Tree realized that she hadn't had anyone to talk to about the way she truly felt since her mom died. Somehow, she could say these things to Carter, and it made her feel better knowing that he heard her—even though he wouldn't remember it tomorrow.

The TV over the counter near their booth cut to a breaking news report, and Tree turned to see the same reporter standing outside the hospital on campus.

I'm standing outside Bayfield University Hospital where suspected murderer Joseph Tombs is being treated for a gunshot wound following a deadly shoot-out this morning that left one officer dead.

Tree stood up and moved closer to the monitor. She called out to the waiter behind the counter and asked if he could turn up the volume.

"What's going on?" Carter asked from the booth. "Tree?"

Tree was glued to the screen as the reporter continued:

Tombs was the subject of a nationwide manhunt that ended after a five-month pursuit across four state lines that left six known female victims.

Authorities are still not sure if Tombs is responsible for the murders of more than a dozen other victims he claims to have buried across the vast deserts of Arizona and New Mexico.

When Tree saw the pictures of the six women Tombs had already killed, she suddenly remembered the policeman sitting at the end of the hallway on the fourth floor. In a flash, everything came together.

"Oh my god," she whispered. "He's been here the whole time."

"What?" Carter didn't understand what was happening, but Tree had no time to explain. She turned around and raced for the door of the diner, leaving him behind at their booth, calling her name.

20

Deena, the nurse, was reading her Harlequin novel when Tree burst out of the elevator on the fourth floor and ran up to her station, shouting at the top of her lungs.

"He's going to escape! Call the police!"

"Who?" Deena yelled back.

"Joseph Tombs! Just call the cops!"

Tree saw Deena grab the phone, but it was going to be close. Rounding the corner, she ran down the hall just in time to see the officer on duty walk into Tombs's room.

"Wait!" Tree yelled, trying to stop him. "Don't go in there!"

He was already gone.

"Shit!"

Tree looked around for any sort of help she could find. Her eyes landed on a big red fire ax in a glass case. After only a second of hesitation, Tree slammed her elbow into the glass, sending shards tinkling to the floor. She grabbed the ax and started making her way down the hall to the room.

Behind her, Deena called out, "Excuse me! What are you doing?" But there was no time to explain.

Tree peered through the window in the door. It was covered with blood spatters, but she couldn't see anyone. Slowly, she pushed the door open and stepped inside.

Across the room was an empty hospital bed with a pair of arm restraints dangling from the guardrails. The fear coursing through her made her knees tremble, but she kept putting one foot in front of the other until she could see the officer's body on the other side of the bed. His throat had been slit, and a pool of red was spreading beneath him, deep crimson against the stark white linoleum. Just as she noticed his gun was missing, she heard something move behind her and wheeled around to see the killer in the Bayfield Baby mask pointing the officer's gun at her.

Tree swung the ax right as Tombs fired, and the bullet ricocheted off the metal blade. The force of the impact knocked the ax out of her hand. Tree screamed and ran for the door as Tombs fired again, this time narrowly missing her head, the bullet tearing a hole in the drywall.

Out in the hallway, she immediately slammed into Deena, who was running down from the nurses' station.

"What are you—" Deena started to ask, but Tree knew there was no time.

"Run!" she screamed.

She tried to grab Deena's hand and drag her along, but Deena pulled back. She didn't understand what was happening.

As Tree turned around to run down the hallway without her, she caught a glimpse of Tombs raising the gun again. *Bam! Bam! Bam!* Tree screamed and kept running as she heard Deena's body hit the floor.

Tree raced to the elevators and frantically stabbed at the button. Behind her, she heard a cold-blooded laugh and turned around slowly.

Tombs had her cornered against the elevators. Slowly, he

reached up and pulled off the Bayfield Baby disguise. Somehow, his real smile was even creepier than the mask's frozen plastic one. A cold chill traveled the length of her spine, and Tree watched, helpless, as he advanced, raising the gun.

Suddenly, out of nowhere, Carter ran around the corner and tackled Tombs, taking him down to the floor. The gun flew out of Tombs's hand, clattering across the floor, and spun to a stop at Tree's feet. She bent down to scoop it up as Carter and Tombs wrestled on the floor.

Tree pointed the gun at Tombs and shouted, "Stop!" as Tombs punched Carter in the face, knocking him unconscious. "Stop right now!" Tree screamed one last warning, and Tombs froze as he caught sight of Tree training the gun at his head.

Without hesitating, Tree took one step closer and pulled the trigger.

Click.

Tree's eyes widened in horror as she realized the clip was empty.

A sickening grin spread over Tombs's face. He began to chuckle at Tree's growing panic as she continued to pull the trigger to no avail, shouting at him to stop.

Click. Click. Click.

Tree watched as Tombs grabbed Carter by the collar, pulling him upright and smiling right at her as he took Carter's head in his hands and twisted.

The sickening snap of Carter's spine made the bile rise in Tree's throat, and she screamed Carter's name. Tombs let his lifeless body fall once more, his head smacking with a dull thud against the floor.

Tree watched through tears she could not control as Tombs came her way. She had no choice but to run, and she raced for the exit Carter must have used. The old wooden double door opened only a few inches—both handles were poorly bound by a chain and padlock—but it was enough. Tree carefully threaded herself through the space.

Tombs stopped behind her. He'd never be able to fit, but she kept moving; those doors wouldn't hold forever. She slipped through a door marked UNIVERSITY BELL TOWER and found herself at the bottom of the stairwell that held the chimes she'd awoken to every morning for what seemed like a very long time. She tripped over something in the dim light and reached down to find a crowbar. A series of loud bangs and the splintering of wood announced that Tombs would not be far behind.

Tree pressed herself into the space behind the door. Moments later, Tombs burst into the tower and roared at the top of his lungs.

"There's nowhere to hide, little girl."

How wrong you are, Tree thought, and she sprang from the shadows behind the door, the crowbar already raised in the air. It was a direct hit straight to his skull.

Tombs went down, and Tree stepped forward to finish the job. She raised the crowbar for one final blow but froze as she watched Tombs writhe on the ground.

"Carter." She said his name aloud.

If I don't reset this day, then he's gone forever.

Tree lowered the crowbar and loosened her grip. It slipped from her fingertips and clanged against the floor.

She stepped over Tombs and ran up the stairs, disappearing into the bell tower. She climbed up the stairs to the very top, and soon she heard Tombs groaning as he followed. By the time he arrived at the top of the stairs, she was ready.

"Hey!"

Tombs stopped and looked up. Tree had climbed onto a thin railing in front of the stained glass clock at the top of the bell tower. She balanced there with the rope to the bell tied around her neck.

"See you tomorrow, asshole."

Then she took one deep breath and jumped. The rope jerked taut, snapping her neck like a twig and pulling the giant bell above. The last thing she heard was the first chime from the bell tower.

When she opened her eyes, she was back in Carter's bed again, and the bell was still ringing.

21

Tree sat up and took a deep breath, adjusting her neck with a soft crack. The scene around her was the same, but she smiled to herself because it was almost like everything inside her was different. She knew who her killer was. Better yet, she had a pretty good idea of who she was.

Carter crawled out from under the desk and smiled nervously.

"Oh, hey. You're up! I wasn't sure—"

Before he could finish his sentence, Tree jumped out of his bed and threw her arms around him.

"I can't believe you tried to save my life!" she said. "Thank you so much!"

Carter patted her back cordially, surprised by her sudden enthusiasm. "Uh, yeah. Yeah, no biggie. I just brought you home."

Tree thought it was so cute the way he didn't remember anything, but he would. She was so excited to get started on one more round of this day. She pulled on her pants while he averted his eyes for what Tree hoped would be the final time.

"Don't know if you remember my name—"

"Carter!" she said with a big smile.

"Yeah," he said with that grin of his that told her he was pleasantly surprised.

She was already running out the door with her shoes in her hand when she stopped short and went back to the bed and grabbed a pillow.

"Do you mind if I borrow this?" she asked.

"Sure."

"See you at lunch." She winked at him and turned to go, pausing for Ryan to enter.

"Dude! You hit that *fine vagine* or wha—?" Ryan froze like he always did when he saw Tree. She ran over, turned him around to face the door, and spanked his butt with her hand.

"You naughty, naughty boy!" she said. Then she stepped into the hall and raised one hand over her head. "Fine Vagine out!" she yelled, and then she headed down the hall, leaving Ryan stunned and Carter laughing.

Tree stepped out of Williams Hall and stood for a moment, surveying the campus before her. She smiled, tossed her heels over her shoulder, and started to walk. As the judgmental art student peeked at her over the top of his sunglasses, she reached over, grabbed them, and put them on.

"Stop global warming?"

The girl with the clipboard held out a pen, and Tree stopped to sign.

"Of course." She scribbled her name and handed back the pen. "You save that planet, gurrl."

She hurried down the sidewalk and yelled at the couple in the grass, "Yo! The sprinklers are about to go off!" They scrambled out of the way in the nick of time, waving and smiling their thanks.

"You're welcome!"

She pointed at the car, and the alarm seemed to start by her command. Tree laughed and hustled toward the frat boys to get in place. As the guy in the baseball cap bit the dust, his head landed squarely on Carter's pillow. Tree even leaned over to plant a kiss on his cheek. As she walked away, every pledge stopped singing and stared at her with their mouths agape.

As she approached the covered walkway, she called out Tim's name.

"I know you're back there," she said with a smile.

When he poked his head around the pillar, she ran up to him.

"Hey, Tim!"

"Hey," he said. "You haven't returned any of my texts."

She stepped up close to him and lowered her voice as if they were planning a top secret mission. In a way, Tree thought, maybe they were.

"Look, Tim, let's get real. I know you don't like girls," she whispered. "Stop trying to be someone you're not. Love is love, right? Now! You go out there and get yourself a fine piece of man ass!"

She patted him on the shoulder and skipped on toward the Kappa house, barefoot and loving it.

She ran up the front porch steps, and when Emily waved at her, Tree waved back.

"Good morning!" she shouted just loudly enough that Emily could hear it through her headphones.

As she reached the stairs to her room, she heard Danielle's voice behind her.

"Oh. My. *God*. You sneaky little bee-yotch."

Tree turned around.

"His name is Carter. No, we did not have sex, but if I finally make it through this day somehow, I'm gonna have his babies. Lots to do. Gotta go."

She ran up the stairs, leaving Danielle to wonder what the hell was going on. In her room, Lori sat at the vanity in her scrubs as always. Tree poked her head in quietly and said Lori's line herself:

"She finally rolls in."

Lori looked up and closed her journal. Tree walked over to where Lori was sitting at the vanity and took a knee on the floor next to her.

Lori braced for the worst. "What's wrong?"

"Nothing." Tree smiled. "Look, Lori. I have been the worst roommate. You've always been there for me, but I've been way too selfish to appreciate it. Can we start over? I promise not to be such a loser."

Lori's eyes narrowed. "Are you high?"

"On life." Tree laughed and pecked her friend on the cheek. She was halfway out the door when she suddenly remembered and turned around. "Oh! By the way! I want to hear about your mystery guy!"

Lori looked a little baffled as Tree winked at her and hurried to class.

Tree threw open the squeaky door at the back of the science lecture hall and poked her head in. This time, instead of slinking to a seat in the back, she interrupted Gregory in the middle of his explanation of extreme agitation.

"Dr. Butler!"

Every head in the room swiveled her way en masse, including Gregory's. He paused with a marker still poised over the whiteboard.

"Can I have a word, please?"

Tree smiled and waited to make sure he was on his way, then let the door close and waited for Gregory in the hall. A moment later, he exploded out of the lecture hall, glowering as he spotted her.

"What the hell do you think you're doing?"

"I'm ending this."

Tree waited as the words sank in and watched his clear blue eyes cloud over.

"Wait. What?"

"I never should have started seeing you," Tree began. "It was wrong, and I . . ." She paused. This was harder than she had anticipated, but she knew it was right. "Anyway, I can't change what I've done, but I can start being a better person today."

Gregory laughed—a short, condescending chuckle. "What lame self-help book did you get that from?"

Tree silently thanked him for making this so much easier.

"You know, you have a wife who loves you so much. So if you can't be faithful to her, at least have the balls to leave."

Tree didn't wait for a response. She was already walking away when Gregory shouted after her, "Don't expect me to let you coast by in my class now!"

Tree laughed but didn't turn around. "Already dropped it!" she yelled back, flipping him the bird as she kept walking. She pushed through the front door of the building without looking back.

22

The Kappa lunch meeting was in full swing by the time Tree arrived. Danielle was holding court, discussing how "totally sad" it was that certain people couldn't even bother to show up for a "mandatory house meeting." Tree rolled her eyes but stayed hidden over near the booster tent full of baby masks.

When she saw Becky arrive with her tray full of food and the infamous glass of chocolate milk, Tree made her move.

As Danielle shamed Becky for her chocolate milk, Becky began to apologize. "I skipped breakfast," she said, the embarrassment written all over her face.

Before Danielle had a chance to respond, Tree plopped down a tray loaded with options far less healthy than Becky's. She immediately began shoveling french fries into her mouth by the fistful.

Danielle stared at Tree as if she were a leper, her mouth hanging open in horror.

"Mmmm." Tree groaned with pleasure as she crammed fries into her mouth. "Oh. My. God. This is so good."

Finally, Tree saw Danielle regain the power of speech.

"What's up with the fat-fest?" she sputtered. "We're Kappas."

Tree picked up a pack of Hostess Ding Dongs and tossed them onto Danielle's table.

"Live a little, hon," she said with a mouthful of fries. "A few calories won't kill you."

"No." Danielle's retort was ice cold. "They'll just turn me into a chunker like Becky here."

Becky was mortified and looked like she wanted to die. She quickly stood up to flee with her tray of food, but Tree touched her shoulder gently and kept Becky in her seat.

Without saying a word, Tree picked up the glass of chocolate milk from Becky's tray and walked over to Danielle. She took the straw out of the glass and dropped it on the patio. Locking eyes with the Kappa president, Tree smiled as she raised the glass over Danielle's perfect hair and slowly poured the entire thing on her head.

Gasps of shock and delight rippled through the assembled sisters as Danielle's disbelief yielded quickly to shrieks. Tree laughed as she watched Danielle turn and run away, mortified.

In the midst of her insurrection, Tree heard someone call her name and turned to find Carter standing behind her. She smiled as he reached into his pocket and pulled out her bracelet.

"Hey," he said. "I just came by to—"

But that was all Tree let him get out. She reached for him with both hands, pulled his face to hers, and gave him a big kiss on the lips in front of everyone.

When she finally pulled away, Carter was smiling, surprised. "What was that for?" he asked.

"I have to run," Tree told him. "But what are you doing later tonight?"

"Nothing."

"You want to take me out for my birthday?"

"What's the punch line?" he asked.

"Look," she said. "I know it's really random, but I promise I'll explain everything tomorrow. Well, assuming there is one." She leaned in and whispered, "Just say yes."

"All right. Yeah." Carter couldn't contain his smile.

Tree took her bracelet out of his hand. "Great," she said. She couldn't contain her smile either.

Tree was over a half hour late to the restaurant where she was supposed to meet her father. He was already waving for his check from his seat on the patio, ready to pay for his coffee.

Tree watched her dad fish out a ten before he looked up and saw Tree standing in front of him.

"Hi, Daddy. Sorry I'm late."

She slipped into a seat across the table from him. Tree could tell by his silence he was hurt. This was the part she didn't know how to handle: the hurt that they shared. Her own hurt she had learned how to manage—not well, perhaps—but enough that it wouldn't sweep her away. Since her mother died, whenever she and her father got together, their burden only seemed to double, and she didn't know how to change that. She tended to grasp for anything safe they could talk about, but safe usually meant unimportant, so they'd usually suffer through as much time as they could endure, talking about nothing at all.

"I like your tie."

Tree regretted the words as soon as she said them. All she could think of was how her mom used to say, *Old habits die hard.*

Her father looked down at his tie and seemed almost surprised by it—as if he'd forgotten he was wearing one.

"Thanks."

The uncomfortable silence filled the air.

"How's school?"

"Fine," she said.

"Like your classes?"

"They're fine. Dad—" Tree paused. *It's now or never*, she thought. "I don't want to do that anymore."

"Do what?"

"Small talk," she said. "It's just that this day is really hard for me."

Tree felt the sadness well up inside her, but instead of trying to push it down or hide it from her dad, she just let the tears fall. "I miss Mom. You know I miss her so much. I miss the way that she smelled. I miss that crazy horselaugh she had."

"Yeah. Me, too."

A smile passed between them as they shared a memory, and Tree wondered if this was how people helped each other with their pain. She hadn't thought about her mother's contagious laughter in forever. She hadn't allowed herself to. Maybe actually talking about the things that hurt was the way to find goodness in them. It felt wonderful to remember her mom's laugh and share it with her dad.

Tree decided she would try to tell him that, the best way she knew how.

"I thought if I avoided all of it—if I avoided you—it'd be easier. But it's been so much worse. All this running and hiding has made me so miserable." She stopped to brush away the tears. "But I think I finally figured it out." She laughed as she said, "It took something totally crazy. But I'm here, and I love you, and I'm so sorry that I hurt you."

Her dad was dabbing at his own eyes now. He reached across the table and took her hand in his.

"Happy birthday, baby."

They sat like that, holding hands across the table and chatting about only big things for another hour or so. Some of the big things were her mom's favorite joke and the time Tree lost her contact lens in the carpet the night before picture day in eighth grade.

These were all little moments.

But none of them were small.

23

When Tree got home, it was time to prepare.

She sheathed a knife that was now tucked into the waistband of her jeans, the handle hidden under her T-shirt.

She synchronized the clock by her bed and the timer on her watch.

She pulled her hair back in a ponytail. Sleek. No-nonsense.

She stopped to check her appearance in the mirror and saw reflected back the eyes of the person she'd discovered herself to be as she lived Monday, September 18, more times than she cared to remember. Her eyes held a message of grit and determination—a message that said she was ready to take control of her destiny.

Teresa Gelbman was going to make it to Tuesday the nineteenth.

Even if it killed her.

The police officer stationed outside Tombs's door didn't have any idea she was standing there until he felt the blade of her knife at his throat. She saw his eyes go wide, and every muscle in his body tensed.

"Shh," she whispered. "Stay calm."

"Take it easy," he said. "Take it easy."

Tree could hear the fear in his voice. She'd been over and over this plan in her head, and she wished there were some way to make the officer understand that she was on his side in this scenario, but there wasn't time. And even if there were, no one would believe her.

Tree whispered her instructions to the officer. "Stand up, slowly."

He did as he was told. She followed him up, the blade of her knife pressed gently against his throat. "Slowly," she repeated.

"This is a really bad idea," he warned her.

Tree nodded grimly. "And so is dying for the sixteenth time."

Tree moved quickly, sliding the officer's gun out of his holster. "Turn around!"

The officer looked back at her right down the barrel of his own gun. Tree saw the terror in his eyes.

"I need you to listen to me," she said firmly. "He's going to escape."

"We can talk about this," the officer pleaded. "Just put the gun down."

"He's going to escape," she repeated, louder this time. "Go get help. Go!"

The officer backed away slowly at first, then turned and broke into a sprint. Tree sheathed her knife again.

So far, so good.

She trained the gun on Tombs as she slowly pushed open the door and entered his room. He was sleeping, his wrists buckled into restraints at his side. But Tree had been killed by this man fifteen times. She could not trust her eyes.

"I know you're not asleep. Open your eyes."

Slowly, Tombs opened his eyes, turning his head ever so slightly. Tree pulled the trigger.

Click.

Tree saw a vicious smile spread slowly across the psycho's face as the panic overtook her. She kept pulling the trigger, but nothing.

Click. Click. Click.

How could this be happening again?

Tombs raised his eyebrows in delight. "Safety's on, little girl."

With that, he hit Tree with a pillow he had been hiding under his blanket and knocked the gun out of her hands. She saw now that his restraints already had been unlocked; his arms were only resting in them, not bound by them.

The gun slid across the floor and out into the hallway. Tree chased after it, bending down to grab it, but Tombs was too fast. He yanked her off the floor and threw her up against the wall, his hand around her neck.

He found the knife in her waistband and pulled it out with glee. "This is a real nice surprise, you coming to visit me like this."

He held the blade to her throat, then ran the tip of it up and down her cheek.

His fetid breath on her face, he pressed his body against hers, and his hand slowly squeezed her neck, cutting off her breath. All of it repulsed and angered her. A burst of adrenaline surged through her. She swung her knee between his legs as hard as she could.

Tombs lost his grip and fell away, roaring in pain. She ducked and rolled just as he swung the knife, burying it in the wooden door where she'd just been pinned.

Tree tried to run, but Tombs was too fast. She felt his hands grabbing her, flinging her across the hall like a rag doll. Her body slammed against the fire hose cabinet, shattering the glass. It rained down on her as she writhed in pain, desperate to escape.

"Whoo! I like you. Damn shame. You're a feisty little shit, ain't ya?" Tombs ripped the knife out of the door and turned back to face Tree, laughing.

She was trying to crawl away from him, but every bone and muscle in her body was on fire. Her hands and knees were covered in shattered glass.

"That's right!" he taunted her. "Crawl, little girl. Crawl!" He watched as she struggled to her hands and knees. "Don't worry. I'll make this one real quick for you."

At that precise moment, the alarm on her wrist went off. The countdown had reached zero.

Tree looked up at Tombs through the pain and gave him a great big smile. She saw the swagger fade from his eyes as the power surged and every single light blinked off. Two seconds later, they came back on, but Tree was no longer lying on the floor in the pile of glass.

Tree stood up slowly behind Tombs, raised the gun, and yelled, "Hey!"

Tombs spun around and jumped away from the gun.

"Safety's off," Tree said. "Thanks for the tip."

She pulled the trigger twice. *Blam. Blam.*

The shots sent Tombs back against the wall, and Tree watched as he crumpled in a puddle on the floor as the first police sirens blared into the drive outside.

24

Back at the Kappa house, Tree lit the red candle on the cupcake Lori had made and placed it between her and Carter.

They were sitting on the rug beneath the window by her bed. The moonlight was pouring in from outside, and the candle was the only other light in the room. Tree realized in a sudden rush of joy that this was the only party she'd ever wanted and the last one she would have asked for prior to today—or prior to sixteen todays, depending on the method of counting.

"So," Carter said. "This has to be strangest birthday you've ever had."

"You have no idea."

"Did you ever figure out how Tombs got free?"

She shook her head. "No. No one knows."

"He's like Houdini."

"I guess." Tree picked up the cupcake and peeled off the paper wrapper.

"What are you going to wish for?"

She thought about it for a second or two, staring at the

glow of the candle. Then she looked across the flame into Carter's eyes.

"Tomorrow."

"Tomorrow?" he asked. "Isn't that kind of a given? Might want to aim a little higher."

Tree smiled. "Nah. Tomorrow's good enough for me."

Then she closed her eyes and blew out the candle.

25

Tree's eyes fluttered open as the bell in the tower tolled the hour.

She felt a little groggy, but after what she'd been through, groggy was something she could live with. Pushing herself upright, she froze as the panic of an unspeakable horror flooded over her.

She was in Carter's room.

The trombone player was being yelled at in the hallway, and her phone began to play the birthday ringtone. She sat up, gasping.

Carter heard her and scooted out from under the desk.

"Oh, hey. You're up! I wasn't—"

"Carter?"

"Yeah," he said. "I'm surprised you remember my name. You were . . . pretty wasted last night."

"No. This can't be happening." Tree repeated it over and over. "This can't be happening!"

She saw Carter frown, clueless as to what she was talking about. This was the nightmare. She didn't know how to go about losing him every day and having to get him back.

"What?" he asked. "What can't be happening?"

"I killed him!" she shouted. "I stopped it!"

"Who?" Carter was growing more alarmed. "What are you talking about?"

Tree was sobbing now as she leaped out of bed.

"What's going on?" Carter asked. He turned around as she started pulling on her pants. "I mean, you were probably just having a bad dream or something. It happens to me all the time when I'm drinking."

Tree ran out the door while he was still turned around to offer her privacy.

It would be better not to have to face good-bye.

Lori was seated at the vanity just like always as Tree threw open the door to their room.

"She finally rolls in."

Tree didn't even respond. She was sobbing, maybe borderline hysterical. On the walk across campus, she'd come to grips with the fact that she might have suffered a mental break. She might need to institutionalize herself.

She immediately began pulling clothes from her drawers and closet, tossing everything in a pile on the bed.

"Going somewhere?" Lori asked her.

"As far away as possible!" Tree was nearly shouting, but she didn't know how to control these feelings.

"What's wrong?"

"I'll tell you what's wrong! Me! I was wrong! I thought if I stopped running, I could beat it! But it's never going to stop!"

"Tree, you're freaking me out."

Tree jammed as many clothes as she could into a giant duffel bag and started wrestling frantically with the zipper.

"Tree, look . . ."

She turned around and saw Lori holding that goddamned cupcake. Candle and everything.

"Happy birthday!"

Lori held the cupcake out to her, but Tree was in no mood. She turned back to wrestling with her luggage.

"Thanks," she said, unable to constrain her sarcasm. "But I finally ate it last night."

Tree froze the instant she said the words. "Oh my god," she said in a whisper. "I died in my sleep."

"What?" Lori asked.

Tree turned around to face her. Suddenly, it all made sense. "You killed me. You poisoned the cupcake, but I never ate it before last night. Remember? Threw one away, dropped it on the floor during the blackout. Never actually got it into my mouth until last night."

Tree frowned as she started working things out. She talked herself through it, right there with Lori listening.

"So you had to find another way. Then Tombs fell right into your lap. He was the perfect scapegoat. You had access to him at the hospital. Did you drug him first?" she asked.

Lori said nothing, just kept rolling her eyes at Tree, quietly shaking her head. But Tree *knew*. And she could prove it.

"You did drug him, didn't you? That way you could unbuckle the wrist restraints. You knocked him out and changed him into that all-black killer's outfit and put the baby mask right on his face. Then you could just leave the hunting knife in the bed with him. You knew he'd wake up and escape. Everyone would just assume *Tombs* killed me. But it was you, wasn't it? *You* were the one killing me."

Lori laughed a little too loudly. "You've totally lost your mind. You actually think I'd try to poison you with a friggin' cupcake?"

"Prove it." Tree took the cupcake out of Lori's hand and blew out the candle. She held it up to her roommate's face. "Go on, Lori. Take a bite."

"You really are crazy."

Tree shrugged. "We'll take it to the police. I'm sure they can tell us what's in your little birthday treat."

Tree headed for the door but didn't get very far. Lori grabbed a fistful of her hair and swung her into the wall. Tree's head hit hard. The cupcake flew out of her hands onto her bed, and she crumpled to the floor in a daze.

Lori slammed their door and locked it. "You stupid little whore," she growled.

"I know I've been a bad roommate, but isn't this a bit much?" Tree asked. "What the *hell*?"

"Oh, I don't know," said Lori. "Maybe because you wouldn't stop sleeping with him."

Tree frowned, trying to understand. Then it dawned on her. "Gregory?" she asked, dumbfounded.

"He just kept choosing you over me," Lori said. "Guess all he wanted was a cheap slut like you."

"Wait. You've been killing me over some stupid *guy*?"

"Oh, that's not the only reason. You're a *dumb bitch, too*!" she roared. "But what I really want to know is, how did you figure it out?"

"Because you've killed me before," Tree said.

Lori smiled like a crazy person and said, "Then I guess I'll just have to do it again."

Tree ran for the window, but Lori grabbed her from behind and tried to rip her fingers into Tree's throat. Tree rolled her back over Lori's bed and threw her off into the corner bookshelf. Lori leaped up and tackled Tree at the knees. Tree flipped over, and Lori wrenched her head by the hair and started savagely bashing Tree's forehead against the floor.

There was a loud knock on the door. Lori stopped her assault and simultaneously covered Tree's mouth with both hands.

"What the hell's going on in there?" Danielle called through the door.

"Everything's fine. Tree just fell. She's okay!"

Lori pressed her hands so hard across Tree's mouth and nose that Tree couldn't breathe. She was trying to scream, but Lori was committed and ready to finish the deed.

Tree jerked her head from side to side to steal some air, but she was fading. To the left, Tree spotted the upturned cupcake lying about an arm's length away.

"Whatever, clumsy hos!" Danielle shouted through the door. "Better see you at the meeting today!"

Tree reached for the cupcake while Lori was busy yelling back to Danielle.

"We'll be there!" she shouted, then turned back to Tree.

Tree was ready. She punched Lori in the throat, hard. Lori's hands came up, her mouth wide open as she gasped for air.

Tree jammed the cupcake directly into Lori's gaping mouth. "Eat it, bitch!"

Lori was hacking and coughing, choking and crying. She was shrieking through a windpipe choking on poisoned cake as she tried to spit it out and scoop it clear with her fingers.

Tree could only watch as Lori stumbled backward in front of the window. Looking up, Tree saw the chandelier. In a flash, she used the last of her strength to jump up and catch hold of the crossbars. Then, yelling like a banshee, she swung through the air, kicking Lori in the center of her chest and sending her flying out their second-story window.

It took a moment for Tree to hear the sickening thud and a piercing scream from Emily, the girl on the front porch with the headphones. Tree limped over and looked out the broken window. Below her on the porch was Lori's crumpled body. Emily was holding her headphones, still screaming. Tree turned and slid down the wall next to the window.

Danielle was already back, pounding on the door. "What the hell was that?"

Tree was too winded to yell back. Softly, she just said, "Lori . . . ate . . . my birthday . . . cupcake."

Then she rested her head on the window seat and passed out cold.

26

That afternoon, after the police reports and the reporters and the coroners and the Instagrammers, Tree sat next to Carter at the counter in the diner on the corner. They ate french fries and watched wall-to-wall coverage of the scandalous campus story the local news had decided to call "Kappa House: A Tragedy in Pink."

Tree had texted Carter about what was going on early in the day. It was a little weird for him, she realized; he'd only known her for a few hours, and she'd known him for sixteen days. Each day was the same day, but the point was that Tree had all these intense memories of Carter that had never happened, as far as he knew. Right now, for instance, he kept referring to things he'd already told her about in a different loop—like the time he accidentally threw his grandma's show cat, Benny, into the dryer with a load of wet towels. Carter started in on the punch line that cracked her up the last first time he told it.

"Benny survived with a chipped tooth and a torn ear—"

Tree jumped in to finish, "But he never walked a catwalk again."

"Oh my god!" Carter's laugh was contagious. "I can't believe you know about Benny!"

Tree tried not to spill all the beans. There were things he'd shared with her in confidence, or in the heat of the moment as they ran from psychopaths, that she'd decided just to keep tucked away. If he ever wanted to share them with her again, she'd "know" them then. If not, well, she could keep a secret.

The good news was that Carter could, too. After her interview with the police detectives, she'd texted him to beg for safe (a.k.a. media-free) passage out of the Kappa house. To her delight, he'd come through with a friend's hockey gear bag that was big enough for her to be zipped up inside of. Carter carried her out to his car with a bag of Tide Pods in hand, telling the reporters at the news vans it was laundry day.

No one batted an eye.

Danielle was back in the spotlight of the continuing coverage of "A Tragedy in Pink." She was wearing her favorite yellow sports bra and black yoga pants, and the longer Tree watched, the more certain she was that Danielle had a big career in small-market news. This was Danielle's first interview, and she was killing it.

"I always knew there was something wrong with Lori," Danielle explained to the in-studio anchor and the viewing audience at large. "She never wore makeup. Never posted any cute selfies. And she literally owned a pair of Crocs. All the signs of a psycho killer . . ."

Carter elbowed her as Danielle turned around to yell at two girls standing in the shot behind her, weeping over Lori's tragic death. Without missing a beat, she shouted, "Hello? I'm trying to get interviewed here."

Tree shook her head. "Oh my god, she is such a tool."

Having quieted the unrest of being upstaged, Danielle continued apace. "Anyhoo, Lori's little plot was super lame.

Poisoning a cupcake? Really? We're Kappas. We don't eat cupcakes."

As the affiliate cut to commercial, Tree's dad called.

Yeahhh! It's my birthday, and I ain't gotta pick up the phone!

She smiled at Carter, who shook his head every time that ringtone played.

"Hey, Dad."

She could tell he was panicked, and it was kind of sweet in a way. Ever since her birthday (for the past sixteen days), she'd been more receptive to building bridges with her dad over the tricky parts instead of just ignoring him altogether. Tree assured him she was just a little scratched up and promised they'd see each other soon.

"I love you, too. Bye."

Carter turned to her after she hung up with her dad. "So, uh, now that your bedroom is officially a crime scene and all . . . where are you planning on crashing?"

She raised her eyebrows and smiled. "Is that an invitation?"

"You sure you want to wake up in the dorm room again?" Carter asked.

Tree smiled. "Only if it's yours."

Carter nodded. He seemed to be deep in thought. "Only, of course, you'll have to sleep in Ryan's bed."

A huge grin spread across Tree's face. This was one of the parts of Carter she loved most. "Of course," she agreed.

He laughed at his own silliness and then blushed a little and stared down at his shoes. "Yeah. We can, you know . . ."

His voice trailed off, and Tree realized that this was one of those things. She'd slept in his bed and changed clothes in front of him for sixteen days in a row now. He'd only experienced that once.

"I almost forgot." Carter reached into his pocket and pulled out her bracelet. "You left this little guy."

Tree looked down and got a little lump in her throat. As she stared at the bracelet in his hand, she realized that this was the last time it would happen. Besides Carter himself, forgetting her bracelet in his room had been the most constant aspect of the last sixteen days. Even when she'd remembered that it was there in his room, toward the end of the run, she'd always left it behind. It was how Carter came to find her on what he considered day one of their relationship.

Now that the killer was dead, the loop would be broken, and tomorrow morning, wherever she stayed, she and Carter would be on day two. No bracelet would automatically be forgotten or returned.

"Thanks."

Tree held out her palm and waited for him to drop the bracelet into her hand. And maybe he did it on impulse, or maybe Carter saw the tears in her eyes and somehow understood. Either way, he took her whole hand in his and interlaced their fingers, pressing the bracelet safely between them.

They sat there for the rest of the afternoon, watching the news coverage and eating french fries. She had some rosé. Carter had some beer, and later if you'd asked Tree what they talked about for hours, she'd probably shrug and tell you about the first subject that arose after Carter held her hand.

"Hey, you know what your little scenario reminds me of?" he asked her.

"What?"

"*Groundhog Day.*"

She frowned. "What's that?"

Carter was amazed. "The movie *Groundhog Day*?"

"I don't know it," Tree confessed.

Now he was alarmed. "With Bill Murray?"

"Who's Bill Murray?"

Just the look on his face had made Tree giggle.

Carter felt this question was an outrage. "Are you kidding me? *Ghostbusters?*" He realized how loud his voice was now and apologized. "Sorry."

"I don't know." She smiled.

"How do you sleep at night? You've never seen *Groundhog Day*?"

She couldn't stop laughing. "You'll have to show me."

27

It was the bell in the tower that woke her up but the ringtone that struck fear in her heart.

Yeahhh! It's my birthday, and I ain't gotta pick up the phone!

Tree sat up in Carter's dorm room and felt like she might be imploding. Her whole body started to fold in on itself as she watched Carter crawl out from under the desk and turn around.

"Oh, hey. You're up! I wasn't sure if you wanted to sleep in or not."

Tree felt the panic of the past seventeen days wash over her, and she scrambled away from Carter, pressing her back against the cinder block dorm room wall. There was no escape from this. Terror gripped her heart with icy fingers and threatened to squeeze the life out of her. Her breath went shallow, and her lips quivered as the tears began to well in her eyes.

Then she saw Carter break into a huge grin.

"I'm kidding!" he said and held up his phone. "It was me. I just called you."

"What?" Tree's throat choked around the word. She blinked at him in confusion.

"It's Tuesday the nineteenth," Carter said with a grin. "You made it."

Tree had never been more ready to strangle anyone. "Oh. My. *God!*" she yelled. "You are such a jerk!"

Carter was laughing as Tree leaped out of bed and grabbed a pillow.

"I'm gonna *kill you*!" Tree screamed. She ran across the room and started giggling with relief as she pummeled him with the pillow.

"Hey! That's enough!" Carter was laughing as he tried to shield himself from Tree's pillow onslaught.

"What is *wrong* with you?"

Carter couldn't defend himself because he was laughing so hard. He finally resorted to a bear hug, wrapping both arms around Tree and the pillow and pushing the whole operation back over to his bed.

Tree collapsed beneath him, still giggling in protest. "That was not funny! You are such a punk!"

Carter leaned in to kiss her, and just as their lips touched, the door swung open.

Ryan appeared, bleached blond, disheveled, and—upon seeing Tree—dismayed.

"She's back?"

"Out." Carter pointed to the hallway.

"I'm not sleeping in my car again. It smells like Hot Pockets and feet."

"Get out." Carter meant business. He picked up the pillow Tree had been hitting him with and threw it at the door.

Ryan pulled it closed to avoid the pillow. Tree heard him yell from the hallway, "I just want clean underwear!"

Tree and Carter both started laughing. She pulled him in closer and said, “Now, where were we?”

“Day two,” he whispered.

Tree smiled as she kissed him. This day was already off to an excellent start.

HAPPY DEATH DAY 2U

■

Though lovers be lost love shall not;
and death shall have no dominion.

—DYLAN THOMAS

1

Ryan Phan stood in his dorm hallway, wishing he could start this day over again. He wished he could rewind and wake up in his own bed, instead of in his car. He wished he hadn't been startled to consciousness by a food truck blasting "La Bamba." But most of all, he wished that Carter would get herpes from that blond girl he was hooking up with right now.

Tree Gelbman was one of the biggest bitches on campus. She'd been known to make football players weep tears of defeat. Even if she was squeaky clean in the STD department, it was only a matter of time before she crushed his roommate like an ant.

Ryan wasn't always this cranky, but the jolt of "La Bamba" was no way to start the day—especially when you were covered in drool and your car smelled like a junior high locker room. If that weren't enough, he'd only barely stumbled from the car when a Pomeranian tried to eat his leg for breakfast. The woman walking it just said, "Jelly Bean! No!" while grinning through her dentures as if it weren't that big a deal; as if it were perfectly fine for her dog to attack strangers—or be named Jelly Bean. Ryan rolled his eyes at the memory. *People are crazy.*

And just as he was recovering from psycho puppy? A homeless dude decided it was the perfect time to ask him for some spare change—which Ryan didn't mind—except that this guy scared the *bejesus* out of him by popping out of the hedge along the sidewalk unannounced. Then, as he recovered from the near heart attack caused by the Spare Change Ambush of September 19, some douchebag on a skateboard nearly ran him over. And did bro-y skater dude bother to stop? Nope. Just kept surfing down the sidewalk (*Isn't that illegal?*) with—get this—a tray of lattes in one hand.

"Sorry, brooooooo . . ."

So, by the time he made it to the entryway of his dorm, where that annoying activist girl with the clipboard had asked him to stop global warming—however *that* was supposed to be accomplished by a signature—Ryan Phan was a man on the verge of a nervous breakdown. He truly wanted to help stop global warming, but he possessed zero bandwidth at that precise moment for human interaction. And so, he did the thing he hated doing more than any other, the thing he saved as his Get Out of Jail Free card for situations where he had come to the end of his rope: he pressed his hands together, bowed to her as he hurried by, and pretended to be a fresh-off-the-boat exchange student who didn't speak English.

That charade made him cringe, but fuck it. It was his prerogative. He was one of, like, four Asian people on this campus to begin with and (as far as he knew) the only student of Vietnamese descent. All he wanted was a shower and a couple of hours of sleep in a horizontal position before he had to go to class.

Instead, he was greeted in the hallway with the endless standoff between Tromboner and Dickwad, the world's most incompatible roommates. He felt for the guy on the horn. The music building was, like, eighteen light-years away by foot. Still, they were called *practice rooms* for a reason. And when was it going to be time to admit that you were probably *not* the guy who winds up playing trombone in the New York Philharmonic? Or . . . any harmonic? *I mean, this asshole is struggling with the Bayfield Babies fight song.*

So, to battle through the last fifteen minutes, and then have his roommate, Carter, throw a pillow at his head? Yeah, fuck that. Ryan ran a hand through his bleached-platinum hair and was about to barge back into his own room when his phone blew up in his pocket.

Oh my god, Ryan! Answer me already!

That was Samar's ringtone. Ryan reminded himself to change that but then realized he'd only forgotten because Samar never called. Ever. Only texted.

You'd better not be in jail right now, you asshole, Ryan thought. Then he sighed and answered.

"Dude! Dude! Get over here now! This is crazy! You won't believe it!" Samar was always excited, but this bordered on hysterical. He was talking eighty miles per minute.

"What? I understood two percent of that." Ryan rubbed his neck and tried to work out the kinks.

Samar's response was basically a high-pitched scream: "*Come now!*"

2

The student physicists of the Bayfield Science and Engineering building had been relegated long ago to the basement. Here, under the cold fluorescent lights, a maze of classrooms, storage spaces, and labs was linked by a crazy warren of corridors that ran through the building's underbelly like intestines.

Ryan was about halfway down the hallway to the lab when Samar, one of his research partners, came barreling up, grabbed him by the arm, and pulled him down the hall.

"Hurry!"

Ryan was running now to keep up. "What?"

"You'll see!"

Samar pulled him through the door of the lab, and Ryan almost tripped over the tangled mess of electrical cables that covered the floor. Samar let go of his arm to scramble over and around the obstacle course of power cords and instruments, joining Andrea "Dre" Morgan, the other member of the team, at the computer terminal panel on the far side of the room.

Dre didn't take her eyes from the screen as Samar joined

her. Ryan took his time. He never got tired of looking at what they created. As he picked his way carefully around the perimeter of the room, he couldn't help but admire the huge globe in the center of the room, crackling with energy: the Sisyphus Quantum Cooling Reactor. It had taken them all two full semesters to build "Sissy"—so many all-nighters and endless weekends stuck in this airless, windowless realm. The premed assholes called them the *mole people*, but Ryan didn't give a shit. It had been worth it. He stopped for a second and took in the glow as Sissy pulsed and hummed. Their quest to build a mini hadron collider had become something even more intriguing and beautiful—a creative event of such inspiration and precision that it had transcended mere experimentation.

They'd applied science and achieved true art.

Now they just had to get it to work.

Dre's head popped up above the monitors, and the look she shot Ryan brought him back down to planet Earth. Something had happened. Something big. He joined them at the terminal, scanning the code on the screens until his eyes landed on a piece of data that made him gasp.

"Whoa."

"Right?" Samar said.

"Point-seven millinewtons of energy." Dre shook her head, short curls bouncing around. "That's like . . . huge."

"When?" Ryan asked her.

She pointed to the time code on their analytics monitor. "Yesterday—12:01 a.m."

Ryan leaned in closer to the screen. He could scarcely believe his eyes.

"We just don't know what set the device off." Samar was so excited he could barely stand still. "Lab was locked. It's like Sissy just decided to fire on its own."

The door crashed open, and Ryan jumped as Roger Bronson, the dean of students, stormed into the lab, his balding head burning Bayfield crimson above his rapidly shrinking crown of remaining hair.

"That's it!" he thundered at them. "I've had it."

Bronson was out for blood, and Ryan thought he might have actually shed their own had he not been caught in the snarl of cables blocking his way. Dre and Samar grabbed their book bags and were already halfway around the opposite side of Sissy by the time Ryan noticed.

"Where are you going?"

"It—It's churro day in the cafeteria," Samar stammered.

Dre rubbed her belly and called out, "Nom nom!" as they scurried past the dean and disappeared into the hallway.

Perfect. Ryan already wanted this day to end, and now it had accelerated from suck to shit in 2.6 seconds.

"Dean Bronson!" he called out in a cheery voice. "Hi! Love the tie. Are those cats?"

The dean paused and glanced down at his tie, confused. "Turkish Angora," he said, then, remembering his rage, barked, "Don't change the subject!"

"What subject?" Ryan knew he couldn't play dumb for long, but any time he could buy was helpful.

"That!" yelled Bronson, pointing at Sissy. "We've had four rolling blackouts, fried electrical circuits, broken bulbs all over campus—and it's all because of your little science experiment."

The way he spat out *little science experiment* like it was a filthy hate crime pissed Ryan off and terrified him at the same time.

"It's my thesis project!"

"It's an abject failure. This university's science department prides itself on pioneering, forward-thinking ideas that yield results. Results that lead to *patents.* Do you see how it works?"

"So it's just about money?" Ryan shot back.

"Yes, Mr. Phan." Bronson wasn't having it. "I hate to shatter your illusions, but somebody has to keep the lights on around here—something you seem hell-bent on stopping. Literally. Consider this joke of a project suspended, effective immediately."

"*What?*" A panic seized at Ryan's stomach. This couldn't be happening. He'd worked too hard. They all had.

"That's right. I already called Professor Boner—"

"I think it's pronounced *Bonner,*" Ryan interjected, but the dean didn't slow his roll.

"—and he's in total agreement with my request. I'm sending security to collect this energy-sucking doohickey by six o'clock today."

It felt like the room were spinning. This was a nightmare, and now all he could do was beg. "You can't just take it!"

Bronson's face twisted into a satisfied sneer.

"Watch me," he snarled. "I suggest you wrap up whatever business you have left here. *Capisce?*"

The dean turned and marched out of the room, slamming the door behind him. Ryan stood there for a second, stunned, then flopped into a swivel chair and let his face drop into his hands. He felt like he might start crying. Or hurl chunks.

This is the worst day ever.

His phone pinged in his pocket, and he grabbed it, ready to kill Samar in a hail of texts, but the message was from an unknown number. He swiped to read it, but there were no words, only a picture.

Of him.

Sitting exactly where he was sitting right now.

Whoever took it had to be standing at the door. He stood up and started picking his way over the cables around Sissy.

"Samar?" he called.

There was no answer. The only sound was the low symphonic hum of equipment—whirring drives, fans cooling drives, electricity crackling through wires.

Ryan swung the door open and listened. No footsteps. No voices. He stepped into the hallway and checked both directions. It was empty. As he stared down the dim corridor, he heard a distant, hollow *bang* at the opposite end. He turned toward the sound and started walking in that direction. The fire exit door that led into the stairwell was open about a foot, and the stairs beyond were completely dark.

His phone pinged again, and he felt his pulse quicken. It was another picture of himself, seemingly at this exact moment. He was standing right there, in front of this fire exit. It must've been shot from the other end of the hall.

"What the hell?"

His own voice was the only sound. When he turned around to see who was there . . . nada.

Ryan headed back down the hall. Now he was getting pissed. Why were his friends being such dicks today? First, Carter put the room on lockdown for that sorority girl who wouldn't have given any of them the goddamn time of day if she hadn't been so blotto the night before. Then, Samar and Dre totally bailed and left him to face Dean Bronson alone. That wasn't the way friendship was supposed to work. Back in elementary school, he'd always been jealous of his classmates with big families. The friends he'd made at Bayfield had become the brothers and sisters he'd never had and always wanted. But enough was enough, and he was calling them on their bullshit.

Ryan flung open the door to one of the larger chemistry labs and scanned the long row of vacant workstations. The only light came from a row of glowing ventilation units lining one side of the room.

"Hey!" he shouted, his voice pinging off the metal surfaces and echoing down the hallway behind him. "While you shit-bags were off eating churros, our project got shut down! Hope you're happy!"

Silence.

A weird bump and rattle sounded from the back of the room, and Ryan froze. He was too tired. He hated being this strung out and jumpy. He started walking down the rows, past a big unit of shelves, each one filled with glass beakers in every size and shape you could possibly need. He loved all the equipment scientists got to use. He was a true nerd at heart. Another time, he might have paused to examine them, but he was on a mission.

If he had paused, he might have noticed the distorted reflection of a Bayfield Baby mask.

But Ryan was too busy trying to flush out his friends and give them a piece of his mind concerning their so-called friendship. He walked with more purpose, increasing his speed when he saw an abandoned janitor's cart and heard the same *rattle-bump*—only louder this time. It seemed to be coming from behind a closed door at the back of the lab.

He reached out and turned the knob. The door squeaked open to . . . nothing. And as Ryan squinted into the black emptiness—

Wham.

A hand landed on his shoulder with such force that he screamed as he spun around, swatting and punching as hard as he could.

Samar screamed bloody murder as he shrank back from Ryan's wild swings, shielding his head from the blows with both hands. "What's *wrong* with you?"

"*Why are you sneaking up on me?*" Ryan yelled back.

"I was bringing you a—" Samar looked down at the

churro he'd just dropped on the floor to avoid being pummeled. He sighed. "Well, now it's covered in bacteria. Two dollars, wasted."

Samar bent down to retrieve the churro, and when he stood back up, Ryan saw a look of raw fear on his face that made Ryan's blood run cold.

His friend's terror was the last thing Ryan saw before he felt an arm snake around him and jerk him back. He caught a glimpse of a Bayfield Baby mask over his shoulder, but before he could scream, the blade of a knife was slamming into his chest. The flash of cold steel and the excruciating rasp of his bones against the blade sent an electric shock of pain blazing through his entire body, and as his eyes rolled back into his skull, all he could hear was . . .

"La Bamba."

He opened his eyes and jerked upright, clutching at the white-hot fire in his chest where the knife was lodged.

But there was no knife.

And no guy in a baby mask.

Just a taco truck rumbling by, with Ritchie Valens's classic turned up way too loud, way too early in the morning.

3

As he pushed open the door to his car, Ryan's heart was still racing. That dream was a little too fucking real.

An avalanche of fast-food wrappers and soda cans tumbled onto the pavement as he climbed out and closed the door behind him. He stretched and rubbed the sleep out of his eyes, then crossed the street to head back to the dorm. The second he stepped onto the curb, a yapping Pomeranian charged at him out of nowhere.

"Jelly Bean! No!"

Ryan whirled around to see an older lady grinning with her big dentures. He rubbed his eyes again. *Am I still dreaming?* Something about the whole thing felt way too familiar.

As he hurried past the woman with the crazy dog, he saw the hedge along the sidewalk and stopped short. Somehow, he knew this part. He took a step back toward the road and glanced around next to the curb until he found a small rock. Eyes narrowed, he chucked it into the bush.

"Ouch!"

Bull's-eye, he thought as a man popped out of the bush and glared at him. "What's your problem?"

The man grabbed the rock and wound up to throw it back. Ryan took off so quickly that he just barely dodged the skateboarder whipping around the corner holding a tray of lattes.

"Sorry, bro!"

Ryan stood slack-jawed and watched him slalom down the sidewalk. *How do I remember all of this?*

The rest of his walk back to his room was an echo. There was the activist with the clipboard just outside, and the kid with the trombone in the hallway, his roommate screaming, "Shut *up*!" at the top of his lungs.

Ryan felt the overwhelming buzz of panic as he raced down the hall to his room, and he felt his hand freeze as he reached for the doorknob.

Please let this be different. What was he doing? He was a scientist. He didn't believe in any grand, guiding hand. This was all a crazy coincidence—his overactive subconscious playing tricks on him, egged on by too many Hot Pockets before spending the night sitting upright in his car. He was exhausted to the point of hallucinating. Ryan tried to shake it off and pushed open the door to his room.

Holy. Shit.

There they were. Tree, stretched out on the bed, laughing, as his roommate hovered over her, their lips just seconds from being in full lock.

Carter glanced over, saw him, and pointed to the hallway. "Out."

He couldn't move. Ryan was frozen, a sinking feeling in the pit of his stomach as his mind raced, trying to comprehend the fact that he was clearly having a mental break.

"Ryan!" Carter was trying to get him gone, but it was no use.

"Dude," he said. "I am trippin' right now."

"Yeah," Carter said, clearly annoyed. "No kidding."

"No. No . . ."

Carter glared at him, waiting, as Ryan struggled to find the words to articulate what was happening.

Ryan couldn't leave. He didn't care how many pillows his roommate threw at him. Maybe no one would believe him, but he and Carter had been through some shit together, and if there was even a remote possibility that another person would listen to him, that person was Carter, hands down.

He took a deep breath and threw himself upon the mercy of the court.

"I'm having that thing. What's it called? When you feel like you've already lived through something before?"

The moment the words left his lips, the blonde on Carter's bed popped up and looked at him like she'd just seen a ghost. No, wait. It was more than that. Like Ryan was the ghost.

She narrowed her eyes and said, "Déjà vu?"

Maybe she was smarter than he'd given her credit for. Usually, he tried not to judge people by the way they looked, but anybody as hot as she was couldn't be smart . . . could they? It was improbable—like Elisabeth Shue playing an electrochemist in that old movie *The Saint*.

"Yes!" he shouted. "That! I feel like I've totally lived through this day already."

She turned to look at Carter, and Ryan saw an understanding pass between them. They'd only spent two nights together, and it was like they'd known each other for weeks already.

"Bill Murray," Carter said.

"What the hell's going on?" Ryan asked.

Before anyone could answer, his phone started playing Samar's ringtone again.

Oh my god, Ryan! Answer me already!

He answered with a weird dread that he'd only experienced when his mom made him take that girl from church to the Valentine's dance his sophomore year because it was *the right thing to do*!

Samar was having the same, overexcited day again, too. "Dude! Dude! Get over here now! This is crazy!"

Ryan forced himself to speak. "I have to call you back."

As he hung up, the blond girl guided him to Carter's bed.

Ryan sank down next to her, his mind racing. He was exhausted and confused. All he really wanted was a bong rip the size of Manhattan and a nap in his own bed, but this girl wasn't about to let this go, and that was probably a good thing. At least she seemed to believe him.

"Okay, listen to me," she said. "The day reset when you died. Right?"

"But it was just a dream." Ryan tried to focus. "Some psycho dude in a baby mask stabbed me."

Tree shared a look with Carter that communicated more than Ryan had ever shared with anyone. *How long have these two* really *been hanging out?*

"Tombs is dead," Carter said.

Tree nodded. "So's Lori."

"Then who's the killer this time?"

Watching the two of them talk, it was like they'd developed their own secret language. Ryan was totally lost.

"Uh, hello?" he interjected. "Would somebody please start explaining what the hell is going on?"

Tree sighed, then took a deep breath.

"Recap," she said. "I was stuck reliving the same day, Monday the eighteenth, over and over, until someone wearing a Bayfield Baby mask murdered me on the night of my birthday. I had no idea who it was because I was such a bitch and so many people hated my guts.

"So, at Carter's suggestion, I made a list of suspects.

Turns out, it was my roommate, Lori, who kept helping a serial killer escape from the hospital, hoping it would look like he murdered me when in fact she was the one all along, and all because she was jealous of an affair I was having with my professor, Gregory, who was married."

Ryan's eyes widened involuntarily.

"I know," Tree said. "Pretty shitty. Anyway, I finally kicked Lori's crazy ass out a window and killed her, which broke the loop, or so I thought, but it looks like I only passed the loop to you, and now you're stuck in this day until we figure out how to stop it."

There was a long pause as Ryan took it all in. He looked over at Carter, then back at Tree, waiting for one of them to burst out laughing.

But they didn't.

That's when it hit him. "Oh my god," he said. "I'm still dreaming."

Carter frowned. "What?"

"It's like *Inception*," he explained. "It's a dream within a dream."

"Dude," Carter said. "This isn't a dream."

Ryan ignored his roommate and stretched out on Carter's bed instead, squeezing his eyes closed.

"What are you doing?" Carter asked.

"Shhh!" Ryan said. "I'm waking myself up."

A sharp pain shot through his chest for a second time this morning, and he sat up yelping and smacking away Carter's hand as his roommate gave him a titty twister.

"See?" Carter said. "Not dreaming."

Tree walked over to the corner of their room and turned around with Carter's baseball bat over one shoulder.

"Show me where you died," she said.

Maybe this was all insane, but Ryan knew for certain what he'd just been through (twice) just today, and he felt lucky as hell that Tree Gelbman (of all people) happened to be standing here. Her presence in his roommate's bed for a second morning in a row was, itself, an unexplainable phenomenon; the fact that she believed him and actually had a plan? Well, that was a miracle on the level of a Hollywood studio actually making *Crazy Rich Asians.*

Ryan jumped up and raced for the door. If this crazy girl had kicked her own roommate out the window, he certainly wasn't going to start disobeying her now.

4

Ryan led Tree and Carter into the dim lab and pointed past the ventilation units and shelves full of beakers to the door of the adjacent room.

"Back there," he whispered.

Tree raised the bat and advanced. When they got to the next room, it was empty, and Ryan nodded at the abandoned janitor's cart.

"Over there. Storage closet."

Tree stepped forward, but she felt Carter's hand on her arm. She stopped and pointed at the bat.

"Here," he said. "Give me that."

"I can handle myself," she said.

"Haven't you died enough?"

She couldn't argue with that. She shrugged and handed him the bat.

Carter took the lead, moving toward the closet with slow, deliberate steps. Tree followed close behind, and Ryan was about to bring up the rear when his eyes fell on the mop sticking out of the janitor's cart. He grabbed it just for good measure.

Ryan could feel his heart pounding in his chest as Carter reached the door to the storage closet. The blood rushing in his ears was almost deafening. The adrenaline coursing through his veins made it impossible for him to stay quiet.

"Bash his head in, Carter!"

"Shhh! Idiot!" Carter hissed. Then he reached for the handle.

The door yawned open with a slow, eerie creak, revealing nothing but darkness beyond.

Carter slipped his free hand inside and felt around for a light switch, but when it snapped on, there was nothing to reveal. The room was empty.

Carter and Tree both turned back around to face the room, and Ryan saw the full whites of their eyes. He'd seen that look before from Samar. Baby Face must be right behind him.

Before he could move, he felt hands grabbing him, and the adrenaline exploded. *Not this time, mothafucker.*

Ryan screamed like a banshee and whirled around, whacking Baby Face across the side of the head with the mop. He heard a voice shouting curses in Hindi as the mask flew off.

"Samar! You asshole!"

Samar was holding his head, a welt fast turning purple across his cheek. "Why did you hit me?" he wailed.

"Why do you keep sneaking up on me?"

"I think my cheekbone is broken!" Samar said, wincing as he ran his fingers gently along his face.

The lights popped on suddenly, and Dre came running into the room. "What's happening?"

"Ryan broke my cheekbone!"

Tree picked up the Bayfield Baby mask and nodded at Samar. "Was it him?" she asked Ryan.

"No. He was here when I got killed."

"What?" Samar was completely lost.

"Where did you get this?" Tree asked him.

Samar shrugged. "It was lying in the hall. Somebody must have dropped it."

A door banged open, and they all turned to see Dean Bronson storming into the room.

"Uh-oh," said Dre.

"That's it!" yelled the dean. "I've had it!"

Samar and Dre were already scurrying away.

"Where are you going?" Ryan yelled.

"It's churro day at the cafeteria," Samar called out as he raced for the door.

Dre was right behind him and shouted, "Nom nom!" as she followed him into the hallway.

Dean Bronson made a beeline for Ryan. "We've had four rolling blackouts, fried electrical circuits, broken bulbs all over campus, and it's all because of your little science project."

Tree looked at him through narrowed eyes. "What science project?"

Ryan loved the effect Sissy had when someone saw it for the first time. He'd never had the experience of taking it all in and seeing his fully formed creation for the first time, and he never would. He'd built it from the ground up with his own sweat, tears, and no small amount of love. He knew every inch of the device pulsing in front of them now, its glow reflected in Carter's eyes as he stood slack-jawed in front of it. What Ryan was no longer sure of was how exactly Sissy functioned. Somewhere along the way, inspiration had taken over, and he'd become fully obsessed. His dreams were filled with equations and the potential of Sissy's power, and he'd followed that vision as it helped lead the project far beyond his original designs. He knew what he'd intended for the machine to do; he'd never considered what might happen if it began to operate outside the realm of his intentions.

Once Dean Bronson had dropped the bomb that he was sending security to collect "your little science experiment" by 6:00 p.m., a stunned silence descended on the lab once more as Tree slowly circled the device, her face a mix of awe and horror.

"The Sisyphus Quantum Cooling Reactor," Ryan said softly. "We call it 'Sissy' for short."

He pointed out the features by way of explanation.

"These are proton lasers. When they fire, they cool the centrifuge, right here, to nearly below one nanokelvin."

Tree stared at him as if he were speaking Klingon. He wiped his palms on his jeans and tried again.

"Basically, we're trying to prove that time can be slowed down on a molecular level. It hasn't worked yet, but we got some promising data after the device fired the other night."

"When?" Tree demanded.

"12:01 a.m. yesterday."

"Monday, the eighteenth." Tree groaned and flopped down on the nearest desk.

"What?" Ryan asked.

She sighed. It was a long, heavy exhalation, and in it, Ryan heard the unbearable heaviness of a bone-deep exhaustion he'd not thought was possible in a white girl whose privilege was as big as her shoe collection.

"You created the time loop, dummy."

With that, Tree stood up and grabbed the baseball bat, picking her way over the canyon of cables as he and Carter hurried to catch up with her in the hallway.

5

They found Dre and Samar in the cafeteria munching on churros and joined them at one of the round tables by the windows, Ryan still trying to refute Tree's theory as she explained it to his friends.

"That's impossible," he said. "Sissy was not designed to do that."

"Maybe we're just discovering what it really does." Samar popped the rest of a churro into his mouth and licked the sugar off his fingers.

"An unintended reaction." Dre considered this. "Maybe we thought we were slowing time, but what if we looped it instead?"

Tree nodded. "And now you're stuck in this day. Congrats. Oh, and by the way? You're going to die. Again . . . and again . . . and again."

Ryan's eyes went wide. "Carter, tell your girlfriend to stop trying to scare me."

"She's not my—" Carter cut himself off, his unfinished thought wafting through the air like a sour burp. Tree shot him a look.

"Wait," he said. "Are you my girlfriend?"

Tree tried to suppress a little grin. (She did not succeed.)

"I don't know," she said. "Kinda."

The smile that spread across Carter's face was so goofy it made Ryan's teeth ache.

"Oh my god!" he said with a healthy dose of sarcasm before he leaned in and turned up the volume. "*Hello?* She just said I'm going to *die*!"

Tree shrugged. "Well, you'd better figure out how to close the loop before the killer finds you again."

"But I don't know how it happened! It just fired on its own!"

Tree opened her mouth to respond but stopped short. "Oh, god."

"What?" Carter followed her gaze across the cafeteria and saw Danielle, Tree's shallow best frenemy and head Kappa bitch, coming at them in a hurry. She was decked out in a tailored school spirit outfit that fit her like she'd been melted and poured into it. From the look of things, he could tell she was on a mission—and she was pissed.

Tree smiled at Danielle as she reached their table. "Hey, Danielle."

"Where were you?" she demanded.

"What do you mean?" Tree asked.

"You ditched our house meeting."

"It was canceled."

"When?"

Tree raised her eyebrows. "Uh, after I kicked my murdering roommate out a window?"

"Exactly." Danielle huffed. "Who's going to pledge Kappa now that we have a death curse? We're in crisis mode, Tree."

Danielle's tunnel vision refocused, allowing her to notice there were other people at the table. Sort of. As her eyes fell on Carter, Ryan, Samar, and Dre, she frowned and turned back to Tree.

"Ew," she said, wrinkling her nose. "Who are these people?"

Ryan watched as Samar's eyes almost fell out of his skull. *Is he actually drooling?*

"I'm Samar," he said, quickly wiping the sugar off his shirt, jumping up, and offering his hand to Danielle, who stared back as if she were unfamiliar with the custom of a handshake.

Ryan noticed Samar's gaze drifting down to Danielle's cleavage. He wasn't the only one.

"Hey, Samosa!" Danielle snapped her perfectly manicured fingers in Samar's face. "My head's the *middle one*."

Samar turned beet red and sank back into his seat, still sneaking glances up at her like a lovesick puppy who'd just been scolded for peeing on the floor.

Danielle turned back to Tree. "Anyhoo, call me as soon as you're done with your creepy little Comic-Con meeting."

She turned and left, her perfect hair flowing behind her like a cloud of glory as she pushed past the peons littering her path.

Samar watched her go, stunned. "Did she just call me 'Samosa'?"

Dre nodded. "Yup."

Ryan was about to come unglued. He slammed his hand down on the table, and everybody jumped.

"Guys. Focus. I really don't want to die."

"Look on the bright side," Tree said. "At least you'll come back. I died sixteen times."

"*Sixteen?*" Ryan shouted and rubbed at his chest. "*Hell* no! That shit hurts!"

Carter held up a hand. "Okay, okay. Listen. I have an idea. I say we just find the safest possible place and wait it out."

"Where?" Tree asked.

Ryan could hear the skepticism in her question. If what she'd told him so far was the truth, it might not matter where they went or what they did. The killer would find him. His invention had created a world where he could make an infinite number of different choices, but the outcome would always be the same: someone would find him and kill him.

According to Tree, his only hope was to find out who the killer was and kill that person first. Still, maybe Carter had a point. Maybe it would be better to find a super-safe place and hunker down with his homies. If nothing else, the odds were better for five of them against one killer than for just Ryan all on his own.

They had lunch in the cafeteria, but Ryan didn't have much of an appetite. He was exhausted and drained, but the fear of being alone, or worse, trapped in a small space with a psychopath kept him from even entertaining the idea of sleep. They all cut their afternoon classes and hung out in the cafeteria, stymied by the virtual lack of anyone who'd want Ryan dead. As Ryan pointed out, he'd spent most of the last four semesters in the basement of the science building. How could anyone want to kill him? No one even knew who he was.

Finally, Carter checked his phone and announced it was time to change venues, so they waited for Samar to get one last churro, and then they followed Carter across campus to the safest place at Bayfield University.

When they arrived at the Bayfield basketball arena, the crowd was already cheering at full volume.

The announcer was calling the starting lineup, and Ryan realized that he'd never actually attended a basketball game once in his two years at school.

If it had been any other time, he might have actually enjoyed it. The energy in the crowd was contagious and exciting, and the cheerleaders weren't terrible to look at. He understood why Carter had thought this might be the best place to wait out the night.

He also understood that Carter had made one small error in judgment. As soon as they walked through the doors, Tree froze and Ryan almost bumped into her. He followed her gaze up at the stands, and a chill ran straight up his spine. The view was a nightmare:

A sea of screaming fans wearing Bayfield Baby masks.

Hundreds of them.

Everywhere.

Ryan turned and glared at Carter.

"Safety in numbers!" Carter yelled over the roar.

Tree just gave a grim shake of her head.

"Who picks a creepy baby for a mascot anyway?" Ryan grumbled. "I knew I should have gone to MIT."

They found their seats just before tip-off. The crowd went wild when Bayfield scored first, and Tree saw Tim sitting a few seats away with a guy she recognized from the track team. They looked like an ad for Beautiful College Men with Perfect Bodies and Square Jaws. She stared just a moment too long, and he looked up and saw her. Tree panicked and gave him a thumbs-up. She was afraid she was being ridiculous about this, but she was proud of him somehow. It couldn't have been easy to come out to his whole fraternity, but here he was, a day later, with a guy who was as handsome and muscular as he was. Only gay men could look that good at a basketball game—or any time, really. It wasn't fair, really, but you couldn't fault them for wanting to hang out with each other.

Tim smiled sheepishly at her and nodded like, *Yeah, he's pretty cute, right?*

Her phone buzzed, and she saw a text from her dad. It was a picture of Tree and her mom a few years ago, along with the message:

I'm really proud of you. She would be, too.

Tree couldn't help but think about her lunch with her dad yesterday. They'd connected in a way she'd thought they'd buried along with her mom. She smiled, but Carter must've seen the tears in her eyes before he glanced down at the picture.

"That your mom?" he asked.

She nodded. "It's ironic. I thought I was stuck in the same day for some big, cosmic reason—facing my mom's death—but it had nothing to do with her. Turns out it was just some scientific fluke."

Carter considered this as the Bayfield Babies called a time-out.

"That doesn't make it mean any less, does it?" he asked.

Tree wasn't sure how to answer.

She'd changed so much living, and dying, the day before again and again. She wished her mom could see who she was now. What good was it to become a better version of yourself if you couldn't be with the one person who loved you the most in the world?

Tree glanced up at the scoreboard and beyond to the *Division Championship* banners hanging from the metal beams that held the roof far above them.

Can you see me, Mom? I hope you can.

She immediately felt like a fool. She'd died sixteen times just yesterday, but each time she came back, there was nothing to tell—no bright light, no hint of an afterlife. If anybody should know what lay beyond death, it was Tree, but she'd always reset the day right back in Carter's bed.

She leaned against Carter's arm a little closer. Maybe he was right. *Does it mean any less if we're just here because of a random act of science?*

"I guess not," she said, staring up at the banners in the rafters.

Carter leaned in, and just as Tree felt his lips on hers, the sirens blared.

6

The fire alarms were deafening. Everybody else in the arena seemed to think it was a prank, but Ryan's stomach knotted up as the announcer came over the PA system:

Students and faculty, please make your way to the nearest exit. This is not a drill. Please exit in a calm and orderly fashion. Again, this is not a drill.

The crowd erupted into groans and boos, and Ryan looked at Carter and Tree. Carter jerked his head toward the door, and they made their way down the bleachers and into the passage leading out of the arena.

The concrete hallway was packed with overhyped, rowdy guys who had clearly smuggled booze into the game with them. They pushed and shoved everybody along the way instead of just waiting their turn like normal human beings.

Ryan felt the terror rise in his throat as he felt the rush of people separate him from Tree and Carter. He glanced up to find that he was surrounded by a group of fans wearing Bayfield Baby masks, and the blood started to race in his ears. His eyes darted around in search of Carter and Tree, Samar and Dre, but he couldn't see them. The masks continued to come at him, fast and thick.

It could be any of them.

The thought made Ryan stop dead in the middle of the corridor, frozen with fear. He took a deep breath and kept turning around, looking for Tree and Carter.

And there he was.

A man was standing stock-still in the middle of the current of bodies. He was wearing a black tracksuit and a baby mask, twenty feet away, right between Ryan and the gate out to the parking lot. The lightless eyes of the mask held Ryan in a hollow gaze.

Then he started pushing his way toward Ryan through the crowd.

Ryan was shaking as he spun around to fight his way upstream against the drunk and excited torrent of fans who were sweeping him toward his certain doom. He felt like he were caught in a wave so large he couldn't tell which way was up. He was in full panic. Ryan couldn't stop holding his breath, until he gasped for air and started screaming for anyone to help. But no one took him seriously. They either ignored him or elbowed him out of their way.

They think this is all a prank.

Ryan glanced over his shoulder and saw the psycho in the mask was gaining ground. Something flashed in the man's hand. Ryan barely saw it for a split second, but he instantly knew it as the glimmer of a sharp blade.

The killer was seconds away from being close enough to grab him, and Ryan's flight instinct finally kicked in. He lowered his shoulder, threw elbows, and fought the flow of bodies with everything he had until he reached a nearby door marked AUTHORIZED PERSONNEL ONLY.

Ryan burst through the door and into a cramped maintenance room. He stumbled along in the dim light, frantic and searching. Finally! Another door at the end. He had just stepped through it when he heard someone following in the first door.

The door slammed shut behind Ryan, and he ran deeper into the large storage room. Long rows of boxed items stacked in disorganized towers lined the rows. It was like somebody's grandpa had been randomly stashing athletic equipment, merch, and supplies in his massive garage. He ran down the rows toward a huge supply cage that rose two stories at the back and slipped inside just as a door banged at the other end of the space.

Ryan moved as quietly as he could past more stacks of Bayfield sweatshirts, banners, flags, and foam fingers. He passed a row of standing mannequins wearing more Bayfield swag, each one with a baby mask. Behind him, he heard the door to the cage rattle and clang, the sounds so close, and Ryan tucked himself behind a stack of boxes in a far back corner. He was crouched under a metal stairway that led to the second level of the cage. He couldn't stop shaking, and he covered his own mouth with his hand, hoping not to give himself away, hoping that he could hear the footsteps of the killer in time to flee.

The first footstep on the metal stairs just above him made him jump, and he bit down hard on his own fingers to keep from yelping in terror. The killer continued to climb, and then Ryan could see him walking across the perforated metal platform that formed the second story of the supply closet.

He was dripping with cold sweat, shivering in terror. He tried to scoot deeper into the corner under the stairs, but as he did, he bumped into something behind him. The killer's footsteps above him stopped instantly at the noise. Suddenly, light from a cell phone flashlight flooded the area beneath the stairs. The killer was trying to find him, flashing the light back and forth, scanning the area all around him. Ryan squeezed his eyes closed and waited for the worst.

But after a couple of booming heartbeats, he heard the footsteps above him move on. The light was gone. Ryan stepped out from the corner beneath the stairs and seized the chance. It might be the last one he ever had. Silently, he doubled back the way he came, keeping his eyes trained on the killer's shape above, watching the psycho in the mask move in the opposite direction.

As he stepped around the mannequins, one of them lunged at him. Ryan screamed as dead eyes opened behind the baby mask, and he felt his body being pinned back. The killer pressed him back against the wall and swung his blade high in the air.

Ryan yelled one more time as the knife tumbled down, down, down . . . and somehow missed him completely.

The knife clattered across the concrete floor as the killer crumpled beside it.

Light flooded the warehouse, and Ryan saw Tree, armed with a heavy bronze trophy.

"Holy shit!" Ryan shouted.

Above him, a voice called out, "What was that?" It was Carter.

"Down here!" Tree yelled.

Ryan heard footsteps racing across the upper platform of the supply cage. It must've been Carter up there looking for him.

Tree dropped the trophy with a metallic thud and reached over to hug him. He was still shaking like a leaf, soaked in sweat, and panting like a dog on a hot day.

"You okay?"

All Ryan could do was nod in shock as Carter bounded down the metal stairs.

"What the hell?" Ryan finally got enough air into his lungs to yell. "I thought you were the killer! Why didn't you say something?"

"I was looking for you!"

Carter glanced down at the killer lying on the floor, out cold. He smiled at Tree.

"Damn. Good job."

"I've had practice," she said without smiling.

"Who is it?" Carter asked.

"Only one way to find out."

Tree bent down and pulled off the mask, flinging it immediately away as she jumped back and all three of them yelled in shock.

Ryan rubbed his eyes and felt his knees start to shake underneath him.

Lying on the floor in front of them was *himself.* Ryan was awake, trembling, and he was also lying at his own feet, knocked out cold.

Tree and Carter both slowly looked up at him, then back down at the version of him on the floor.

Ryan wanted to tell them that this was a dream; that this was impossible.

But he could only muster two syllables:

"Da *fuuuuuuck?*"

7

After a brief moment of extreme freak-out, Tree was finally the one to insist that Carter and Ryan stop trying to figure out why or how or what the actual hell was happening; they only had to snap the fuck out of their paralysis and accept that this was *a thing*. If Ryan #2 woke up, he'd try to kill Ryan again.

As usual, she was correct. *Thank god somebody around here has a bias for action,* Ryan thought. And of course it would be Tree. She was the one who had just lived yesterday sixteen times in a row.

They put the mask back on Ryan #2, and somehow Ryan and Carter managed to carry him back to the science lab.

They tied him up in a chair in the glow of Sissy. Then they all collapsed in a sweaty panting mess and tried to catch their breath and figure out what the hell to do next.

Carter broke the silence. He was still trying to reach for the most reasonable solution.

"You sure you don't have a twin brother?" he asked. "Maybe you were separated at birth?"

"Of course I'm sure!"

Ryan had decided somewhere between the gym and the lab that this bonkers bullshit was his new normal now. Still, he was unprepared for the moment when Ryan #2 started to stir. As he came to, eyes blinking hard, the impostor seemed to realize the gravity of his situation.

And then, he spoke. "Oh, shit."

"*Oh, shit* is right!" Ryan yelled at him. "*Who are you?*"

"Who do you think I am, dummy?" Ryan #2 shot back.

"He's you," Carter whispered, clearly trying to wrap his brain around the warped universe he now inhabited.

It didn't help that Ryan shouted, "*Duh!*" at the top of his lungs—in perfect unison with his doppelgänger.

Tree was on a mission. "What the hell is going on?" she asked Ryan #2.

He briefly struggled against the power cords holding him but then gave up and answered her.

"I was trying to close the loop, but I somehow got knocked into a parallel time loop! We're all in serious danger! The longer we exist in the same dimension, the worse things will get! It's a butterfly effect! You have to kill him!"

Ryan was on his feet now. "*Me?*" he yelled.

Ryan #2 ignored him and kept talking to Carter and Tree. "He's going to create bigger problems if you don't stop him! Kill him! Now!"

"Screw that!" Ryan said, trying to get his friends' attention. "Kill *him*!"

"You're wasting time!" Ryan #2 told them. "Do it!"

"Dude! I'm your friend, not him!"

Ryan was on the verge of hysteria now as Carter and Tree looked back and forth between them, a couple of deer caught in headlights.

Ryan had to act fast. His only help in this whole bananas day had come from Carter and Tree. If they got confused or gave up on him now, he was on his own, and that was something he wasn't ready to deal with. The only way out of this was to reset and send them all back to the beginning.

"Screw this," he said. He reached over to the control console and powered up Sissy. His invention crackled to life with a hum that made the whole room vibrate as the asshole version of himself that was tied up in the chair started yelling, "Stop him!"

"Wait!" Tree turned to him. "Ryan, maybe you should stop."

Ryan couldn't believe they were listening to this jerk.

"Forget him!" he told her. "He's crazy! I'm the one who designed this! I know what I'm doing!"

He hurried over to the computer, furiously punching in code. The lasers started to fire in individual quadrants as Ryan #2 started to pitch and rock, trying to drag himself to the controls and free himself.

"*You don't understand what you're doing!*" Ryan #2 shouted.

"*Shut up, Fake Ryan!*" Ryan shouted back.

The power started to surge, the lights overhead pulsing as Sissy pulled power from the grid.

"Uh, this doesn't feel right." Carter looked pale, and Ryan only had a few more seconds.

"Ryan! Stop!" Tree was getting worked up now, but Ryan ignored them both and kept typing commands into the control console.

The door flew open with a bang, and Samar and Dre appeared, mid-debate:

"But a parsec is a measure of distance, not time!" Dre said.

Samar scoffed at her. "Are you calling Han Solo a liar?"

They both suddenly became aware that they weren't alone and froze mid–nerd fight.

When Ryan #2 turned and looked at them, Dre let out a quiet, "Whoa."

Samar did a triple-take, then stared hard at the bottle of Yoo-hoo he was drinking.

At that precise instant, the lab door banged open again, and Ryan saw Dean Bronson storm in, flanked by a pair of burly campus security guards.

"What did I tell you about turning that thing on?" the dean bellowed.

Ryan ignored him and kept entering commands as fast as he could. All the lasers were firing now. It was just a matter of a few more seconds—and that's exactly what he got when Bronson and his buddies realized there were two of him in the room.

"Turn it off! Now!" Bronson was trying to get to him, but now he couldn't take his eyes off Ryan #2.

Ryan stayed right where he was, willing Sissy to power up faster.

When Bronson saw that he wasn't budging, he yelled, "Get him!" at the campus cops, who sprang into action, climbing through the mass of electrical cables as fast as they could.

Ryan reached behind the console and grabbed a giant wrench they used to tighten connections on the machine. He started swinging it in an arc around his open flank while he continued to type commands.

Come at me, dudes. I can code with one hand tied behind my back.

Only Samar realized in the moment what he was doing at the computer, and he shouted at him, "Ryan! What are you doing?"

Ryan #2 was rocking back and forth now like he were riding a bronco, about to break the chair they'd tied him to, but Ryan was almost done. The device was reaching critical mass. The entire room hummed with an energy that made his hair stand on end while the lights flickered and surged like the Vegas strip at midnight.

"Almost there!" Ryan shouted over the dull roar, right as he saw Ryan #2 rock free with a violent lunge that finally undid the cords.

Quick as a flash, Ryan #2 turned, grabbed the chair, and charged at Sissy, apparently ready to smash the sphere into a million bits.

"*No!*" Ryan shouted as he saw Ryan #2 raise the chair over his head and swing it . . .

A *boom* radiating out from Sissy sent every person in the room flying backward away from it, the very air around them shimmering like it was made from interdimensional spider webs.

Ryan was lifted along with them, and in that split second, as they all hung suspended between the molecules of Earth, he saw the floating stream of Samar's Yoo-hoo curling toward the air in a beautiful, liquid ribbon. He saw the chair, ripped from Ryan #2's grasp, tumbling upward against gravity, away from the sphere it was meant to destroy. He saw the look of defeat on Ryan #2's face as the shock wave leveled the room, sending all of them hurtling toward the perimeter of the lab, Dean Bronson's jaws flapping like a dog who had stuck his head out the window on the highway.

Both security guards were thrown backward toward the door, one of the glass panels exploding from the blast, and as the roar filled his ears, Ryan saw one final thing before they were plunged into total darkness:

Tree and Carter, flying through the air, each still reaching for the other's hands across all of space and time.

8

The only thing Tree could hear was the ringing in her ears from the explosion.

Her whole body buzzed from the energy that had pulsed through the lab, and she was afraid to move. She wasn't sure how long she'd been out, but as she lay there, trying to determine if anything was broken, the ringing became less of a squeal in her ears and began to sound more like . . .

A bell.

Her eyes flew open with shock and horror, and she shot straight up in Carter's bed.

There he was, rummaging around under his desk as her phone started ringing on his nightstand.

Yeahhh! It's my birthday, and I ain't gotta pick up the phone!

Carter pulled himself out from under the desk.

"Oh, hey. You're up! I wasn't sure if you wanted to sleep in or not."

Tree felt the shock in the pit of her stomach explode into anger. "No. Fucking. Way."

Carter stood there, looking flustered. "I . . . uh . . . folded your clothes—"

Tree leaped out of bed and marched straight to Carter's door. Flinging it open, she yelled over the trombone player at the end of the hallway, "*Ryan! Get in here right now!*"

After a moment, Ryan slunk into the room.

"You two know each other?" Carter asked.

"*Yes!*" Tree shouted at the same moment Ryan shouted, "*No!*"

Carter frowned, confused. "Huh?"

Tree was so pissed off she couldn't even begin to explain it all again to him. Instead, she turned on his roommate with the white-hot rage of a thousand suns and did her dead-level best to murder him with her voice.

"Ryan, you dumb-ass! You sent me back!"

"What?" He blinked at her.

"It's Monday the eighteenth!" she yelled.

"Uh . . ."

"I can't believe this! I just got out! How could you do this to me?"

Ryan turned to Carter, completely weirded out. "Who's this crazy white girl?"

Tree stomped over to the dresser and yanked her clothes on. She felt like she might disintegrate—fall apart at the seams and just cease to exist, which, in this moment, would have been fine with her.

"Maybe you just had a bad dream." Carter was trying to help. Of course. As always. But Tree couldn't contain the bile that boiled up inside her.

"You're right. It is a bad dream. It's a nightmare! This sucks the hardest mega-balls in the history of shitty ball-suckery!"

She grabbed a pillow off Carter's bed and smashed her face into it, muffling the loudest scream she had ever attempted. It lasted for a while, and when she ran out of air and pulled the pillow from her face, Carter and Ryan just stood there, staring at her, possibly afraid. She had to pull it together.

Tree took a deep breath.

"I'm okay," she said.

"You sure?" Carter wasn't convinced.

She nodded. "Yes. He just needs to fix this. Now."

Ryan cocked his head and considered her for a moment. "This is a joke, right?"

Calmly, Tree walked up to Ryan and got right up in his personal space. She meant business, and she lowered her voice to a serious level so he would know she couldn't be trifled with.

"I wish," she said. "Ryan, we need to go back to your lab, turn on Sissy, and figure out how to send me back."

He frowned. "How do you know about Sissy?"

Tree just couldn't *even* anymore.

"Let's *go*!" she said, and marched out the door.

She was three steps down the hall when she realized they hadn't come along. With a sigh, she walked back to their room, poked in her head, and snapped her fingers.

"*Ándale*, people!"

This time, they followed her. She led them out of the dorm and right into yesterday.

All over again.

The creepy art student who checked her out was right on time. Tree passed him and barked like a dog. He jumped like she'd tased him, and she just didn't have the bandwidth for the student activist.

"Stop global warming?"

Tree sidestepped the girl's clipboard in a hurry, but she did say "Sorry," and she actually was.

As she led Carter and Ryan across the quad, the day unfolded with her greatest hits:

Sprinklers.

Car alarm.

The singing pledges on the lawn.

Tree passed them all without hesitation, not even pausing when Tim popped out from behind the arch of the covered walkway.

"Hey, you haven't returned any of my texts—"

"You're gay," she said without breaking her stride.

He stood there stunned, but Tree remembered the handsome guy he'd be with at the basketball game tomorrow and felt assured in the confidence that she'd done the right thing.

Ryan was practically running after her. "You're going the wrong way. The lab's back there."

"I have some business to take care of first," Tree explained.

She didn't say another word until they'd reached the Kappa house. Carter and Ryan followed her up the stairs, past Emily in her headphones on the front porch. She waved at Tree, and Tree tried to smile an acknowledgment, but she was on a mission. She briefly considered telling Emily that she might want to move away from the window above her, but she was already opening the front door, and she wanted to get this over with.

She motioned for Carter and Ryan to follow her upstairs, but after she got to the middle landing, she stopped. A frown slowly crossed her face as she waited for Danielle to appear in her yellow sports bra, as she had every time she'd relived the day.

But Danielle wasn't there.

"What's wrong?" Carter asked.

"She was supposed to be here," Tree said.

"Who?"

Tree shrugged it off and headed back up the stairs.

When she opened the door of her room, Lori was seated at her vanity as always.

"She finally rolls in."

"Where is it?" Tree asked.

"Where's what?"

Lori glanced up as Carter and Ryan walked into the room and stood in the doorway, fidgety and unsure.

"Oh, hey, Carter."

"Hi," Carter said with a smile.

Tree looked at Carter and tried to quiet the nagging doubt in her stomach. Since when did these two know each other? *What the fuck is happening?* She turned back to Lori.

"Where's the cupcake?"

Her roommate-slash-murderer let out a little laugh, pretending to be confused. "What cupcake?"

"The one you made for my birthday," Tree said sweetly. "The one you poisoned."

Lori played along. "*Oooohhhh.* That one."

She laughed again, grabbed her black duffel bag, and started packing it with gym clothes.

"I'm serious!" Tree said.

Lori paused. "Look, Tree, I don't know what stupid joke Danielle put you up to, but there's no cupcake. Sorry. I'm pulling a double for Jen. She has the flu. Happy birthday, though. Toodles!"

Lori zipped her bag and walked out the door.

And then she was gone.

Tree felt like the ground was shifting under her feet as she listened to Lori walk down the stairs and out the front door.

"What's going on?" Carter asked.

"I have no idea." She shook her head. "It's all different."

9

Tree finished her explanation and slurped the last few drops of her Diet Coke through a straw. Carter and Ryan both sat with their mouths hanging open at what, over the past two days, had become Tree's favorite table in the cafeteria. The soft light poured in through the trees, and she watched as students wound their way across the quad, unaware that there was an actual wrinkle in time occurring as they hurried to class.

"There were two of me?" Ryan seemed sort of excited about the possibility.

"Yes," Tree said. "That's how this whole thing started."

"This reminds me of *Back to the Future Part II*," Carter said.

"Totally!" Ryan held up his hand, and Carter gave him a high five.

They both turned to look at her for affirmation. The baffled look on her face said it all.

Carter started giving her clues. "Marty McFly? The DeLorean?"

Tree shrugged. "Sorry."

"Are you serious?" Carter sounded almost personally offended. "You've never seen *Back to the Future*?"

A terrible realization struck Tree like a thunderclap.

"Oh my god." The panic returned to the pit of her stomach. "Does this mean there are two of me?"

"It's possible," Ryan said, "but only if you were knocked into a quantum-cyclic dimension. Otherwise, you're probably stuck in a holographic multiverse where there's just one of you."

Tree blinked at him. "Oh. Okay. Thanks for clearing that up, Ryan. Super helpful."

"You've never heard of the multiverse theory?" he asked.

"No."

Ryan grabbed a napkin and folded it, then poked a hole through it with a pencil. "This is our universe. But look—"

"Dude," Carter said. "You're not doing the folding paper universe thing, are you? It's such a cliché."

"Shut up," Ryan told him. "I'm mansplaining."

He folded the napkin again and again, lining up the holes.

"In theory," he continued, "the universe has six dimensions. If what you're saying is true, then maybe you woke up in the same day but not the same dimension. That would explain the anomalies."

Tree thought about this for a second. "So, how different are we talking here?" but before Ryan could answer, she saw Danielle heading their way. "Oh, shit. I missed the house meeting."

As Danielle walked up, Tree wasted no time apologizing. "Danielle, I'm so sorry. I just—"

"Hey, babe," Danielle interrupted her.

Tree realized that Danielle wasn't even looking at her. Danielle was looking at Carter, who stood up and smiled back at her.

Babe?

She didn't have time to process as Carter leaned over to Danielle and kissed her.

Tree felt the planet grind to a screeching halt beneath her. It was the feeling of whiplash while sitting totally still.

What. The Actual. Fuck?

For a moment, she thought she might scream at the top of her lungs, then tackle Danielle and try *being* the killer for a change.

When Carter and Danielle finally came up for air, Danielle looked at Ryan and for the first time didn't wrinkle her nose. Instead, she smiled and gave him a little fingernail waggle.

"Hey, Ry."

Tree saw Ryan blush like a smitten puppy. If he'd had a tail, he'd have wagged it until he piddled on the floor in excitement.

"Hi, Danielle." Ryan could barely make eye contact with her, but Tree could stare at nothing else. She was watching the slow-motion car wreck of her worlds crashing into one another. She looked Danielle up and down. Was that a copy of *The Miracle Worker* on top of the books she was carrying? Aliens must have landed and replaced Danielle with a perfect replica of her former self—only this version was capable of a healthy relationship with a good guy and being kind to nerds.

Just when Tree thought she'd seen it all, Danielle whipped out a pair of dark sunglasses and put them on. She waved her arms in front of her like a lost Muppet and began "feeling" her way to an empty seat. They all watched her clearly having a mental break until Danielle dropped the act and grinned at them.

"Did that look real?" she asked. "I'm auditioning for this year's production of *The Miracle Worker*. Did you know Anne Frank was blind and deaf?"

Carter frowned. "Uh . . . Helen Keller?"

"Excuse me?" Danielle said.

"Anne Frank was in the attic," Carter explained.

"Oh! Whatever." Danielle laughed. "All I know is, *acting* blind is probably harder than actually *being* blind. It's crazy."

Maybe this is *the same person*, Tree thought. Perhaps some things never changed.

As if she'd heard Tree thinking about her, Danielle turned and gave her a singsong scolding.

"Well, *somebody* missed our house meeting today."

Tree started apologizing as if by reflex. "I—"

"—totes *kidding*." Danielle winked at her. "Birthday girls get a pass. Anyhoo, we picked this year's charity. Ready for it?" Danielle paused for effect. "We're doing the Special Needs Art Fair again!"

She started clapping for herself, and Tree couldn't get over how genuine Danielle's excitement appeared to be.

"Nice!" Carter said.

Ryan started tripping over himself to give her compliments. "You do so much good, Danielle," he finally managed. "I really admire that."

"Please." Danielle modestly waved her perfect manicure through the air. "It just warms my heart seeing those little faces. I mean, don't get me wrong, sometimes they try to hug you for too long and it gets a little uncomfortable, but you just get used to it. And at the end of the day, there's no greater reward in life than the love of a child."

Carter put his arm around Danielle and gave her a squeeze.

Tree tried not to throw up in her own mouth.

"Tree?" Danielle was looking at her now, concerned. "You okay?"

"Yeah . . . I . . ."

As she desperately tried to form a sentence, Tree's phone rang.

Yeahhh! It's my birthday, and I ain't gotta pick up the phone!

For the first time ever, she was happy to hear that sound. *Saved by the ringtone.*

"Hey, Dad," she said. "Sorry. I'm on my way. I'll be there in ten." Tree stood up and grabbed her bag.

"Wait," Carter said. "You're leaving?"

She stopped and stared at Carter. Something about his question split her heart right down the middle. She had to get out of there before she started crying.

"I'm supposed to meet my dad for a birthday lunch," she explained, then turned to Ryan. "I'll meet you in the lab at three. We're figuring this out before it gets any worse."

Tree glanced back at Carter before she turned to go, and it was a mistake. He was looking right at her over Danielle's head. Maybe it was her imagination, or maybe it was this whole screwed-up universe, but there was something in his eyes that looked to her like longing, and now as she tried to keep herself from running as she left the cafeteria, there was something in her eyes, too. By the time she pushed through the doors onto the quad, the tears were spilling down her cheeks.

There was nothing to figure out in the lab at 3:00 p.m. There was no way to keep this from getting any worse. Teresa Gelbman finally understood that there was only one thing worse than dying over and over again.

Living with a broken heart.

10

Tree knew the exact table where her father would be, and she hurried past the hostess stand to the outdoor seating on the spacious deck that ringed the building. She'd fixed her makeup in the bathroom, but her eyes were still red from crying and she felt the need to apologize—to everyone, it seemed, even her father.

"Sorry I'm late. I've just had a crazy day."

Her dad smiled. "It's okay, sweetie. Everything okay?"

"It's fine."

Tree looked down at the menu and braced herself for the small talk she was certain would come.

Right on time, her dad started in. "How's school?"

Tree didn't know if she had it in her to broach the conversation about her mom again. She'd been so pleased with the place they'd gotten on that yesterday so many days ago, but somehow the fresh pain of seeing Carter and Danielle together had dulled her pain over anything else. She'd never understood before that fresh heartbreak hurt worse than old scars.

If she wanted to get through lunch with her composure intact, she'd have to put off the talk with her father for another day. It was days like these when Tree missed her mom the most. She'd had a way of sensing exactly what Tree needed—to talk, to go to the movies, a good cry and a hug, a bag of Sour Patch Watermelons. The sadness of not having her mom to talk to made the pain of what she needed to talk about that much heavier.

Her father sat watching her, waiting for an answer about school. He was clearly worried. Tree took a deep breath.

"Are you ready to order?" A waitress had appeared out of nowhere, and her dad held up a hand.

"We're waiting on one more."

"Okay. I'll be right back."

Tree idly watched the waitress head back inside the restaurant. "One more?" she asked. "Who else—"

Tree couldn't speak anymore. Or even remember what she'd been saying. The waitress had stopped in the doorway to let a customer through.

Tree's mother stepped outside.

Time stood still.

The outdoor seating at the restaurant was crowded, but Tree no longer heard the voices or the clank of silverware. All she could hear was her own breathing. She watched as her mother scanned the length of the deck filled with diners. Then their eyes met, and she smiled.

Tree was running toward her now, intercepting her mom before she got even halfway to the table. She was almost sobbing as she threw both arms around her in the middle of the weekday lunch rush.

Her mom laughed, that perfect, crazy horselaugh that Tree knew she'd never hear again.

"Whoa. Hi."

Tree gasped for breath. “You’re here!”

“Of course I’m here. It’s our day.”

Tree saw her mom look at her father with that *What’s wrong?* look she used to give him when Tree had been in high school and upset about something when her mom got home from work.

“Are you okay?”

It had been years since she’d heard those words, and the joy that rushed through Tree was like a white, healing light, sewing up wounds, erasing scars, soothing fears.

Tree wiped away her tears. “Yeah. I’m just . . . I’m just really happy to see you.”

Tree hugged her mom again—more tightly than ever before. A burst of laughter flooded from both of them now, and Tree felt every part of her coming back to life. She drank in that special comfort that can only be found in the arms of a mother who loves you no matter what, and she decided she would never let go again.

“Five . . . four . . . three . . . two . . .”

Tree could hear Ryan’s voice counting down in the lab as she reached the lower level of the science building. Sissy was humming, and the whole building seemed to shake and rattle as she raced to the door and yelled, “*Stop!*” at the top of her lungs.

Ryan punched a key, and the lasers powered down as Tree bent over, her hands on her knees, gasping for breath.

“Leave it,” she choked out.

“You told me to—” Ryan began, but Tree held up a hand and cut him off.

“I changed my mind.”

She looked around the room: Dre, Samar, Ryan, and

Carter. All of them stared back like she had gone insane. Maybe she had, but her mom was alive. Somehow, someway, in this dimension, she had her mom back. If dying all those times was what it had taken, it was a small price to pay. She smiled at all of them, nodded her thanks, and walked back out the door.

She was halfway to her car when she heard Carter's voice calling out behind her to wait. He fell into step beside her.

"Why the change of heart?" he asked.

"Everything's different now."

"Different how?"

She stopped and turned to face him. "When were you going to tell me?"

"Tell you what?" he asked.

"About Danielle."

Carter frowned. "You guys live in the same house. I thought you knew."

"Uh. No," Tree said. "I definitely didn't know. The bigger question is, does she know?"

"About what?"

Tree rolled her eyes. "One of her closest friends woke up in your bed this morning. You don't think that's newsworthy?"

"Nothing happened," he said. "I slept in Ryan's bed."

"So why take me home?"

"I was afraid you would choke on your own vomit like Janis Joplin."

Tree groaned. "Look, it's fine. This is the way it's supposed to be. My mom's okay. Lori isn't trying to kill me—"

Carter held up a hand. "Wait. In this other dimension. We weren't . . . ?"

Behind Carter, Tree noticed Professor Gregory Butler leaving one of the buildings with his wife, Stephanie. It looked like they were having a heated conversation. Then, right in the middle of it, Gregory looked up and noticed Tree staring at them.

"I have to go," she said.

Before Carter could protest, Tree headed off in the opposite direction from Gregory and Stephanie.

At least in this dimension, that was one mess she could avoid.

11

The video felt familiar, but as Tree sat on her bed, watching on her phone, she couldn't help but notice weird differences. She was there with her mom singing, "Happy Birthday to Us," but the cake she expected to see on the counter was replaced with a huge cinnamon roll with a single candle in it. There were now a whole trove of memories of which she, herself, had no memory.

She was about to tap the screen to watch it again just as the expected knock came at the door, and Danielle breezed in with her hair up in fat curlers, wearing Tree's top.

Some things never change.

"I know." Danielle rolled her eyes. "I'm just borrowing it for tonight. What time are you going to the party?"

"Sorry," Tree said. "I can't make it. Something came up."

"*What?*"

In the sudden anger that passed over Danielle's face, Tree saw a flash of the person she knew so well. Then, all at once, the new Danielle was back, all smiles.

"I mean, we've been planning this for weeks, Tree."

Tree sighed. "I know it's a surprise birthday party, and

I'm sorry. It's just . . . my parents are in town. I have to see them."

The lights surged, and the room plunged into total darkness. The blackout was right on schedule.

"Ugh," she heard Danielle say for what felt like the thousandth time. "Our tuition dollars at work!"

Tree blinked as the lights flickered on. It all felt so familiar again.

"So who told you about the surprise party?" Danielle asked. "Was it Lori? I swear, that girl really needs to learn how to keep a secret."

Danielle was still talking, but Tree bolted over to the TV and grabbed the remote. When she pressed the button, *Teen Mom* filled the screen, and Tree changed the channel until she saw the thing she'd been so afraid to see. There was the local news report. Serial killer Joseph Tombs's mug shot filled the screen, followed by the reporter standing outside Bayfield University Hospital.

"Oh my god," Tree whispered. "He's still here."

One more time, Tree raced down the fourth-floor hallway to the nurses' station, shouting at a startled Deena.

"He's going to escape!"

"Who?"

"Joseph Tombs! Call the police!"

Tree turned to see the police officer stationed outside Tombs's room already up and on his way into the room.

"Wait!" she yelled. "Don't go in there!"

But it was too late.

She ran down the hall and stopped to shatter the glass case that held the fire ax with her elbow. One careful step at a time, she approached the door of Tombs's room and swung it open. This time, the bed was empty.

There was no sign of Tombs or the cop, and she felt the familiar rush of her own blood in her ears as she crossed the space with cautious steps, the ax gripped in her trembling hands. As she stopped to peer behind the bed, she heard the . . .

Flush.

The bathroom door swung open, and Tree spun around, the ax raised to strike.

"Whoa!"

Tree froze as the police officer grabbed his gun from the holster and trained it at her chest.

"Drop the ax!" he yelled.

"Wait!" she cried. "I can explain!"

"*Drop it! Now!*"

Tree obeyed and put her hands in the air. "He's escaped! He's going to kill someone!"

"Face the wall!" he commanded. "Hands behind your back!"

"You don't understand! Lori let him go!"

He jabbed the gun toward her for emphasis. "I'm not asking again!"

Tree turned around and put her hands behind her back. The officer stepped in and cuffed her as she begged him to pay attention.

"Please. Listen to me. My roommate works here. She let Tombs go so she can blame him, but she's going to kill me."

"Lady, I don't know what kind of bad shit you're on, but Tombs is down in the OR right now. They just took him."

"Who took him? Was there a tall girl?" Tree asked. "Dark hair in a ponytail?"

The cop grabbed her by the arm. "Let's go."

As he pushed her out the door and into the hallway, the police officer spoke into the walkie-talkie mounted on his shoulder.

"Dispatch, this is Officer Ramirez. I've got an 11550 over at the hospital. Need immediate assistance."

Through a crackle of static, Tree heard the dispatcher say, "Copy that. Available units, please—"

Bam!

The killer in the Bayfield Baby mask burst through an open doorway and slammed into the cop. Tree screamed as the killer pinned Ramirez to the wall. The glint of the blade flashed once before finding its mark over and over. As the cop slid to the floor in a pool of crimson, Tree made a run for it as best she could, the metal of the cuffs roughly pinning her wrists behind her back.

At the end of the hall, she rounded the corner to the elevator bank and backed up to the call button, frantically pressing it as the masked psychopath stepped around the corner and stopped.

"You can lose the mask!" she yelled. "I know it's you, Lori!"

The only response was the killer raising the bloodied knife.

Ding!

The elevator doors opened right behind Tree. She whirled around and came face-to-face with Lori.

Tree froze for a split second as her brain tried to wrap itself around this new development, but Lori was already jabbing the button and pulling Tree into the elevator with her. The killer charged at them with the knife raised high, hitting the elevator with a thud as the doors closed in the nick of time.

She stared at Lori, stunned. "I thought you—"

"Are you okay? What the hell's going on? Who was that?" The terror in her eyes was real.

"Tombs escaped!" Tree said, gasping for breath. "He's trying to kill me."

"Tree, that's not possible. I just helped them take him down to the OR."

The elevator suddenly jerked to a stop as the lights overhead flickered and died. It was almost pitch-dark now, and Tree felt the familiar terror of her own impending death return with a vengeance.

"What's happening?"

Lori was stabbing at the lobby button, but nothing was happening. "It's stuck."

"He cut the power."

"Just stay calm," Lori said, but the panic in her voice belied her words. She grabbed the emergency phone and held it to her ear, jamming the receiver hook in search of a dial tone that didn't exist. "Shit!"

Lori turned and started prying apart the doors, inch by inch, opening them up until they could see the darkened hallway.

She whispered, "C'mon!"

Tree had no choice but to follow.

12

Lori helped Tree jump down out of the elevator, which had stopped a couple of feet higher than the floor. The handcuffs were making her fingers prickle now, and Tree scanned the hall looking for an escape.

The entire floor was under construction and deserted this late at night, leaving only the dim glow from a few work lamps and exit signs to light their way.

They had to get out fast. Large plastic tarps were draped over every door and hung from the ceiling in other areas to minimize dust during the remodel. It was impossible for Tree to tell where they were or which way they should go.

Lori got her bearings quickly and pointed down the hall. "There's an emergency exit at the other end. Come on."

Tree had to trust her. The sheets of hanging plastic blocked her view of any exit, but she did see a sledgehammer leaning up against a wall.

Tree nodded to it. "Wait. Grab that."

Lori picked it up and, shoulder-to-shoulder, they made their way down the long corridor. Every door they passed through was covered with plastic sheets, and Tree knew that each one could be hiding a killer. Above them, every few feet, a ceiling panel had been removed, and bundles of thick black cables hung down in their way. Lori swept them aside with the sledgehammer and held them for Tree so she could get by without the use of her hands.

As they forged ahead, one of the plastic sheets covering a doorway in front of them billowed out toward Tree. She stared into the dark room, expecting to see the baby mask at any moment.

Ahead of her, Lori approached another thick bundle of cables and stopped suddenly as if she'd heard something. Tree stopped behind her and listened.

"What?" she whispered. "Did you hear something?"

Lori turned around slowly, her eyes wide with shock. Tree watched as her lips parted gently and a thick bead of blood rolled down the corner of her mouth.

Tree looked down in horror and saw the handle of a knife sticking out of Lori's chest. Her roommate dropped the sledgehammer with a metallic thud, then collapsed beside it.

The bundle of power cables hanging in front of her began to move as a hand pulled them sideways, revealing a Bayfield Baby mask. The killer spotted the sledgehammer next to Lori's body and picked it up. Playfully, he spun it around in his hands and said nothing.

"All right, asshole," Tree challenged him. "Let's see what you got."

The sledgehammer flew toward her so fast that she was barely able to dodge the blow. It smashed deep into the drywall, buried with such force that it got stuck.

Tree seized the moment and ran.

With two tugs, the killer dislodged the sledgehammer and barreled after her.

Dodging plastic panels and power cords with her hands still cuffed, Tree found the emergency exit and slammed into the door, but it didn't budge.

"*Come on!*" Tree yelled.

The killer was closing in on her. Tree took a step back and kicked the door open just as the killer swung again. As Tree jumped out of the way, the momentum of the sledgehammer pulled him past her and through the door, into the stairwell, sending him down a flight of stairs. He tumbled to a stop on the landing below.

"Ha!" Tree shouted, triumphant.

The killer popped back up to his feet.

"Shit."

She turned around and ran up the stairwell. Up, up, up she went, losing track of how many flights or which floor, until finally she banged open a metal door marked ROOF ACCESS.

Tree pushed through the fire exit door onto the roof and felt a blast of cool air. She paused just in time to see the killer charge out after her, and she took off running across the rooftop. She glanced back over her shoulder, but the killer stopped cold and even seemed to tilt his masked face at her like a confused dog. For a moment, she couldn't understand why.

The confusion didn't last long.

Her next step landed on air, and Tree ran right off the edge of the building.

Tree wasn't sure how many stories she fell (seven? eight?), but as she jerked awake in Carter's bed to the toll of the bell tower, one thing was certain.

This might be a new dimension, but she was right back where she'd started.

13

R*ookie move, Tree.*

As she waited for Carter to get out from under his desk, she couldn't believe she'd been stupid enough to run off the roof of a building.

"Oh, hey. You're up! I wasn't—"

"What dimension am I in?" Tree asked.

"Huh?"

Tree tried again. "Danielle."

"My girlfriend?"

"Ugh," she moaned. "Same one."

As her dad's ringtone played, she rolled out of bed and started getting dressed. Her whole body ached.

"You okay?" Carter asked her.

"I'm fine," she said. She looked up at him and changed gears. Something had been bugging her since, well, the last time she lived through this day.

"I mean, no offense," she said, "but how could you possibly end up with her?"

Carter shrugged. "Well, I mean . . . she's really nice."

Tree laughed. "*Nice.* Ha."

"Wait. Isn't she, like, one of your besties?"

The door swung open before she could answer, and Ryan appeared, mid-yell: "Dude! You hit that fine vagine—?" He saw Tree and froze.

She looked at Carter. "Hmm. Interesting."

"No. I wasn't trying to—"

Tree wasn't buying it. "Not as innocent as you look."

She turned to Ryan. "You—meet me in the lab in an hour."

"Huh?" Ryan blinked at her.

"I've got to get out of these disgusting clothes."

Tree grabbed her bracelet and phone. As she made her way down the hall, she heard Carter's voice and smiled. "Nice one, dickhead."

It took some time to do the recap for the whole gang at once. As Sissy hummed in the background, Carter, Ryan, Samar, and Dre asked question after question as Tree tried to remain patient. She'd had plenty of practice at telling the whole damn story in a way that would get Carter to believe her quickly. It was the endless questions from Ryan, Samar, and Dre that really bogged things down. She'd finally remembered to tell Ryan to check the reports. Once he saw the anomaly at 12:01 a.m., they were all as convinced as they needed to be.

Wrapping up, Tree told them the most important point of the story.

"Listen to me carefully," she said. "I have to stay *here* in this dimension. Just close the loop."

"Oh, sure," Ryan scoffed. "No problem. Even though we have no idea how this even happened in the first place!"

"You're all brainy science people, right?" Tree said. "Figure it out."

"We're messing with forces we have no business touching," Samar said with a solemn nod.

"Maybe you should have thought of that before you built this big, dumb thing." Tree took a breath. "Just do me a favor and try, okay? Please?"

Ryan looked at Samar and Dre. They shrugged and nodded. He turned back to Tree.

"Look," Ryan said. "This is going be a trial-and-error situation. We have to rule out every variable in order to narrow down the correct algorithm that will close the loop."

"Okay . . ." Tree said.

Dre tried to lay it out for her. "It could be days, maybe weeks of work. And if what you're saying is true, there's no way to keep a record of our progress."

Tree frowned. "I'm not following."

Samar stood up and walked to the dry-erase board, which was covered with code.

"Look, say we test dozens of variables," he said, circling a huge swath of the code on the board. "By the end of the day, the loop will reset, right? So everything we learned gets erased."

He wiped away all the code he'd just circled with an eraser. "We can't track our progress because we won't remember what we learned."

"We'll be back to square one."

Tree sank into a chair. "Then I'm screwed."

A hopeless silence hung in the air until Carter snapped his fingers. "I've got it!"

They all looked at him with what seemed to Tree to be extreme skepticism.

"Everything resets, but your memory doesn't," Carter said. "Right?"

Tree nodded.

Carter grinned. "So you'll have to be a living record."

"You mean memorize everything?" she asked.

Samar jumped up. "That's genius!"

Tree couldn't believe what she was hearing. "No. No, it's not genius! I'm not a scientist! And *hello*? You do realize there's a psycho killer after me. I'll have to die over and over until you figure out how to close the loop."

They were quiet for a moment. Then Samar spoke up. "I guess you could always kill yourself before the killer finds you."

Tree rolled her eyes. "Another genius idea."

"Beats getting chased by some crazy dude in a baby mask," Dre said.

Tree groaned. This was not what she'd had in mind. These science geeks had broken her life. Why the hell couldn't they fix it?

"Do you have a better idea?" Carter asked her.

Tree sighed. "I knew you'd say that."

14

For the next few weeks, Tree studied harder than she ever had in her life. The truth of the matter was that she wasn't a bad student; she'd just stopped trying after high school.

When her mom died, Tree no longer had an interest in studying anything. Why should she be knocking herself out to learn a bunch of stuff that she'd probably never use again anyway? Her mom had done all of that: gotten the degree, pursued the career, had a family. And for what? To die at fifty? What was the point of that? Tree decided then and there that if she saw a shortcut, she'd take it every time. On her deathbed, her mom hadn't looked back on her life with satisfaction because she'd aced statistics in college. Tree swore she'd have all the fun she wanted, and if that meant a C– here and there, that would be just fine. Since then, college had been an experiment in the bare minimum. Tree was smart enough that she could party as hard as she wanted and coast by on quick wit and SparkNotes.

With the exception of Dr. Butler's biology lab, she'd never signed up for any class she didn't have to take. Bayfield only required two science classes to get a communications degree. She'd knocked out geology her freshman year. "Rocks for Jocks" hadn't been that hard, and there were lots of field trips to a nearby quarry for extra credit to keep her GPA from tanking. Astronomy was her sophomore year, and "Stars at Bars" involved fake IDs and pitchers of beer on the patio at a bar called the Deadwood. She and Danielle had taken that class together and met there every Tuesday night to copy notes from the guy who Tree had been hooking up with at the time—precisely for access to his notes. He was sort of a douche, but he had excellent handwriting.

Gregory's biology course was tougher, but she'd only signed up to be close to him. He'd given her the grade so she'd keep coming back. Telling that asshole she'd already dropped his class had been one of her finest moments back in her old dimension. Tree smiled at the memory as she sat in the lab copying the equations she had to memorize in today's cram session.

Samar was at the dry-erase board writing an endless string of numbers under the label FAILED ALGORITHMS while Dre and Ryan worked on the next set of codes they'd try. Carter was surprisingly helpful. He was always bringing her Diet Cokes or going out to grab food and churros for the gang. He had a calming effect on Ryan, who tended to get worked up about the endless number of equations they still had to try.

With every reset, it never got easier having Carter around because Tree knew he'd be going to meet Danielle later, but the thing was, he made her smile. As long as she had to twist her brain memorizing equations and symbols she'd never even seen before, she figured she might as well have some eye candy nearby. Tree finally decided that she wanted Carter in her life any way she could have him, and if that was friendship, well, his presence was better than his absence.

Every morning, when Tree woke up in his bed, she'd check to see if Carter was still with Danielle. He always was, but she figured it couldn't hurt to ask. Things had a way of shifting around in this dimension, but she eventually gave up hope that this would be one of them.

After she climbed out of bed, Tree would open the door and call Ryan into the room. She'd spend the next half hour convincing the two of them she was stuck in a time loop by telling Ryan things he hadn't even discovered about Sissy yet and, as they walked through the quad to the lab, pointing out exactly what was about to happen the second before it did. This blew Carter's mind, adorably, every time.

Once they were both onboard, she'd sit them down in the lab, grab a marker, and start writing out the algorithms that had failed previously. Dre and Samar would stand there stunned, watching the blond alpha bitch scribble the information on the dry-erase board while Carter and Ryan explained what was going on.

After the gang determined which equations to try next, Samar would walk her through them while Ryan got to work writing the code. Once he was done, he'd enter it into the system, and Sissy would rev up.

So far, Sissy had glitched fatally on every attempt. The machine would power down with a slow whir, and the screen at the terminal would flash *Sequence Failure.*

That was Tree's cue to memorize the latest equation that didn't work. She'd study by writing it out herself, asking Samar and Dre to explain to her (again) what the symbols were, how they were supposed to work, and why they didn't. At first, she could memorize the equations by rote—just a string of numbers. But after a few failed days, it became too hard to remember that many characters in a row without any context.

If she had to tell the truth, Tree was curious. As long as she was stuck in this day, she might as well understand the science behind it. The whole process required an intense amount of focus—not unlike going through rush, only this time to join a club exclusively for them. She was being inducted into this weird science sorority, one where the Greek letters she'd worn for years *actually meant* something.

When she could write from memory that day's failed algorithm in addition to all the equations that had come before, Tree would head out to have lunch with her mom and dad and enjoy what was left of the day before it was time to reset the loop.

Usually, she'd stop for a cherry Slurpee on the way back to campus. At the Kappa house, she'd been helping Danielle run her lines for *The Miracle Worker* by making videos of her clumsy blind walk. Tree found that Danielle did better when she could see herself, and she was helping her tone down some of the movements so Danielle didn't look like a crazy person trapped in a kitchen mixer.

Usually, Carter would join them for the rehearsal before he and Danielle went to dinner. Tree would excuse herself after a little while and head upstairs to her room to study a little bit more. Hanging with Carter in the lab was one thing, but watching him flirt with Danielle was too hard.

Every day, even though she'd tell herself not to, she'd go to her second-story window and watch the two of them kissing down on the porch. A few repetitions back, she'd gotten so annoyed she'd held her cup out the window and poured her Slurpee on their heads, but most days, she was able to control herself.

When she was positive she could remember everything she had to write on the dry-erase board the next day, all she had to do was find a new way to get back into Carter's bed. It was insane, and Tree knew it, but it was also her new normal. Sometimes, she just ran a bath and relaxed for a while before turning on the hair dryer and dropping it into the water. Or she'd stage a public display and drink a bottle of liquid drain cleaner in front of a startled customer at the supermarket.

Subtle things continued to shift every now and then. Once, as she was leaving the Kappa house to go meet her parents for lunch, she noticed Gregory's Mercedes slow down and follow Lori until she stopped and got in it. Dr. Butler and her roommate proceeded to have a heated discussion, and Tree wondered if perhaps Lori had gotten her wish in this dimension.

It was super strange to walk through her day knowing that some of her actions had zero consequence, while others—learning the equations, especially—were a matter of life and, well, death.

As she began to accept the routine, she realized how much pleasure she was taking in the simplest things. It turned out she was a lot smarter than she'd given herself credit for being. The more she learned about physics, the more she wanted to know. Her deep dive into the field of quantum mechanics was expanding her mind, and as it did, she was seeing new possibilities for herself.

Tree actually began to enjoy the whole process—well, the science, not the suicides; but even those had a silver lining. She was experiencing life and death without fear, and it made her feel invincible. As she climbed the stairs of the bell tower one night, reading over the day's failed algorithms for a final time, she couldn't help but smile at the absurdity of her college experience so far—and the hope it gave her about what she might accomplish if she ever lived to see a new day.

If I can live through this, I can do anything.

Tree tossed the notebook on the landing at the top of

the tower and slipped the rope that would soon snap her neck over her head. Stepping out onto the ledge in front of the clock's massive hands, she spread her arms, took a deep breath, and did a glorious, ten-story swan dive right into Carter's bed.

15

Tree sat up rubbing the back of her head as Carter came out from under the desk and started his routine.

"Oh, hey. You're up!"

Tree said what he was saying right along with him.

"I wasn't sure if you wanted to sleep in or not. I folded your pants for you last night. You know, I wasn't sure if that material . . . gets wrinkled." She pointed at the desk he was just searching. "And anyway, what are you always looking for under there?"

Carter reached into his pocket and removed a white plastic half circle. "Mouth guard," he explained. "I grind my teeth at night."

"Mystery solved." Tree was too disappointed with this answer not to be sarcastic.

She hauled herself out of bed and winced in pain.

"You okay?"

"Yeah," Tree grunted. "Never better."

She started for the door, but another stab of pain made her stop and grab for the desk.

"Are you sure?" Carter looked worried.

Everything started to go white in front of Tree's eyes. "Actually? I'm probably going to pass out."

She felt herself start to drop like a rock and felt Carter's arms around her at the last second.

Ryan burst through the door to yell about fine vagine, then stopped short and gasped up at Carter.

"Is she dead?"

Carter struggled to keep Tree from slipping to the floor. "A little help here?"

When Tree slowly came to at the hospital, the first face she saw was Carter's.

"Hey," he said softly.

She smiled. "You still came."

"Yeah. Of course. Why wouldn't I?"

Tree smiled at him, but she had to fight the tears in her eyes. Of all the pain she felt in her body, her heart still hurt the worst.

"Oh, hey," Carter said, "we just got ahold of your parents. They're on their way—"

"No!" Tree said. "They can't come here. It's not safe."

The lights flickered before Carter could answer, and the hospital was plunged into a blackout.

In the darkness, Tree realized Carter had no idea what was happening. She'd fainted this morning before she'd had a chance to explain anything to him.

Carter had no idea about Sissy, or the algorithms, or the loop. He didn't know that in another dimension, the two of them were falling in love.

Right now, he wasn't even sure if she remembered his name.

Of course, this time, Carter was with Danielle. Maybe he didn't care if she knew his name or not.

Tree wanted to pull him close and tell him that he was the last thing she thought about every day. He was the reason she had the strength to do what she did. She found the courage to end every night because it brought her back to him every morning.

A second later, the lights flashed back up, and Tree saw Gregory had stepped into the room behind Carter.

"Can I help you?" he asked.

Carter jumped. "Jesus!"

"It's okay," Tree told Gregory. "He's a friend."

Gregory smiled, but not with his eyes. "Visiting hours are over."

Carter nodded and turned to go.

Tree called out, "Thanks, Carter," and just like last time, he stopped in the doorway, turned around, and smiled.

"Feel better," he said.

And for just a split second, with his eyes locked on hers, she did.

When Carter left, Gregory turned and closed the door.

Tree realized she'd only seen him twice in this dimension: once with his wife, and once with Lori.

"Well," she said. "I guess now you know why I missed your class today."

"Sorry?"

"Advanced bio?"

He frowned and looked down at the name on her chart. "I'm sorry," he said. "Are you in my class? You don't look familiar."

Apparently, some good choices did follow you into a parallel universe. Tree smiled. "My mistake."

Gregory offered her his hand. "I'm Dr. Butler."

He had no idea who she was.

"Nice to meet you."

This is so weird, Tree thought as Gregory pulled up a chair.

"Miss Gelbman, I've been having a hard time pulling up your medical records—"

"I know," Tree said, cutting him off. "I should be dead." Gregory looked shocked. She continued, "My results? They don't make sense, right?"

"Uh, yes," Gregory said. "Highly alarming, to be honest."

Something about that word *alarming* triggered Tree's mind, and she remembered that Tombs was in this very building. She sat bolt upright and said, "She's about to die."

"Who?" he asked.

"Lori!" Tree shouted. "He's going to kill her!"

"What?"

"Listen to me. You need to stop her from going down to the OR."

"Excuse me," Gregory said. "I don't know who you're talking about."

Tree stopped short. "Really? Well, maybe your *wife* does."

Gregory froze. The look on his face told Tree she'd been right. Tree pointed at the door and yelled, "Go!"

The minute he was gone, Tree quickly sat up, pulled the IV line from her arm, and climbed out of bed. There was one gun in this hospital that she knew of, and it belonged to Officer Ramirez, who was standing guard over Tombs.

Tree poked her head out of her own room, then silently raced down the hall.

16

Deena was reading the same book she was always reading on September 18. She didn't even notice when Tree sneaked past her at the nurses' station.

When Officer Ramirez came out of the bathroom, Tree was ready. As the cop walked through the door zipping his pants, Tree stepped out and whacked him over the head with one of the heavy old telephones that were still in every room.

As the officer crumpled to the floor, Tree reached down and grabbed his gun.

"Sorry," she said.

Then she headed back into the hall, moving like a pro, room by room, clearing each one as she went.

A nurse came out of one of the rooms ahead, and Tree stepped back into the doorway to let her pass. Once the coast was clear, she continued down the hall until she stopped short. There was a trail of bright red liquid on the floor. Blood. Tree's heart began to race as she followed the drops to another door. She raised the gun and entered the room.

There were beds in this room, the privacy curtains drawn around each one. A patient gown was lying on the floor, and nearby, fresh blood led Tree to the back corner.

Tree took a deep breath, pointed the gun, and ripped back the curtain.

It was Lori.

Her roommate was still alive but barely, bleeding out into a puddle spreading beneath her. In a few seconds, it would all be over.

Tree turned her head to look away and saw a reflection in the polished chrome of a medical cabinet. The sadistic grin of the Bayfield Baby mask leered just behind her, the knife poised above her, ready to slice her out of the day and sentence her to live this moment all over again.

Without missing a beat, Tree spun around and unloaded three rounds into the killer, blowing him off his feet. He hit the linoleum with a bone-crunching smack.

She bent down and tore off the mask to reveal Tombs, still alive but barely.

"Who set you free?" Tree growled at him.

He tried to speak, but all he could manage before he died was a choked gurgle of blood and then a final silence.

Tree held up the mask in her hand, staring at its cruel grin. She couldn't see the curtain behind her move, and by the time she sensed someone behind her, it was too late. As she was pulled into a chokehold, she glimpsed a second baby mask looming above her. She tried to raise the gun, but the killer grabbed her forearm. Reaching back, she tried to pull off the mask with her free hand. Choking and defiant, she was able to spit out, "*Who are you?*"

When her attacker didn't answer, she made a decision. She was tired of dying alone and afraid.

With her last ounce of strength, Tree aimed the gun at one of the oxygen tanks in the room and fired.

There was a deafening *kaboom* as the whole room exploded into a ball of fire and threw Tree directly into . . .

. . . Carter's bed.

She sat up as the flash of the flames receded, and heard Carter say, "Oh, hey. You're up!" as she silenced the call from her dad.

Tree rolled her eyes. "I'm so done with this shit."

She had to get back to the lab.

17

The dry-erase board was covered in dozens of equations, and Tree was almost finished. She spoke the last one aloud as she wrote it from memory:

"Multiply the Euclidean vector by the square root of pi to the seventeenth power, we get an axiom of 0.004, which then gives us a linear-plane vector of 8.2."

Tree put the cap back on the marker and turned around to see Carter, Ryan, Dre, and Samar all staring at her in silence, their mouths hanging open.

"Daaamn, girl," Carter said quietly.

Samar and Dre approached the board almost reverently and scanned the equations.

"If these are all the failed algorithms—" Dre turned and looked at Samar, who nodded.

"Then there's only one possibility left," he said.

They both looked at Ryan. As if reading their minds, he jumped up and moved to the computer, furiously punching in code. He hit Enter, and a message popped up:

DATA COMPLETE—SYSTEM READY

Ryan looked up at Tree in shock.

"Holy shitballs. You did it."

Samar and Dre gave each other a high five.

Carter turned to Tree and hugged her. She tilted her mouth up toward his by reflex, forgetting where she was for just a second. She could feel Carter sense it, too. This was chemistry in a physics lab.

Tree held his gaze until she felt it slip, until finally, it evaporated into awkwardness.

It was Ryan who broke the weird silence that followed by throwing his arms around both their shoulders.

"Let's do this!" he shouted.

Samar and Dre were already double-checking Sissy's cables and wires as Tree and Carter hovered over Ryan at the terminal. Ryan paused to look at Tree.

"Just so we're totally clear: this algorithm is bifurcated by parallel Cartesian coordinates."

Tree held up a hand. "Ryan. English. Please."

He nodded and tried again. "One variant closes the loop in this dimension. The other one sends you back to your original dimension and closes that loop. It's decision time: Do you want to stay here or go back?"

Tree looked at Carter, and for the first time, her confidence faltered. She closed her eyes for a moment and shook it off.

"I'm staying here," she told Ryan. "Final decision."

Ryan nodded once. "Okay. Here we go, then."

He hit Enter, and Sissy crackled and hummed. As the machine started to fire up, lights began to flicker, and soon the whole room was pulsing and vibrating.

Tree could feel Carter's gaze on her, but she couldn't look at him anymore.

The device seemed to be building to a crescendo, when all at once it powered down on its own.

"What happened?" Tree asked. She could tell from the crestfallen looks on everyone's face that this latest effort had also just failed.

Dre studied the analytics. "The vector's off," she said.

"But you said this was the right one!" Tree was beginning to feel like she might fall apart.

"The math was right," Dre said. "Something's off."

"Guys!" The tone of Tree's voice left no choice but to look at her, and once she had their attention, she continued. "I've been literally killing myself to memorize all this shit for you. Failure is not an option."

Tree noticed Ryan glued to the screen at the computer. He hadn't said a word. She walked over and saw the grave look on his face.

"What's wrong?" she asked.

"Something in the hard drive," Ryan said. He pointed at the screen. "It must be a virus."

"Dude!" Dre yelled at Samar. "Did you open spam porn on the computer again?"

"No!" Samar shouted back, but it was fairly obvious he was lying.

Dre rolled her eyes, and Ryan threw up his hands.

"Great," he said. "I'm going to have to manually reenter all this code."

"How long?" Tree wanted to know.

Ryan shrugged. "Six, seven hours?"

"Ryan, look at me," Tree said. "I'm already on borrowed time here. Get. It. Done. Understand?"

"Uh . . . yeah. I'm on it. Jeez."

Tree left before the hopelessness of the situation paralyzed her. She was beginning to wonder if the loop was something that couldn't be undone.

Tree was already at the lunch quad when Carter caught up with her. She had hoped that if she kept ignoring him, he would leave her alone. She was staying here, and she was going to need a little break if they were ever going to be friends. Things had shifted, just not in the direction Tree had wanted. It was too hard for her to be near him and not touch him now.

Ignoring him didn't work.

Carter fell into step with her as they passed the Bayfield swag table.

"Get your school spirit on before the big game. Twenty percent off with your student ID." Keith Lumbly was doing his best to sell more crimson sweatshirts and baby masks—hopefully, Tree thought, not to psychopaths.

"Tree, hold up a sec."

She stopped and turned to face Carter.

"Are you sure about this?" he asked.

"I'm sure."

"But what about the killer? You said people are going to die tonight."

Carter paused. He shoved his hands in the pockets of his jeans and stared down at his tennis shoes. When he looked back up at her, Tree felt her knees go wobbly.

"If the loop closes," Carter said, "and we don't help them, then aren't they dead . . . for good?"

"I can't go back to that hospital," she said. "It's too risky."

Carter squinted up at the bell tower behind her. "So that's it? We walk away and let a bunch of innocent people die?"

Tree sighed. "People die every day, Carter. I can't be responsible for everyone. I know how selfish that sounds, but it's true."

Carter's eyes filled with a disappointment Tree had never felt pointed in her direction.

"Yeah," he said. "Actually, that does sound pretty selfish."

Tree's eyes filled with tears, but she refused to let them fall. "That's not fair," she said. "You don't know how hard this is for me. I don't want to have to choose between you and my mom, but I have to."

"What do you mean 'choose' between us?"

Tree had wanted to tell him so many times and sworn that she never would. Now that the moment was here, there was no way to hold back.

"Carter, we're together. In the other dimension."

For what seemed like hours, Carter just stared at her, totally in shock.

"Us?" he whispered.

"Yes. Us. I woke up in your bed, just like today. I did it over and over and over until I fell in love with you. But that version of us is back there. And my mom is alive here. So I've made my decision."

The tears she swore she wouldn't cry finally slid down her cheeks. A sad, listless silence hung between them until Carter reached up and gently tucked a strand of hair behind her ear.

"What if you're wrong?" he asked her. "Maybe this isn't the life you're supposed to have."

Tree wiped her cheeks with her hands. "Really?" she said. "So what? I'm supposed to go back to the other dimension where my mom's dead? I'm not going back. I can't lose her again."

"You just said it yourself: people die. We can't stop that no matter what. How we keep living is what matters."

Tree heard someone calling both their names and turned to see Danielle at the outdoor lunch tables, waving and smiling. Her house meeting was in full swing.

"Your girlfriend wants you," Tree said. "Better go."

Walking away from him was one of the hardest things Tree had ever done.

As she turned away, she heard Carter jog over to Danielle to say they were just talking about "school stuff." Tree shook her head and walked away, picturing the pout on Danielle's face as she begged for help on her American lit paper until he finally agreed, and she could go back to the Kappa business at hand.

Tree didn't turn back to look, but she knew if she did, she'd see Carter's eyes following her, watching until she disappeared around the corner at the other end of the quad.

18

Tree arrived at the restaurant later than usual and found her mom and dad already seated on the back deck. Her mother smiled and waved from the table, but as Tree walked toward them, she felt doomed. It must've been written all over her face.

Her mother was instantly on her feet. "Sweetie, what's wrong?"

"I'm okay." As she said it, another spasm of pain shot through her. She grabbed at her stomach and steadied herself against the back of a chair.

"You don't look okay."

Her mom frowned and felt Tree's forehead, looking for a temperature.

Tree gently pushed her mother away. "Mom, I said I was fine."

"You're cold as ice." Her mother was growing more alarmed by the moment. "I think we should go to the hospital."

"No! We can't go there!"

The words flew out of her mouth just a little too loudly.

Her parents exchanged a worried look. Tree tried her best to soothe them and appear calm.

"Look, I don't want to freak you guys out," she said softly, "but I need to get as far away from campus as possible."

Her father looked alarmed. "Theresa, what is going on?"

Tree shook her head. "Dad, please. I can't explain right now. I just need you to trust me."

Her father must have seen the desperation in her eyes, because he stopped trying to argue or force her to talk. He just nodded a single time.

"Okay," he said. "Let's go."

As Ryan sat at the computer entering the last bit of code, Samar and Dre checked all the device's connections, making sure everything was plugged in and secure. Finally, Ryan stopped typing and sat back with a relieved sigh.

"Done. Finally. You guys ready?"

They gave him a thumbs-up.

"Okay. Let's close this loop once and for all."

With a single keystroke, he fired Sissy up. The glowing proton lasers hummed to life, aimed at the centrifuge.

Tree sat alone in the back seat as her dad drove, one hand on the wheel, the other twined with her mother's. The road was deserted, and Tree gazed out the window, feeling better with every mile they put between their car and the Bayfield campus.

As they sped past the Bayfield power station, a massive stand of glowing electrical towers surrounded by a high chain-link fence, her mother's voice brought her back to the present.

"Hey." Tree looked up to find her mom's infectious smile

as she turned around to face her from the front seat. "Know what I'm craving right now?"

"What?" Tree asked.

"Those giant cinnamon rolls from that bakery in Morrow Bay."

Tree couldn't return the smile, and a sense of dread grew in her chest. She only knew their birthday tradition as an eerie video that played on her phone, an enviable memory that belonged to this other version of herself, and she couldn't escape from the true memory of *her* mother from *her* dimension being dead.

"Our birthday last year?" Her mom paused. "You don't remember? You ate two of them."

"That wasn't me," Tree whispered.

"What, honey?"

Her dad interrupted them.

"Hey, girls, it's getting late. How about we turn in somewhere for the night?"

"Sure." Her mom yawned. "I think we're all pretty pooped."

As her dad pulled off the road, Tree felt a deep unease settling over her like a dense fog. She couldn't put her finger on it, but being alone with her parents suddenly felt wrong—like she was an impostor in her own life.

They pulled up to a '60s-style motel. A neon sign illuminated their rental car, alone in the parking lot. The whole place was a shrine to kitsch.

Her dad got a room, and Tree sat with her mom on the bed, watching bad TV.

Her phone chimed, and she picked it up. It was a text from Ryan:

About to start over here. Fingers crossed . . .

Her dad crossed the room carrying an ice bucket.

"Going to find some ice," he said. "Be right back."

As he walked out the door, Tree's mom grabbed the remote and hit the mute button. "Okay. Just tell me one thing," she said. "Are you pregnant?"

Tree laughed out loud. "What? No. Mom, it's not like that."

"Sorry." Her mother breathed a deep sigh. "I had to ask."

Tree wished she could explain. She'd thought about it a lot on the drive, approached it from every angle she could imagine. How could she tell them about any of this? How would she ever convince them?

"It's about a boy, isn't it?" her mom asked.

"No. Yes. I don't know," Tree stammered. "It's complicated."

Her mom smiled. "Trust me, I can do complicated."

Tree studied her face, trying to summon the right way to explain the inexplicable.

"Have you ever wondered what your life would have been like if you couldn't be with Dad?" she asked.

"What do you mean?"

"What if you had to choose? What if being with him meant you'd lose someone really close to you? That you'd never be able to see that person again?" Tree paused. It was hard to talk around the lump forming in her throat. "What would you do?"

Her mom thought for a moment, then she took a deep breath. "We all have to make hard choices, Tree. That's life. Sometimes the past is pulling us in one direction while the future is calling us somewhere new. But if I had to choose, I'd pick your dad. Every time." Her mom reached over and squeezed her knee. "Without him, I wouldn't have you, right?"

"But how did you know he was the one?" Tree asked.

"I didn't." Her mom smiled and shrugged. "I took a chance and followed my heart. That's how love works, you know? It's a leap of faith."

For one perfect moment, Tree existed with her mother. Her heart was full, and her eyes were glowing with the image of the woman she would one day be. For just a little while, the whole multiverse—with all its endless dimensions—fell away, and it was just the two of them, side by side, lit only by the glow of the television.

And then Tree realized what was on the screen, and she leaped for the remote. The news report that was news to everyone but her was playing out on the local broadcast. She turned up the volume just as the in-studio team went live to the reporter Tree had seen so many times before.

This time, though, her story was different.

I'm standing outside Bayfield University Hospital where a terrible tragedy continues to unfold. Details are still coming in, but so far we can confirm two victims: a nurse and a police officer. Another man is in critical condition and fighting for his life after attempting to subdue the attacker.

A photo of Carter flashed onto the screen, and Tree's eyes filled with tears.

"No." It was the only word she could muster.

"Tree?" Her mom sensed the panic coursing through her. "Tree? What's going on?"

Tree grabbed her phone off the nightstand and called Ryan's number. Every ring felt like an eternity, and the icy fear in her stomach reached her limbs as she quietly prayed for Ryan to pick up.

For the first time, Tree knew with certainty that Carter was worth everything. He'd put it all on the line for her before, and tonight, he'd run directly into harm's way for people he hardly knew—to do exactly what she'd refused to do. If anything happened to him, it would all be her fault.

Her mother was right. Moving forward meant following her heart. It meant going back to her dimension, where she and Carter could take a leap together, even if her mom would only live in her memories.

As the phone rang endlessly in her ear, Tree Gelbman was finally ready to leave the past behind.

Her future was calling.

19

Back in the lab, no one could hear Ryan's phone buzz as it clattered across the table. The screen flashed Tree's number beneath *Crazy White Girl,* but the hum of the machine had turned to a dull roar and filled the lab, drowning out the vibrating phone.

Ryan stood nearby, holding his laptop as he helped monitor Sissy. Samar and Dre darted around the lab, checking various monitors and devices. As the ignored phone logged "1 missed call," the monitor at the computer began to flash:

COUNTDOWN SEQUENCE INITIALIZED

Tree yelled into the phone as soon as the beep sent her to voice mail.

"Ryan! Don't close the loop! You can't—"

She was interrupted by a robot's voice:

I'm sorry. The mailbox is full and cannot accept . . .

Tree was paralyzed, her mind frozen on the image of Carter's face on the news. She felt like her head might just crack trying to figure out the impossible: how to keep Sissy from working one last time.

"I can't let him close it," she said.

"Tree! What is going on?"

Her mother was alarmed, and Tree couldn't blame her. Without context, her mother probably thought she was having a nervous breakdown. But there was no time to explain. Tree had to do something, and do it right now, or she would be faced with being stuck in this dimension. It was a future where she would lose Carter—either forever, or to someone else—and carry always the unbearable regret that if only she had gone back to the hospital one last time, everything would've been different.

How could she keep Ryan from closing the loop? If only she could get back to campus in time to pull the plug on Sissy and—

Pull the plug.

In a flash, she remembered the electrical station they'd driven past on the way here.

Tree spotted her dad's car keys lying on the table. She raced over and grabbed them. Her mother called her name, but if Tree paused, it would be too late; she would either lose her resolve or run out of time. She threw open the door to the room and barreled into her father, who nearly lost his grip on the bucket of ice.

"Tree?"

Tree blew past him without a word, running to the car. She slammed the door and roared out of the parking space, accelerating past her stunned parents and out of the parking lot.

Pedal to the metal, Tree pushed the car as fast as it would go. She put her phone on speaker, but she got Ryan's voice mail again. She yelled a curse to no one and stomped on the gas.

The whole lab trembled as the proton lasers reached maximum intensity.

Dre and Samar backed away from Sissy, keeping their distance. Ryan wondered what was keeping Carter. He said he'd be back because he wanted to see this, but they couldn't wait any longer. Dean Bronson could come back at any moment, shut down the machine, and screw up the universe forever. The excitement Ryan felt as he watched this amazing machine reach its full potential surged through him like the energy popping through the cables at his feet. He glanced at the countdown clock on his computer screen: *7 . . . 6 . . . 5 . . .*

"Here we go!" he shouted.

Tears ran down Tree's cheeks as she pounded on the steering wheel, willing the rental car to go faster.

"*Come on!*" she yelled.

Up ahead, the sign for Bayfield Utility Power Grid flashed into view. Tree stomped on the gas and yanked the wheel. The tires skidded onto the drive leading to the entrance. Ahead, the access gate was chained and padlocked. Tree white-knuckled the steering wheel and closed her eyes, urging the car to go even faster, and blasted through the gates of the perimeter fence. She kept going and aimed the hood for what looked like the base of a tower. The rental car was a full-throttle missile that slammed at top speed into the structure with a deafening *boom!* Tree's world became blue flame and white-hot sparks as the car collapsed around her like an accordion and her tortured body once again was crushed into oblivion.

20

Tree sat up in Carter's bed as the tower bell tolled 9:00 a.m., relieved like never before to see him digging around under the desk for his bite guard.

"Oh, hey. You're up!"

"That's the last time I'm dying for you."

"What?"

Tree just smiled at him. Happy he's alive.

A few hours later, Dre and Samar were checking all the connections to Sissy as Tree watched the screen over Ryan's shoulder. He'd been working at the terminal for quite a while.

"How long will this take?" asked Tree.

Ryan smiled at her. "Thanks to your crazy memory, shouldn't take long at all. I can have Sissy ready to go in just a few minutes."

"I need a little more time," she said. "There's something I need to do." She nimbly skirted the pile of cables and headed for the door.

"Tree?" Ryan called out.

She stopped for a second and looked back.

"Are you sure you want to go back?"

Tree paused and gave him a sad smile. "I can't spend my life living in the past," she said. "I have to take a leap of faith."

Tree got to the Kappa house just as Lori was leaving with her bag slung over one shoulder.

"She finally rolls in."

Tree smiled. "Lori . . . hi."

"Big night?" Lori asked.

"You could say that." Tree changed gears. "Listen, Lori, I just wanted to tell you that it's good to see you."

"Okay?"

Tree followed Lori's gaze and noticed Gregory's car idling curbside. Gregory stepped out of the driver's side and tried to look casual.

"He's not worth it," Tree whispered.

Lori looked stunned. *How does she know?*

"Trust me," Tree said. "I know what it's like to get involved with a married guy. Living a double life. Feeling like crap every time they leave. But it's never too late to change."

Lori just stared at the ground. Tree waited until her roommate looked up, then reached out and took her hand.

"Somebody once told me that every day is a chance to be someone better. This is your day."

"Okay . . ." Lori waited for Tree's usual sarcasm to drop but heard something different and real. Tree meant it. "Thanks."

Tree reached out and wrapped both arms around Lori. "Take care of yourself," she whispered.

Tree slipped inside and made her way to Danielle's bedroom—prominently marked with a Bedazzled sign that read DANIELLE. She knocked twice, but no one answered, so she opened the door and poked her head inside. At that exact moment, Danielle walked out of the bathroom wearing a silky robe, surprised to see her.

"Tree!"

"Look, Danielle," Tree began. "I feel bad. I've misjudged you, and—"

She stopped short as Nick, the frat guy with the Pleasure Dome, followed Danielle out of the bathroom. He was shirtless and wet, wearing only a towel. When he saw Tree, a sly smile crossed his face.

"Nice! Three-way!"

Danielle looked like she was frantically searching the room for someplace to hide.

"He's kidding," she told Tree.

"No, I'm not—"

Danielle cut him off. "Nick's shower was broken, so I said he could use mine." Tree saw her staring daggers in his direction. "*Right*, Nick?"

He frowned at her. "My shower's fine," he said.

"Right," Tree said. "Never mind. Sorry for interrupting."

Tree hurried out of the room before Danielle could stop her. She could hear them arguing all the way down the stairs. She smiled to herself and shook her head.

Some things never change.

Tree rounded the corner at the restaurant and spotted her parents sitting at the far end of the patio. This is how she wanted to remember them, laughing and talking, ready to celebrate together. She took a deep breath and started making her way toward them between the crowded tables.

"There's the other birthday girl!"

Her dad jumped up and gave her a hug and a kiss. "Hey, Dad. Do you mind if I talk to Mom alone for a minute?" Tree smiled up at her father. "Just some girl talk."

"Sure," he said. "I can make a couple of work calls."

"Thanks."

He grabbed his phone and headed off with a smile. Tree sat down across from her mom.

"Everything okay?"

"Yeah. Fine," Tree said. "Everything's fine."

She sat there digging deep for the courage she needed to get through this. She didn't know what to say or how to say it.

"Mom." Tree's eyes welled up just saying the word. "I really want you to know how much I love you."

"Aw. I love you, too, sweetie."

"No. I'm serious," Tree said. "People say 'I love you' all the time, but you never really know how much it means until you can't say it to their face anymore. You're so beautiful and amazing, and I just hope I become half the woman you are one day."

Tree could see her mom was touched. She smiled that beautiful, infectious smile, and Tree felt warm all over.

"Are you kidding?" her mom said. "I'm the woman I am because I had you. I mean, I've never really told anyone this, but when I was pregnant with you, I was scared shitless."

Tree laughed. "Why?"

"I was afraid I was going to suck at being a mom. But then I held you for the first time, and something inside me changed instantly. You unlocked parts of me I never knew I had. The best kind of love does that. It changes you. Makes you a better person. Someday, when you hold your baby, you'll know what I mean."

Tree's eyes welled up with tears. "I'm so stupid. I really thought I could have it all. But I can't."

"Nobody can," her mom said with a smile. "But guess what? That's okay. You'll get what you need."

Tree dabbed at the tears on her cheeks with a napkin. "I hope so."

Her mom opened her arms. "Come here."

Tree got up and sat gently on her mom's lap. Her mom brushed a tear from Tree's cheek.

"Am I crushing you?" Tree asked with a smile.

"Nope. You're my little girl."

They held one another's gaze for what seemed like a long time, but in her heart, Tree knew it could never be long enough.

From here on, Tree would carry this moment forward into her future, so she took it all in—the way the sun filtered through the leaves over the patio, the aroma of the restaurant's grill, the endless blue of her mother's eyes, and the soft kindness of her smile.

Tree's mother had taught her so much over the years: how to tie her shoe, ride a bike, and make a budget. Her mother's love *had* made her a better person; it was the kind of unconditional love that made you feel worthy. It left no room for you to see yourself otherwise.

You taught me how to love myself.

It was the truest gift anyone could ever give her. Now, she'd given Tree one final gift.

You taught me how to say good-bye.

Tree heard singing and turned as her dad approached the table with a birthday cake. There was just one candle on it, and Tree and her mom finished the song together.

Her mother smiled at her. "Make a wish."

Then they closed their eyes and blew the candle out together.

21

This was the moment of truth.

Dre, Samar, Carter, and Ryan were circling Sissy like sentinels when Tree arrived at the lab.

"You ready?" Ryan asked.

Tree nodded, and Ryan reached for the master switch.

"Wait!" she said.

Ryan paused. Tree looked around at each one of them.

"I know how confusing this must be. I mean, you've only known me for a couple of hours, but I've known you guys for weeks. You all worked really hard to try to send me back home, so thank you."

"Well," Samar said, "the jury's still out on whether you're totally nuts, but happy we could help."

Everybody laughed, and then Tree said, "Ryan, light her up."

Ryan hit the master switch, and Sissy started purring. Lasers started firing. The room began to vibrate. Ryan darted back to his computer, and Tree saw the countdown clock at fifteen seconds again.

Dre and Samar made themselves busy running diagnostics and checking the equipment for safety.

In the middle of it all, Tree found herself alone with Carter for a moment.

He looked over and smiled at her, then stared back at the sphere full of lasers. "In this other dimension, do we know each other?" he asked.

Tree smiled. "Yeah. You can say that." He was so cute when he blushed just a little bit.

The lights overhead began to flicker, and Ryan yelled, "Seven seconds!" from the console. "Six! . . . Five! . . ."

Bang!

Dean Bronson stormed into the room flanked by the same pair of burly campus rent-a-cops.

"What did I tell you about turning that thing on!" he shouted over the roar.

Tree's stomach dropped.

"Wait! This isn't supposed to happen now. You're not supposed to come until tomorrow!"

"Turn that thing off! Now!" the dean thundered at Ryan.

"No! Please!" Tree begged him.

The countdown clock ticked to 1. An enraged Dean Bronson managed to find the master power cable and ripped it out of the wall socket. Once again, the lasers powered down. The dean triumphantly dropped the cord to the floor.

Tree was pissed. "You can't do this!" she yelled.

The dean looked at her with a sneer. "And who are you?"

"I'm a student here."

"Keep this little attitude up," he told her, "and we'll change that." He turned to the guards. "Get that thing out of here."

Dre looked stricken. "Where are you taking it?"

"My office," said Dean Bronson, "where it will remain under lock and key."

There was nothing left to do except watch and feel helpless as Sissy was rolled out of the room. A defeated silence hung in the air.

"That's it," Tree said. "I'm screwed."

Carter spread his hands and made an appeal. "Okay. It's a setback. I get it. But you can reset the day. Try again, right?"

Tree shook her head. "No. You don't understand. I keep getting weaker every time I come back. I don't know how many chances I have left. For all I know, this could be it. If I die again, I might stay dead."

"Ooh," Samar said. "That's a problem."

"No shit," echoed Dre.

They all sat in silence for a bit, the futility and frustration washing over them.

Suddenly, Tree flashed a wily grin. "Unless we steal it back."

"Steal it?" Ryan asked.

Tree shrugged. "I mean, it's not even really stealing if it's your property."

"Whoa, whoa, whoa," Samar said. "I don't know about this. If we get caught and I get expelled, my parents will hang me by my nut sack."

"I'm with him," said Dre. "Except for the nut sack part. Obvi."

Carter stood up and shook his head. "I don't mean to throw a bag of dog shit on your porch, but as far as I'm concerned, you guys owe this to her. You created this whole situation, so it's your obligation to help her. If she dies, that's blood on your hands."

"Okay," said Samar. "That's a little dramatic."

"He's right." Everybody turned to look at Ryan. "This is our fault, so we fix it. That's what scientists do. We solve the problem."

Samar suddenly leaped to his feet and shouted, "*Hell yeah!*" at the top of his lungs.

Everyone froze and looked at him like he was crazy.

"What?" he asked. "Too much?"

"A tad," said Dre.

A half hour later, the whole crew gathered around their usual cafeteria table as Dre unfolded a brochure with a map of the campus and started circling locations and tracing routes from Dean Bronson's office to the lab.

"So check it out." Samar pointed at a path running through the quad toward the science and engineering building. "Dean Bronson spends every evening knitting in the faculty lounge here."

"He knits?" Carter was incredulous.

"It's his thing." Samar tapped the building with the faculty lounge. "Anyway, all we need to do is get the keys to his office, sneak over to admissions, break into the dean's office, grab Sissy, wheel her back to the lab without anyone from security seeing us, get Dean Bronson's keys back to him without him knowing they were ever gone, power up Sissy, run diagnostics, flip the switch, and *bam*! Tree's back in whatever whack-ass dimension she came from, and we just saved the damn day." Samar dropped his pen like a mic.

"Okay," Tree said. "Sounds awesome. How do we do it?"

Samar shrugged. "I have no idea."

Everybody sighed or groaned. Faced with Dean Bronson's confiscation of Sissy, the general consensus was clear: *We're toast.*

Carter wasn't giving up. "We need a diversion," he said. "Some way to distract the dean."

On cue, a Facetuned photo of Danielle popped up on Carter's phone, serenaded by a ringtone of James Blunt's "You're Beautiful."

"She picked the ringtone," he mumbled with a blush,

grabbing his phone and avoiding any and all eye contact. He swiped and answered. “Hey, babe!”

Tree could hear Danielle yapping at Carter a mile a minute. She couldn’t quite make out what Danielle was saying, but she sounded like a very pissed-off version of Charlie Brown’s parents.

“I’m just hanging out with Ryan—”

Tree was disgusted watching Carter dealing with Danielle’s type A jealousy. She was such a . . .

That’s when it hit her: *Drama queen.*

Tree reached over and grabbed the phone out of Carter’s hand.

“Hey!”

There was no time to explain.

“Danielle! Hiiiii. So, we have a little favor to ask you . . .”

22

Roger Bronson sat alone in the faculty lounge, knitting a scarf in the colors of the Bayfield Baby, crimson and white. His ex-wife used to laugh at him for knitting, and so he'd taken to keeping his hobby on campus. Now that she'd left him, knitting by himself in his own living room was an option, but it was depressing to be at home alone. The house felt strange and empty. Instead, he came here and put Sean Hannity on TV to keep him company while he practiced both knit and purl stitches for a ribbed scarf to wear to the football games. The rhythmic monotony of his clacking needles freed his mind from the endless litany of issues to be addressed: student retention, discipline, and the unremitting havoc wreaked by those snotty-nosed little bastards with the experiment he'd confiscated. As of tonight, there'd be no more rolling blackouts.

The door of the faculty lounge swung open, and Dean Bronson looked up expecting to see Hank, the night janitor, making his rounds. Instead, a young woman in dark glasses appeared, tapping and swinging a red-and-white cane in front of her. The dean performed a swift inventory of the sight-impaired students currently on the rolls. This young woman was certainly not on it. He'd have remembered. Blind or not, she was stunning. Whoever was helping her get dressed in the morning was doing an excellent job.

"Can I help you?" he asked.

The young woman whirled toward the sound of his voice. "Oh! *Pardon.* I appear to be very lost."

Her accent was . . . French? But a dialect with which the dean was as of yet unfamiliar. It made sense, though, that she was foreign. Her bone structure alone was evidence enough of her European heritage.

He jumped to his feet and tossed his needles down. He was quite eager to help this damsel in distress.

"I'm Dean Roger Bronson," he informed her.

She smiled. "*Bonjour.* My name is Amélie . . . Le Pew."

"Oh!" It all made sense now. "You must be with the exchange program."

"*Oui, oui.*"

Out in the hallway, Tree and Carter watched the whole debacle go down through a small window in the door to the faculty lounge. When she had asked Danielle to distract Dean Bronson and swipe his keys, this was not what Tree had anticipated.

"She's really into her drama class," Carter explained.

They watched as Danielle reached out into the air as Dean Bronson approached her.

"*Monsieur,* may I know your face?"

"I'm sorry?" he asked, but there was no more explanation to come. Danielle started aggressively rubbing her hand all over his face. The dean felt bolts of lightning coursing through him. His knees began to tremble.

"Such strong features," Danielle said.

"Thank you." Dean Bronson was beyond smitten, and he breathed in deeply to capture the aroma of the moment.

"You must be French," he said, nearly panting. "Your hand smells like cheese."

Watching from the hall, Tree had to clamp both hands over her mouth to smother a laugh as Danielle, without any hint of an accent, shouted, "I don't eat cheese!"

Flustered, she quickly tried to recover with a flurry of mumbled high school French and a strong accent on the words *lactose intolerant*.

She set off thwacking her stick around the room and was clearly pleased to see Bronson following her like a puppy looking for a treat.

"Where are you trying to get to?" he asked her, practically panting by now.

"*Le café*."

Tree could tell that Danielle was searching the room frantically for Bronson's keys, knocking that cane against furniture as if her life depended on it.

"You must mean the cafeteria," Bronson said. "I'm happy to show you."

Danielle froze when she spotted the keys sitting on a nearby table. Her only problem was getting the dean off her back for long enough to grab them.

"Here," he said. "Allow me."

Tree and Carter watched as Dean Bronson tried to take Danielle by the arm. As he did, Danielle stumbled forward and slammed her entire body into another little end table, toppling a fake flower arrangement. As it fell to the ground, the vase exploded in a torrent of glass marbles that immediately rolled and bounced all across the room.

"Oh no!" Danielle shrieked.

Smelling a lawsuit and an international incident brewing, Dean Bronson flew into action. "Don't move!" he shouted. "You'll trip!"

With the dean on all fours chasing marbles, Danielle ran

like a gazelle to the table, snatched the keys, and leaped to the door where Tree and Carter were standing watch. She slapped the keys in Tree's waiting hand, who immediately spun around with Carter and made a run for it.

The dean groaned to his feet to find Danielle standing near the door, looking almost like she was, well, looking out into the hall. But before his doubts could take solid shape, she snapped back into the part of fumbling blind girl.

The dean shot forward to intercept her before she could demolish anything else.

"Pretty quick there, aren't you?" he said. "Hold on now. I just need to grab my keys."

Danielle knew he couldn't go looking for his keys this soon or they were all busted. She gave it everything she had and tripped, launching herself toward a large hanging tapestry. She closed both hands around the fabric and yanked as hard as she could. The fabric ripped away from the hanger and landed on top of her as she fell to the floor.

As Danielle struggled under the fabric, crying out for help, a flustered Dean Bronson raced to her aid.

"Eeet is so dark!" Daniel cried out.

The dean tried to help. "Look for the light!" Even as the words left his mouth, he regretted them. "Oh. Jeez. That was inconsiderate. I'm sorry."

Danielle continued to flail, pulling the curtain over her head.

"You're making it worse," Dean Bronson said.

Perhaps this poor young woman was newly blind and still getting the hang of it.

"I cannot breathe!" Danielle shouted, continuing to tear at the curtain, tangling it further.

The dean continued to pull at the fabric wondering how someone so beautiful could be so helpless.

Ryan, Dre, and Samar were already waiting outside Dean Bronson's office as Tree and Carter came racing up.

Carter immediately started trying keys in the lock.

Ryan was dancing back and forth from foot to foot like a little kid needing to pee. "Hurry up, dude!"

"Got it!" Carter said.

Finally, the handle turned.

He swung open the door and flipped on the lights. There, on a dolly in the corner, was Sissy. Samar and Dre rushed over and immediately began wheeling the device out of the room.

Back in the hallway, Carter quickly closed and locked the door of Dean Bronson's office. Ryan, Dre, and Samar took off with Sissy. Then Carter flashed Tree a smile, and the two of them sprinted off in the other direction.

When Roger Bronson finally untangled the flailing young exchange student from the tapestry, her hair was a disaster. The beret she wore was barely hanging on now, and as she attempted to right herself, she smiled beneath her dark glasses and, in the French accent he still couldn't place, said, "*Gracias.*"

As the dean bent down to retrieve her cane, Danielle saw Tree and Carter arrive back at the door. Oblivious, Dean Bronson handed her cane back to her.

"*Merci,*" she said.

He smiled. "Okay. Shall we?"

He turned and walked toward the door, Danielle tap-tap-tapping behind him, when he suddenly paused.

"Forgot my keys again."

As the dean turned to go back to the table where his

keys should've been, Danielle realized that this was her big moment. She wasn't going to be another actor with perfect cheekbones and killer lips; she would be a star. Without hesitating another moment, she did the only thing she could. Her cane swung up and down so fast it made a *pffffwht* through the air before she whacked Dean Bronson as hard as she could in the face.

The dean yelped in shock, holding his nose with both hands. Blood was already gushing out between his fingers.

"Christ almighty!" he roared in pain and anger. "Be careful with that thing!"

"*Oh no! Mon dieu!*"

"Oh god!" he shouted. "I'm bleeding!"

As Bronson attempted to stem the bleeding with his Angora cat tie, he stumbled over to the table under the flat screen and began opening the cabinets for a tissue.

Watching from the hallway, Carter pushed open the door and tossed the dean's keys to Danielle. She caught them and dashed across the room, setting them back on the end table, and then pirouetted and landed on the sofa in an impossibly casual pose.

Bronson turned just a split second after Danielle hit the couch. Was she *smiling* at him?

Bronson had reached a boiling point. "Do you want to go to the cafeteria or not?"

Danielle gave him a sexy, "*Oui, oui,*" but Bronson was done.

He stormed over, grabbed Danielle by the wrist, and marched her toward the door.

"Don't you have a dog or something?" he asked.

Danielle set her mouth in a sexy pout. "My dog died."

Bronson shook his head and kept walking. First thing in the morning, he'll be setting new academic standards for exchange students.

23

Ryan, Samar, and Dre were busy reconnecting all of Sissy's electrical cables when Carter and Tree burst into the room.

"How's it going?" Carter asked.

Ryan ran back to his computer, firing up the diagnostic software. "We're on it!"

Tree glanced up at the clock. It was already 9:13 p.m. "Guys, we've got less than three hours to make this happen."

"Not gonna lie," Ryan said. "It'll be close."

"Shit." Tree shook her head and turned to Carter. "Stay here."

"Why?" he asked.

"Just promise me you'll stay here?" Tree grabbed her jacket and pulled it on.

"Where are you going?" Carter wanted to know.

Tree spotted a toolbox near Ryan's desk. She grabbed a long flat-head screwdriver.

"I need to borrow this." She tucked the screwdriver behind her back and ran out of the lab.

She heard Carter call her name, but she didn't look back.

At the hospital, Tree slipped directly into Tombs's room while the cop was still using the bathroom. She still had time. She sneaked behind him and slid the gun out of his holster while he was still peeing. His stream slowed to a sad, messy trickle as he twisted around to find her aiming the barrel at him. He awkwardly raised his hands.

"Sorry," she said. "Bad timing."

"Just take it easy," he said.

"You can put it away," Tree told him.

The cop tucked and zipped his pants. Slowly, he turned around.

"Lady, you're making a big mistake."

"There's a killer on the loose." Tree kept the gun trained on him. "Go get help."

"What?" he asked.

"Go!"

The cop backed away before bolting from the room. Tree heard him yelling in the hallway.

"She's got a gun!"

Tree took the elevators down to surgery. She ran down the hall and blew past the emergency exit door before slowing down as she approached the OR. She raised the gun, then walked into the room. Lori was standing over Tombs's gurney.

"Lori, move!" Tree shouted.

Lori jumped out of the way, revealing Tombs, already sitting up, wielding a knife.

Bam-bam! Tree blew Tombs off the gurney.

Lori was frozen in shock. Tree grabbed her.

"Come on!" she said. "We have to move!"

"What the hell is happening?"

"I'll explain later!" Tree pushed her toward the door. "Move!"

Over in the lab, Ryan typed commands into the computer until he thought his fingers might fall off. Finally, Sissy started to power up. Carter, Dre, and Samar moved around the perimeter of the room, double-checking the device.

At that same moment, Dean Bronson, his bloody nose stuffed with Kleenex, was guiding the crazy, beautiful, blind exchange student down the hallway to the cafeteria when the lights began to flicker overhead. The whole building was experiencing an all-too-familiar power surge, the kind of power surge he'd definitively stopped with authority when he'd confiscated that ridiculous science gadget . . . and Roger Bronson knew that he'd been had.

"What is this?" he growled, spinning Danielle around and ripping off her sunglasses. "You're not blind!"

He yanked the cane from Danielle's hand and tossed it to the ground as if it, too, were not really a cane. As Dean Bronson took off running toward the science building, Danielle fished her phone out of her purse and dialed. It only rang once before Carter picked up.

"We've got a problem," she said.

It only took Bronson a few minutes to get there, but Carter had helped Dre and Samar be ready. As Sissy glowed and the lights flickered, Dean Bronson and his guards came flying around the corner only to find the lab door locked from the inside.

"Get it open! Now!"

One of the guards grabbed his keys and unlocked the door, but the door still wouldn't budge.

On the other side of the door, Samar and Dre leaned against a desk Carter had jammed under the door handle.

"Keep them out!" Ryan shouted from the computer.

"We're trying!" Dre called back.

Samar was sweating, his eyes wide with panic. "If I get expelled, my parents are going to disown me."

Each time the guards rammed the door with their body weight, the desk quaked beneath them. With every hit, the door inched open a little bit more.

"*We can't hold them much longer!*" Samar shrieked while Ryan typed. He was almost done.

"Come on, come on . . ." Ryan whispered at the screen.

It was one part plea, one part prayer.

Tree led Lori down the hospital hallway, sweeping the area with the cop's gun as they went. A couple of doctors and nurses fled the scene or hid beneath desks, terrified that there was an active shooter in the building.

"Will you please tell me what's happening?" Lori begged.

"At first I thought he was trying to kill me. But it's you he wants."

"*Who?*"

Tree froze. At the far end of the hall was the killer. He was wearing a Bayfield Baby mask and holding a long knife.

Tree took aim. "It's over, Gregory!" she shouted.

Gregory reached up and pulled off his mask.

"What?" Lori gasped. "Why?"

"His wife was on to him about your affair," Tree explained, loudly enough for Gregory to hear. "So he stole a page from your old playbook. He set Tombs free so everyone would think Tombs killed you, but it was him . . . and the secret of his affair would die with you."

Gregory walked down the hallway toward them and gave Tree a slow clap for her explanation.

"Bravo," he said. "Whoever you are."

Tree rolled her eyes. "Once a slimeball, always a slimeball."

"Do I know you?" Gregory asked.

"Stay back, asshole, or I shoot."

Gregory didn't stop. He kept moving. Tree fired a warning shot at the ground near his feet. Now he froze.

In the silence that followed, they could hear the scream of approaching sirens.

Tree smiled. "Hear that? You're going to rot in prison."

Gregory started walking again, a slow sneer taking shape across his face. "I don't think so," he said. "See, there's one little detail you failed to recognize in all this."

He was bluffing and Tree knew it. "What's that?" she asked.

A voice behind her said, "Me."

Tree turned around to see Gregory's wife, Stephanie, standing behind her and Lori.

Stephanie raised a gun of her own and pointed it at Lori. "Did you really think I would let a little whore like you ruin my life?"

And she shot Lori.

Tree screamed at the blast, and her roommate collapsed to the ground. She was hit, but she was alive.

"Lori!"

Tree turned her gun on Stephanie, but the next thing she knew, Gregory had tackled her, and they both slammed into the ground. Her gun flew out of her grip and skidded away. She struggled with him on the floor, but he was too strong. He pinned her down, grabbed her head in both hands, and smashed it into the floor. She tried to fight back, but the darkness was already seeping into her vision.

Tree's head shook like the campus bell after it rang. She could barely focus on Stephanie walking over and picking up the gun she had taken from the cop.

Tree struggled to stand, but her limbs wouldn't obey her. A puddle of blood was seeping away from Lori, growing bigger. Gregory stood above both of them, and Stephanie approached him, holding a gun in either hand. She offered one to Gregory.

"Would you like to do the honors?" she asked.

Her husband smiled at her. "Don't mind if I do."

Gregory pointed Tree's gun at her.

"Oh, wait. I almost forgot," Gregory said. He turned the gun on Stephanie and shot her point-blank in the chest. "Sorry, hon. I want a divorce."

Stephanie's eyes went wide as blood blossomed across her blouse. She hit the floor, her head bouncing with a sickening thud. She was dead. Gregory turned the gun back on Tree. "Now, where were we?" he asked.

"*Hey!*"

From somewhere above her, Tree heard another voice, and Gregory spun around and started firing his gun wildly down the hallway.

Tree was in no shape to fight, but it was now or never. She muscled her way to her feet just in time to see Carter running headlong down the hall toward her, ignoring the hail of bullets.

As she stumbled through an open doorway, Gregory turned and fired, barely missing her head. Tree's heart raced and her head pounded, but she pushed on, through a door leading to the MRI room. Gregory was right behind her. She ran down a short hallway and pushed past another door leading into a small viewing chamber. There was a computer terminal in front of a large glass window. She could see the MRI machine in the next room, but there was no other way out. It was a dead end. As she turned around to flee, Gregory blasted through the door.

Tree grabbed a lamp off a table in the corner and swung it with everything she had, whacking the gun out of Gregory's hand. She tried to hit him again, but he caught her wrist and overpowered her. She felt him lift her off the floor.

No, no, no!

But it was too late. Gregory hurled her through the glass observation window. She crashed through the glass and tumbled to the ground on the other side of the wall in the next room, where the MRI machine was housed. Glass shards shredded her clothes, palms, knees, and elbows.

Gregory retrieved his gun and opened the door beside the broken window. Tree saw a flash of the large warning sign on the door. It read:

CAUTION! STRONG MAGNETIC FIELD. NO METALS.

Gregory casually walked into the room and circled Tree as she slowly stood. She could feel the blood running freely down her cheek and making her palms slick. The bloody glass crunched under her feet.

Gregory turned his back to the MRI machine and raised the gun at Tree. With a shaking hand, Tree reached behind her back and pulled the screwdriver out of the waistband of her jeans. Her hand shook as she held it out in front of her. This was the end. This was the night that Gregory killed her. It was a futile gesture, but it was defiant. She might die tonight, but she wasn't going to quit. She'd be back, and she'd get it right.

Gregory looked at her and laughed.

"Look who brought a screwdriver to a gunfight."

Gregory aimed his gun at Tree, his finger itching the trigger.

"Wait!" Tree yelled. "There's something I need to tell you."

"What's that?" Gregory's face was a mask of pure derision.

Tree smiled back at him. She could taste blood on her

teeth, but it was all about to be over. Nothing tasted sweeter than having the last word.

"You suck in bed," she said.

With that, she reached out and slapped the main power button to the MRI.

The machine whirred to life, and Gregory's hand was ripped away from Tree as the powerful magnet sucked the gun back against the machine. He yelled in pain and surprise as his right hand was stuck beneath the pistol. He reached out with his left hand to try to peel his right hand away, but the stainless steel Rolex on his left wrist got pulled into the same magnetic field. For a moment, he was stuck there, pinned to the machine like Christ on the cross. His eyes zeroed in on Tree's hand, trembling as it tried to hold the screwdriver.

"No! Wait!" he yelled.

Tree released the handle, and the long metal blade flew across the room like a rocket, finding the shortest distance to the powerful magnetic force of the machine—directly through Gregory's chest.

His eyes went wide, and he let out a last gasp. When Tree was sure he was dead, she pushed the power button again, and his lifeless body crumpled to the floor.

24

The hospital was a blur of activity as Tree raced back to where she'd left Carter and Lori. Sirens wailed in the parking lots, and the hallways were swarming with police in Kevlar vests, shouting, pointing, and stringing caution tape. A trauma team raced by with a cart of equipment, and Tree followed them through the mayhem until they reached Carter, who was helping Lori to her feet.

"Are you okay?" Tree asked her.

Lori managed a weak smile as several nurses eased her onto a gurney.

"This is a pretty good place to get shot," she said.

Tree grabbed her hand. "Lori. I'm so sorry."

"For what?" Lori asked. "You just saved my life."

"I just wish . . . I wish things could have been different."

One of the nurses urgently pushed her way between them. "I'm sorry," she said, "but we need to move her." And then Tree's grip on Lori's hand was broken as they wheeled her away.

She heard Carter's voice calling her.

Tree turned around to find Carter standing there, nursing his head with some gauze, but smiling.

"I thought I told you to stay put," she said.

He shrugged. "Sorry. Couldn't help myself."

Carter glanced up at the ceiling, distracted. The lights above them suddenly began pulsing like crazy.

Tree ignored it; she'd had enough of blackouts and flashing lights and killers and that goddamned Bayfield Baby. She stepped up to Carter, and their eyes locked.

"I hope you know I'm only going back for one reason."

Carter smiled at her. "In this other dimension? Are we . . . ?"

Tree nodded. "Yeah. We definitely are."

Without a moment's hesitation, she leaned in to kiss Carter. As he wrapped both arms around her, his lips found hers for the first time (today), and Tree knew beyond the shadow of a doubt that this was a love that existed beyond the bounds of time and space.

This was a love that lived in every dimension.

While Tree and Carter locked lips in the hallway at the hospital, Dre, Samar, and Ryan were under siege in the science lab.

Bronson and his security goons finally forced open the door and burst into the lab. Dre fell backward, but Samar was standing by with the fire extinguisher, and he sprayed the intruders in a blinding fog. *Every second counts,* he thought as the powdery-white plume engulfed them all.

Ryan stood guard over the computer, counting down from five . . . four . . .

The lights overhead started to surge, getting brighter and brighter . . .

. . . *three* . . .

Dean Bronson stumbled from the white cloud and reached for the nearest, thickest electrical cord.

. . . two . . .

Ryan looked up and smiled.

. . . one.

Sissy fired another huge electrical pulse.

The shock wave rocked the entire lab as every overhead lightbulb exploded, even the ones across campus in the ceiling of the hospital above the couple kissing near the OR. Glass broke, tubes shattered, and shimmering gold sparks rained down around Carter and Tree.

As the lights flashed and faded, as the dimensions expanded and contracted, nothing and no one would ever pull them apart.

In the dark aftermath of the surge, when all was quiet in the rubble of the lab, Ryan opened his eyes. His face was covered in dust, and as he lay there, remembering who and where he was, his eyes went wide to the sound of distant coughing, and his first thought was, *Oh. Fuck.*

The giant magnetic pulse had left more than smoke and dust in the air. Ryan sat up and surveyed the scene of debris and destruction. But the whole gang was here, so that was promising: Tree, Carter, Ryan, Samar, Dre, Dean Bronson and his henchmen.

One by one, slowly but surely, they all woke up.

Samar was covered in Yoo-hoo but none the worse for wear.

Carter sat bold upright, immediately searching for . . .

Tree. She was sitting behind him. A little scraped up, but she was really super-duper happy to see him.

"What just happened?" he asked.

Tree smiled, and her eyes filled up at the same time. "A whole lot," she whispered. "A whole lot."

25

A week later, Tree, Carter, Ryan, Samar, and Dre milled around the quad wearing bright orange safety vests picking up trash with pokers. Their probation with the school was all about garbage collection and keeping their science experiments intro-level. Somehow, Danielle had escaped punishment, but Dre was more focused on figuring out exactly what the hell they'd all just experienced.

"It doesn't make sense," she said.

"Yes, it does," Ryan said. "It acted like a slingshot. When she jumped back into this dimension, the vacuum created by the centripetal force closed the loop."

Samar poked a churro with his trash poker thingy and raised it off the ground to eye level. "Who throws away a perfectly good churro?"

Tree hit Carter's poker with her poker, knocking his piece of trash off the pointy end.

"What are you doing?" he asked.

"Starting a sword fight with you," she said with a grin. "Come on."

She whacked his poker again, and he laughed and said, "Bring it."

Ryan was done. It was bad enough to watch them do this shit in his dorm room. But in public? On the quad? He had to speak up. "Ugh," he said. "Get a room."

"Why?" Carter asked. "Wanna sleep in your car again?"

"Ha. Ha," said Ryan, just as two black SUVs screeched to a halt in front of them. The plates were government-issue, and a team of men in well-tailored suits spilled from the doors, led by an older, distinguished-looking scientist in a tailored gray suit.

"Uh-oh," Samar said. He had barely recovered from the night they'd closed the loop. "This looks bad."

The lead agent stopped in front of Ryan.

"Ryan Phan?"

Ryan glanced both ways. "Maybe," he replied.

The man in the gray suit flashed a badge. "I'm Dr. Isaac Parker. I'm here on behalf of DARPA."

"Sweet!" Dre couldn't help but overhear, and it was impressive.

Dr. Parker smiled and nodded. "We'd appreciate it if you'd come with us to answer some questions," he said. "All of you."

"Are we in trouble?" Tree asked.

"No, ma'am," Dr. Parker assured her. "We are just . . . curious."

All five of them shared a nervous look.

All five of them climbed into the SUVs anyway.

The DARPA headquarters was an imposing monolith. *This,* thought Tree, *is the definition of tax dollars questionably spent.*

After hustling down a long staircase that descended into

a massive, bustling lobby, Dr. Parker led the gang down a long, sterile hallway flanked by more men in dark suits. They also passed robots. Samar had to really keep it on lockdown to avoid freaking out.

They finally arrived at a hive of activity. Men in lab coats milled about performing experiments that Tree was fairly certain the general public was never allowed to know about.

And there, on its own slightly elevated platform like a work of art and connected to a streamlined network of computers, was Sissy.

"Holy shit," Ryan whispered. Sissy had never looked better.

"Hope you don't mind us borrowing her," Dr. Parker said.

They gathered around the device, and Dr. Parker continued to explain. "What you've created here is truly remarkable."

Samar leaned into Ryan's ear and whispered, "Suck it, Dean Bronson."

"We've been having some difficulty understanding how the device operates," Dr. Parker explained. "We figured you could help."

Dre piped up right away. "We have no clue how—"

"Of course. Happy to help." Ryan cut her off—not because it was a mansplaining thing but because he smelled an opportunity. He looked over at Dre and mouthed the words, *Shut the fuck up*.

"There's just a lot of code that needs to be written," he explained to Dr. Parker.

Tree stepped forward. "I think I can help with that part."

Everybody stopped and looked at her like, *You can?*

Dr. Parker seemed pleasantly surprised by their willingness. "Great," he said. "So we just need to find a test subject."

Carter frowned. "You want to force someone into a time loop? That's pretty harsh. It'd have to be someone who really deserves it."

The minute the words left his mouth, Tree knew. *Ding!*

Tree smiled at Dr. Parker. "I might have the perfect recruit."

Danielle was fast asleep in a pink, tangled mess of down and silk. She wore a velvet sleep mask and didn't wake up until she heard her phone ring. The ringtone was Guns N' Roses' "Welcome to the Jungle."

Danielle peeled her sleep mask off and sat up with a biiiiiiig stretch.

She smiled.

Today is the first day of the rest of my life, she thought. *Who knows what it might hold?*